A _____
Born Carpenter

Mark + Kayla,

Where are the Duanes.
See you at dinner.
Soon as they get back.

With love to 1 special
friends

Thom
20 Aug. 1986

A
Born Carpenter

a novel

Thom Roberts

WEIDENFELD & NICOLSON
New York

Copyright © 1988 by Thom Roberts

Published by Weidenfeld & Nicolson, New York
A Division of Wheatland Corporation
10 East 53rd Street
New York, NY 10022

Published in Canada by General Publishing Company, Ltd.

The author gratefully acknowledges permission to reprint from "Fire and Ice," in *The Poetry of Robert Frost*, edited by Edward Connery Lathem, © 1969. Published in the United States by Henry Holt and Co., and in England by Jonathan Cape Ltd. Reprinted by permission of the Estate of Robert Frost, Edward Connery Lathem, and the publishers.

Library of Congress Cataloging-in-Publication Data

Roberts, Thom.
    A born carpenter.

    I. Title.
PS3568.024748B67   1988   813'.54   87–37191
ISBN 1-55584-071-X

Manufactured in the United States of America

Designed by Irving Perkins Associates

First Edition

10 9 8 7 6 5 4 3 2 1

for Jeanne, Mark, Wyatt, Bryan and Adam

He was a born carpenter. For all the exacting hunger of his heart, for all the disorder in the rhythm of it, he had not merely a respect for his trade but a passion for it, an obstinate probity, an almost manual joy in the thing he was shaping. . . .

—Romain Roland,
Beethoven the Creator

Part One _____

Demons

I _____

I'm in the Duck & Dog, a popular Irish bar, or pub, as the Woodstock locals like to call it, listening to the strangest story I've ever heard. The storyteller is a wiry little man named Rob Dawson. He's one of the locals, but I don't know him very well. Just well enough to say hi when I see him on the street or in the Duck & Dog. Usually I try to avoid him, not because I dislike him, but because he's a drunk and a general nuisance, and he has never spent more than two minutes with me without asking for a job. I'm a contractor here in town, and it's not unusual for local carpenters to ask me for work, especially in the winter months like now when things are slow. But Rob is not a carpenter. As I said, he's a drunk, and not a very good one at that.

But tonight he has a story to tell, and I'm his audience. It's funny, in a perverse sort of way, because I'm also his subject, and he's telling the story as though I were someone else. It's not that he's drunker than usual and doesn't know who I am. It's that he has chosen to tell it in the third person.

"Boy, did I hear a funny story about old John Noble," he says as I try to slip past him and go to the other end of the bar.

"Hi, Rob," I say.

He grabs my jacket at the shoulder and says, "Come on, let me tell you this great story I heard." He's much smaller than I am, maybe five-three and no more than a hundred pounds, but he manages to pull me down to the empty stool next to him.

He speaks softly, as though he wants to tell me a secret, which I guess he does. "I heard a funny story about you, John."

"Yeah? Where'd you hear it?"

He gulps his bourbon, wipes his lips with a frayed denim cuff and says, "Just around, you know, it's a little town and people are always tellin' things."

"Right," I say, knowing all too well how stories pass from mouth to mouth in our town and how they get progressively better with every telling. "So what's the story you heard?" I'm annoyed, but I'm also curious. Who wouldn't be?

"See, it was, I don't know, 'bout twenty years ago, this guy, John Noble, split from his wife and decided he was gonna kill himself."

Shit. I know the story he's going to tell. I don't think I want to hear it. "You're going pretty far back," I say.

He ignores me. "John was in his twenties, I guess, and he had this little Volvo sports car. But he was all broke up about his old lady leavin' him, and there was a kid, too."

Audrey. Hearing him mention her sends chills through my body. My daughter, now only a little younger than I am in Rob's story. I haven't seen her since she was not quite three.

"So John decides to go upstate to this old house he has and knock himself off."

"It wasn't exactly like that," I say, but Rob continues to ignore me. It's his story and he doesn't want me to interrupt it.

"It's up in some little farming town, north of Troy."

"Easton," I say. He glares at me. His eyes are watery and somehow impish and menacing at the same time. They are clearly telling me not to interrupt.

"This old house up in Easton, New York, was built around 1776, and it had a big central chimney with a lot of fireplaces coming off of it."

"Six."

"In the center of this chimney there was a secret room. It was for the people back then to hide in when Indians came around and caused trouble."

"It was also for hiding from British soldiers," I say. He doesn't want to hear a thing.

"So John buys a bottle of good Scotch and gets in his fancy sports car and goes up there. He has a book of poems by some poet who committed suicide . . ."

"Sylvia Plath."

Rob downs the rest of his bourbon and slams his glass on the bar. Pat O'Ryan, the bartender, takes it as a sign to refill the glass, which it is, but I know it's also a sign for me to shut up.

"He reads this book for a while. Then he starts drinkin' the Scotch, and when he's gettin' a little glow on, he decides it's time to do his thing. But he has his own way of doin' things. Guess it must have been the Scotch and gettin' all romantic about death from this poet."

I think I'm angry, not just with Rob, but also with whoever it was who told him the story. Only a few people know about it, or at least only a few people did. I order a bourbon from Pat, too. Rob goes on with his story.

"So old John takes all his clothes off and turns the oven on, but he doesn't light it. It's the gas he's goin' after, just the way the poet lady did. So he gets some cushions or somethin' from the couch and puts them on a little bench in front of the oven. Then he covers them with a white sheet, and bare-assed as a baby, he lies down and sticks his head in the oven. But then he gets scared or somethin' and decides to have some more Scotch. He's feelin' pretty loose and's probably not sure he really wants to kill himself. So he drinks more Scotch and reads some more poems, and thinks that maybe he doesn't have to stick his head in the oven, that maybe the gas will just fill the room and slowly put him to sleep. I mean kill him easy-like."

"Dammit, that isn't the way it happened." If the story's going around, after all these years, I want it to be told the way it happened. The funny thing is, I'm not really angry. I guess "bemused" is the right word. Bemused and curious. He's got the basics right, but the truth is off. I had actually turned the oven off. I wasn't so sure I wanted to die after all. But Rob isn't interested in that part of the story.

"Old John's sittin' there, guzzlin' the booze and readin' the poems, when he hears a car comin' up this long dirt driveway. 'Shit,' he says, lookin' out the window. It's a cop car. Someone had figured out what he's doin' and has called the cops. Here he is, half drunk, bare-assed and readin' poetry by a dead poet, and this cop car's comin' up his driveway. Then he gets this idea. The secret room. He runs downstairs and moves the trapdoor, which goes to that secret room. He climbs inside and pulls the door shut about the time the cops come in the house. Here's the good part. There's these loose bricks in the fireplaces. Old John, he can move them and see what's goin' on in any room on the first floor of the house, but the cops, they can't see anything. John's standin' there in this little secret room, hoping like hell those cops, there was two of them, don't know anything about this room. He felt pretty ridiculous standin' there with no clothes on and sure didn't want the cops findin' him like that, if you know what I mean."

"I do know what you mean," I say. "This is the only part of the story you've gotten right so far."

He still isn't interested. "So those cops, they're about to shit when they smell gas and see the cushions by the oven. They first think he's already killed himself, but then one of the cops—and this is when things get funny—one of the cops realizes if he'd killed himself, there'd be a body there. There's this talk about how maybe he gassed himself and then staggered outside, where there are about two thousand acres of summer corn growin'. Maybe he got enough gas, then went out to die, the way dogs do sometimes, just creep out in the woods or someplace and die alone. So that's what these cops start to figure. Then one of them picks up this book of poems and for some reason knows this poet killed herself."

"That's not at all true," I say. "The cop had never heard of Sylvia Plath."

"So the cops get all mystical, thinkin' this guy, old John Noble, really has killed himself, and instead of leavin' a suicide note has left this book by some dead poet as a clue. One of the cops says, 'Yeah, he was supposed to be a book nut, that's what they said. Went to college.' The cops talk and decide maybe John's still alive, but know they'll never be able to find him if he's out in the middle of the cornfield. So one decides they should radio for more cops and a dog to search him or his body out. Now, what you gotta understand is John's seein' and hearin' all this, and he's gettin' sober fast as hell. He's hidin' in this chimney, thinkin', 'What the fuck am I gonna do now,' when he hears one of the cops say, 'We'd better park out by the road so they can find us. This isn't the easiest place to find.' So that's what they do. John hears them talkin' on the radio, then he hears their car pull away. Now he's got his chance, and he knows what he's gonna do. He gets out of that secret room and puts his clothes on. Then he goes outside and gets in that fast sports car of his. He figures he'll pass the cops at the end of the driveway and outrun them."

I interrupt again and try to explain that I didn't know the cops were going to be at the end of the driveway. I thought they had left, because I didn't hear them say anything about calling for more help. Rob is glaring at me. His eyes are very watery. I don't know if it's from the liquor or if it's because I'm interrupting his story. It's strange, but I'm feeling sorry for him, and I decide to try and let him tell it his own way. We both finish our whiskey and order fresh drinks from Pat. I pay for this round.

Rob downs his drink in one gulp and doesn't bother to wipe his lips this time. Misty bourbon spews onto the bar as he tells me what happened.

"So John's drivin' down that long dirt driveway, just prayin' those cops haven't blocked it where it meets the highway. But his prayers don't do any good, because when he gets there, the car's parked right in the middle. John thinks real fast and figures he can get past them if he guns his car and shoots past the cops through the corn growin' there." Rob smiles, anticipating what he's going to say next. I grin, too. He doesn't have it exactly right, but he's close enough.

"Those cops nearly snap their heads off when they hear that little car and then see a streak of yellow shoot through all that corn. The one cop who's drivin' gets so excited about goin' after John that he stalls the engine, and by the time he gets it goin' again, old John's halfway to Troy. The cops turn the siren and red lights on and take off after him. They probably know they can't catch him, so they radio on ahead to some other cops. Least, that's what I'd do."

I feel the liquor now and I laugh and say, "I'm glad you feel you can speculate a little."

He gives me a look of disgust when he says, "They'd never have caught him if John hadn't wanted them to. That's where John outfoxed them, if you know what I mean."

I do, but I don't say anything.

"John, he was playing a game with them now, sort of jerking their chains around. Just as those cops figure they'll never stop him, John slams on the brakes and pulls over. The cops are goin' so fast they nearly pass him. But they finally get stopped next to the little Volvo, and the one cop who's ridin' shotgun says, 'Get out of the car.' But John doesn't move. The cop gets out of his car and goes over to John. He has his hand on his gun. John still doesn't move. 'Okay, buddy, get out of the car,' the cop says. This is where John gets him. He just sits there and says, 'What you gonna do if I don't, shoot me?' The cop pulls his gun and says, 'That's right,' and John shrugs his shoulders and starts laughin'. 'Okay,' he says, 'that's what I'm here for.' "

Rob's laughing and wheezing as he tells this part of the story. I can't help myself, and I laugh, too. I see Pat standing over us behind the bar, and I think he's going to cut us off because we've had too much to drink. He's a good-natured Irishman, about sixty-five, and while he can put his liquor down as well as anyone can, he tends to think of some of his patrons as his responsibility, if not his children. He expects people like Rob Dawson to get drunk to the pass-out stage, but I guess he works to protect the dignity of the rest of us.

Anyway, when I think Pat's going to cut us off, he starts laughing, too, and says, "Well, by Jesus, if that's what you said to the cop, I'll drink to it, and I'll buy the next round for you very fine gents as well." He pours, and Rob, delighted to have so distinguished an audience now, goes on with the story.

"You get it?" Rob says, laughing and gulping simultaneously. "He says, 'That's what I'm here for.' You should have seen the expression on that cop's face, and on the other cop's face, too. He got out of the car soon as he saw his partner draw the gun, and he knew that wasn't right."

Even I have to admit that Rob is convincing. He's telling it as though he had been there, and he's got my attention. I no longer want to interrupt him and tell him what really happened. His version is better than mine could ever be, and it's not that far from the truth.

"So this other cop, the one who doesn't have his gun out, tells his buddy to put his away, and then he starts talkin' in a nice way to John. He says, 'Look, there are some people down in Woodstock who are worried about you. We're worried, too, and we want to help. Just talk if you want to.' John looks at him, and he's not laughing now. He knows this cop's a nice guy. He's older, probably in his fifties, and he's, I don't know, like some kind of father figure to John then.

"The other cop, the one who pulled his gun, puts it away and lets the older guy do the talkin'. John's feelin' pretty mixed up now, and he realizes he does want to talk. So he gets in the cop car and they just drive around the countryside and talk. John tells them about his lady and little girl and how upset he is about losin' them and all, and the cops just talk to him in a nice way and make him feel better."

Rob's crying as he tells the last part of the story. "You know what those guys did?" He wipes his eyes with his cuff. I'm feeling a little teary myself now, because I clearly remember what they did. "Those guys, especially the older one, you know the one who seemed a little like a father, they said they'd take John to a shrink if he wanted to see one, but then the older one, he said, 'We'll take you if you think you need one, but I don't think that's what you really want, do you?' John shook his head, and the cop said, 'I got a great idea. You know where we're goin'? We're goin' to the county fair. We'll just have ourselves a hell of a time.' "

Now Rob's smiling again. So are Pat and I. "That's just what they did, too. John went to the county fair with those two cops. They rode on all the rides together, ate a bunch of cotton candy and popcorn, and did all the things kids and their parents do at county fairs. That's the honest-to-God truth. After the fair, they took John back to his house, and the old cop said, 'You gonna be all right here? Want us to stay with you?' John says, 'No, I'm fine now.' And he was."

Rob's through with his story now and is asking Pat for another drink. Pat asks if I want one, and I shake my head no. Reluctantly, he gives Rob a drink. I get up from the bar stool, realizing I've got to get home while I can still drive. Rob turns to me and says, "What I want to know is, why didn't you kill yourself? I mean, before the cops came?"

I shrug and say, "You tell me. It's your story."

Rob Dawson is very drunk now, but he still manages a grin when he says, " 'Cause if you were dead, I couldn't ask you for a job."

I'm suddenly fond of this sad little guy, and that's why I offer him the job.

Of course, he never shows up for work. I'm not surprised, but I'm sad about it. At least I was finally able to offer him the job, and I guess that's all he really wanted.

II _____

My two sons have heard me talk about Leslie Summers, and they know they have a half sister somewhere in California, but they don't know this in a concrete way. To Jack, the ten-year-old, Audrey is only a name that sometimes comes up, usually when I'm a little drunk and being sentimental. To Mike, who's fourteen, she's less abstract. Once when we were talking about her, he said, "I think of her as being like someone in a movie I've heard about but haven't seen. I know she's somewhere in California, but she doesn't mean anything to me. Guess I'll have to see the movie first." I don't think my wife, Kay, gives any thought to Leslie or Audrey. To her, they're a dead part of my past, just as her first husband is a dead part of hers. Kay is a practical woman. To her, life moves forward. I'm not so practical, and I tend to take frequent excursions backward. Kay is warm and understanding, but I don't think she realizes how important it is for me to find my daughter and get to know her. Rob Dawson's story made it more urgent. I don't know exactly why but it did.

I'm forty-nine, and as far as I know, I'm not senile, nor am I particularly forgetful, yet I often find that I confuse my day-to-day life with my past, as well as with my dreams—my literal sleeping dreams. I sometimes try consciously to sort these things out, but I usually end up with a blur of vignettes.

Being honest is easier now, but I still catch myself wanting, and maybe needing, to polish the edges of my memory. For example, there's something vague and wispy in my brain that makes me want to believe that I met Leslie Summers on the day John Kennedy was assassinated, although I know it was actually six or eight weeks earlier. Like everyone who is old enough to remember Kennedy's murder, I can remember virtually every moment of that day: I'm a twenty-four-year-old journalism major at the University of Colorado in Boulder, and I have a morning job with a weekly newspaper in Denver, so I'm in my office when my mother calls to tell me the president has been shot. I hang up the phone and turn the office radio on. Kennedy is being rushed to a Dallas hospital. As I drive back to Boulder in my beat-up '49 Chevy, the radio tells me Kennedy is dead. This was *my* president, the first presidential candidate I'd been old enough to vote for. I pull to the shoulder of the Denver–Boulder Turnpike and cry.

This is when I wish I had met Leslie Summers. Leslie changed my life the way Kennedy's death changed America, and I want to be able to remember clearly everything that led to my change as I remember everything that led to America's.

But I can't. Not without making things up. I sometimes blame my dishonesty on Leslie Summers, because she was a natural liar; however, it took me a long time to realize it. She told stories to fill the spaces. She couldn't stand voids in logic, so she rearranged facts in order to make sense of her life.

III _____

I love wood. I like to shape it, sand it and finish it. If I had more patience, I'd be a good furniture maker. But I don't have that kind of patience. It's not that I don't take my time to work the wood so it's just right. I get a great deal of pleasure out of that. It is, rather, that I like big projects. I like to design and build houses—big houses. Whenever possible, I like to build with native lumber, which in upstate New York is most commonly white pine, hemlock, maple and oak. It used to be my dream to own or at least lease several hundred acres of wood lots and have my own mill. I wanted to cut my logs and mill the lumber myself and then let it season out in the open, the way the early English and Dutch settlers did it. But that was only a dream. When I was younger and had the energy for such an enterprise, I didn't have the money. Now that I do have the money, I have neither the strength nor the time.

But still I like to use native lumber when possible. This isn't for practical reasons. I suppose it's for ethical reasons. I like the idea of taking wood from a forest, shaping it, and then returning it to the forest from which it came. I buy from local mills, usually a year or so before I'm going to use it. I sticker it, which means I put spacers between the planks and leave them outside where the air can get to them. This natural seasoning is much better than kiln drying. Once the lumber has seasoned, I run it through a large planer. I do

13

this even with framing lumber. Most builders don't do this. By running it through the planer, I can get it to the exact dimension I want, and I can make certain the dimension is true.

If the lumber has been planed to exact dimensions, it's going to be easier to handle when construction begins. The men who work for me are not going to be spending half their time digging splinters out of their hands. Also, the framing members are going to be uniform. There's nothing more exasperating for a carpenter, a good carpenter, than framing a building and later discovering the studs, rafters, joists and collar beams are uneven. When this happens, nothing farther down the line fits perfectly. This early care doesn't appeal to a lot of builders and customers, because it seems as though nothing is happening. Most people want instant gratification. It is exciting to see walls go up in a matter of hours, but it isn't so exciting later on when nothing fits right.

There's another reason for doing things right, for making certain every structural member of a building has its integrity. This is obscure and personal, but it's also very important. Every building, be it a small shed or a huge mansion, reflects lives. People construct these buildings, people use them. People are conceived and born in some of them, and people die in them. Buildings are wombs for the living and, if allowed to stand long enough, epitaphs for the dead.

Several years ago I was hired to remodel the top two floors of an old apartment building in New York City for a young married couple. Included in the project was cutting a hole through a wall and installing a maple butcher-block counter between the kitchen and dining room. First I had to chisel the plaster away. Then I had to cut and remove the wood lath. And finally I had to cut out several studs. These studs had been buried for over a century, and now fate and good timing were allowing me to uncover them.

There was a ghost in this wall, and for a moment I thought I might be the reincarnation of this ghost. Except for the nail holes and the plaster and lath markings, the studs looked as though they had just been set in place. But more important was that they had been planed to perfection, not by a modern machine like mine, but by a loving carpenter's hand planer. Even before I checked with my tape measure, I knew what the dimensions of these studs would be. They were true 2x4s. The carpenter of the 1880s who framed this section of the building was not under orders to take such care with the wood he used, at least not with the framing materials. I know this because later in the project I cut into other walls which had been built by different carpenters, and the studs were what I expected: rough-cut and *close* to being true.

There was another bonus for me in this wall. The carpenter who had so carefully handled and shaped his materials had also left a gift for me, for the carpenter of another century who would uncover his work. On one of the studs there was a pencil drawing of a woman's slightly plump leg, complete with frilly garter and a laced Victorian boot. The drawing gave me a companion who worked and joked with me throughout the project. I'm sure the young couple I was working for will never be aware of this, but the work my ghost and I did for them is as close to perfect as carpentry can be. If in another century this building is remodeled again, some carpenter may be fortunate enough to chance upon one Victorian leg as well as one slim naked leg from the late twentieth century.

I wish I had known about good carpentry twenty-five years ago when I met Leslie Summers. I don't remember the exact circumstances of our meeting. It had to be in either September or early October of 1963, because I remember fall colors in Boulder, where we were both students, and I also remember Leslie's deep tan and sun-bleached hair, which showed it hadn't been long since she had been stretched out on a beach on Long Island, where she said her family had a summer house. I think my roommate, Yanish Johnson, met her first, but I may be making this up because it seems logical. Yanish almost always met girls first. He was my height, about six-two, but that's where the similarity ended. Unlike me, he had an athlete's lean and well-developed body. I'm not good when it comes to recognizing what women find attractive in men, but I always knew what it was in Yanish. He had a clear, healthy, boyish face, with deep-blue Nordic eyes that somehow drew you into them. And he had an almost too perfect smile that showed off his even white teeth. Yanish simply looked the way most men would like to look.

That's why I think he met Leslie Summers first. She couldn't have helped being attracted to him. I don't know how I ended up being her boyfriend unless it was because of persistent determination on my part. I was in love with her the first time I saw her— from the first time Yanish brought her to our small apartment.

She was trim, about five-six, and almost always wore well-tailored clothing, which I thought of as very feminine and New York chic. Although I can't remember the time and circumstance now, I can clearly recall what Leslie was wearing the first time we went out on a date, which was actually a study break: a colorful madras skirt, a pale-blue blouse with a button-down collar and long sleeves, brown Bass Weejun penny loafers. I can close my eyes even now and bring her image to my mind. Her face is almost Indian-looking, especially with her tan. Her cheekbones are high and have a fine sculpted look. Her eyes are black and intelligent-looking; they somehow suggest there is a lot going on, that there is a quick mind behind them. She has shoulder-length blond-brown hair which is baby-fine and hangs straight except for a little wisp which she constantly brushes away from her right eye. Her smile reveals beautiful, straight white teeth. I notice teeth frequently, because my own have always given me trouble.

Our first date was short and simple. We had coffee at a café on the Hill, a block of shops, 3.2 beer bars, restaurants and book-stores near the university campus. I don't remember much of what we talked about, but I do know Yanish was mentioned several times, and I was jealous. I wanted to tell her he was a bastard when it came to girls, that he wanted only one thing from them, and when he got it, he dropped them and went on to the next con-quest. But I didn't say this. Instead, I praised him, said he was a good guy, a great roommate and all that sort of thing. I had a kind of what-the-hell attitude, because it seemed clear that she was out with me just so she could get more information about him. At least that's the way I saw it, and since I didn't think I'd get anywhere, I didn't see any sense in ruining Yanish's chances.

When I took her back to Farrand Hall, the dorm where she lived, she did something that screwed me up for weeks. With absolutely no warning, she put her arms around me and kissed me on the mouth. Then she said, "Thank you for a wonderful evening, John." She went inside and I didn't see her again for over a month.

That kiss still haunts me. I can feel her firm body against mine and I can taste the moisture of her lips. There was a momentary and mutual frenzy about the impulsive kiss, and I should have treated it as a warning, but I didn't. I didn't because I was in love.

I tried to call Leslie Summers several times the next day, but there was never an answer. The following day was equally fruitless, so I finally called the dorm's housemother, who curtly told me it was against university policy to discuss a student's whereabouts.

"But this is urgent," I protested.

"Are you a member of her family?" she asked with a tone that made her sound like a funeral director.

I almost said I was her brother, but ended up replying, "No."

The bitch hung up on me.

A week went by and I still couldn't reach Leslie. I loitered around Farrand Hall, hoping I'd see her. I asked other girls if they knew her. But nothing worked. It was as if she didn't exist, and I almost began to believe I had made her up. I checked in the admissions office, but was given the same story about university policy. I finally told Yanish I was in love with Leslie. I expected him to turn on me, but he didn't. He was in pursuit of another girl and had almost forgotten Leslie Summers.

More time passed. Days and then weeks. Sometimes I'd wander around campus aimlessly, hoping I'd run into her. Other times I'd go to the café where we'd had our date, and I'd sit at the same table, thinking she'd appear, as if she'd just gone to the bathroom and was coming back to join me. I began cutting classes and sat for hours at a time by the phone. I went to the phone company and got a directory for Manhattan, because that was where she'd said her father lived. There were forty-nine listings under the name Summers. I tried all of them, even the business numbers, by making person-to-person calls for Leslie. No one had ever heard of her. I tried Somers and Sommers, but still didn't have any luck. I did get a Leslie Sommers who turned out to be a lonely woman from Sweden who wanted to talk.

I began getting notices from my instructors, asking why I hadn't been attending classes. After about three weeks, my mother called and said she was getting notices, too. I explained that I had been sick, which wasn't entirely a lie, but that I was better and had started going back to class. I tried to talk to Yanish about what was going on, but he didn't take it seriously. He had no conception of what it was to be in love with a girl, and he certainly didn't understand what it was to have problems with one.

I began hallucinating. The first time it happened I was in Denver, where I was still managing to go to work most mornings. I was walking toward the post office when I began to feel light-headed. There was a humming sound and I lost my peripheral vision. Yellow spots were darting back and forth in front of my face, and I fully expected to die without ever seeing Leslie Summers again. Then I saw her. She was sitting on the post-office steps about half a block away.

I began running toward her, calling, "Leslie!" She was just sitting there, calmly eating an apple as I approached her.

"Leslie," I said, standing in front of her, trying to catch my breath.

"What the fuck you want, mister?" said the old woman who was sitting in Leslie's place, rummaging through a King Soopers grocery bag.

I could only stare at her. She had been Leslie, but now she was an old woman, wearing a filthy blue stocking cap and a tattered gray overcoat.

"Go on, get the fuck outta here."

I said, "I'm sorry," and walked on.

After that, I began hallucinating frequently, usually while I was trying to sleep. Leslie would float through my bedroom wall and approach my bed. I'd call out to her, but she'd put a finger to her lips and say, "Ssh." I'd reach for her as she got closer, but then she'd laugh and turn away. I'd try to get out of bed and go after her, but there were always weights around my ankles and wrists.

In my deepest moments of depression, I lost all hope of ever seeing Leslie Summers again. Sometimes I would make myself believe she was a dream, one of those dreams one tries desperately to go back to. If I could only catch another glimpse of her, I thought, I could hold her forever. But she refused to appear, and I had to admit that she was not a dream. Sometimes I would think I'd never see her again because she was dead. I'd tell myself I should have known when she kissed me that she was desperate and anxious, even suicidal. Then I would blame myself for not being more sensitive. I imagined a dark and secretive past for her, and I was reminded of my own childhood suicidal obsessions. Demons started coming in my sleep when I was five or six. They'd laugh and point to a long, high black wall over which I could see bright, colorful lights, and they'd tell me that was where I should be. They'd tell me my father was on the other side of the wall, and I'd beg them to take me there, to the other side. I knew Germany was on the other side of the wall. Germany was where the war was, and that was where my mother said my father's plane had been shot down. If I could get to Germany, I'd find my father.

I would try to ride my bicycle to the wall so I could look over, but no matter how hard I pedaled, the wall remained in the distance. When I knew I couldn't make it on my bicycle, I'd try my pogo stick. I would start jumping up and down on it. When I got going, I could see our whole neighborhood, all the plain brick houses and neat yards on our block. Then I'd go higher and I could see all of Denver, with snow-capped mountains to the west. Far below, I could hear the demons shouting and laughing, and then I'd turn just slightly and see the wall. It didn't matter how high I jumped, the wall was always higher. Germany would always be on the other side, and there was only one way for me to get there and be with my father. The pogo stick would slowly bounce to a rest on earth and the demons would be there, shaking their heads in amusement and saying, "We told you so."

Now those demons began following me again everywhere I went. If I could have thoughts of suicide, why couldn't Leslie have them, too? Maybe she was braver or more desperate than I, and maybe she had acted on her thoughts, or desperation. Would I ever be that brave or that desperate?

Eventually, my what-the-hell attitude returned, and that, of course, was when Leslie Summers reappeared in my life. I was gloomily walking across campus to my geology class, thinking about sea gulls, wondering why there were so many in Boulder, which is around twelve hundred miles from the nearest ocean. I didn't really care about the answer.

But sea gulls were what my mind was occupied with when I heard a cheerful voice say, "Hi, stranger."

I froze. This wasn't another of my hallucinations. I knew that, but still I was wary. She materialized, hooked her arm in mine and continued walking with me. "Hey, aren't you glad to see me?" she asked. She was smiling broadly. Her gorgeous white teeth glistened in the sunlight, and I realized I hadn't noticed it was a beautiful autumn day.

"Of course I'm glad," I managed to say. I wanted to take her in my arms and kiss her, but I didn't. "Where have you been?"

My tone must have sounded hostile, because she said, "I meant to call you, but I couldn't."

"You don't owe me anything."

"Hey, come on," she said, pulling away from me. She was laughing now and playfully punching me. "I had to go home for a while, and I just couldn't . . . Okay, I didn't call. I thought about you, though. Does that count?"

"Sure it counts." I was beginning to loosen up. She didn't, in fact, owe me anything, and she didn't know what I had been going through.

"Where you headed?"

I lied and said, "Just wandering." Going to class was the farthest thing from my mind.

She held my hand and said, "Mind if I wander with you?"

That afternoon we bought a six-pack of Coors and drove my old Chevy up to Flagstaff Mountain, which looks out over Boulder and the eastern Colorado plains. There are numerous parking areas on Flagstaff, which have been popular with high school and college lovers for generations. Leslie and I found one of the more secluded spots. I was, of course, curious about her trip home, but she dismissed my curiosity with "I had some personal business to deal with." Then she manipulated the talk to questions about me.

I told her my younger brother and I had been raised by our mother, who had been widowed during the last days of World War II, when our father's plane was shot down in Germany. Leslie was interested in knowing more about our mother, why she had never remarried, and how she had raised and supported us.

"I don't know why she never remarried," I said. "She was very young and good-looking when my father died, and I remember there were men around in those days. I don't know for sure, but I think it had a lot to do with the fact that she had to work hard to support Bob and me. When she did have free time, she spent it with us. You know, Cub Scouts, Boy Scouts, all that."

"Where does she live now?"

"Denver. We've lived there all my life. Since I was a baby, I mean. I was actually born in Wyoming, but Mom and my father moved to Denver before the war. That's why I'm here at CU. I'm a resident."

Leslie laughed and asked, "Why'd you start school so late?"

"I didn't exactly," I said. "I did begin right out of high school in '57, but dropped out after the first semester. I really didn't know what I wanted to study, and there was the problem of money. Also, I guess I had wanderlust."

She edged closer to me and rested her hand on my knee. I wanted to put my arm around her, but I didn't, not then, because I didn't want to do anything that might scare her off.

"What do you mean by wanderlust?" she asked. "Did you just take off and travel?"

"No, not exactly. I went to New Orleans, where I have an aunt and uncle and some cousins, and stayed with them while I tried to join the Merchant Marine."

"Really?" She squeezed my knee. "That sounds exciting."

I should have detected something then in her tone that suggested her life had not been filled with excitement, at least not with pleasant excitement, but I didn't. I was too busy trying to make myself sound interesting to her. "At first, it wasn't at all exciting," I said. "I used to hang around the union office at the shipyard every day. I was always told the same thing: 'You can't get your papers without experience, and you can't get experience without your papers.' I was discouraged at first, and I almost gave up, but then I met a guy one day. He was a ship's cook. We got to talking and ended up getting drunk together in the French Quarter. He said he needed a cook's assistant and promised to see what he could do about helping me get my papers. The next day I had a bad hangover and realized that everything this guy had told me was probably bullshit, and I almost didn't go to the union office that day. Thank God I did, though, because when I got there, this guy at the front desk who had been discouraging me for so long said, 'Hey, Noble, these are for you.' He handed me some papers, and that was it. All I had to do was pay my union dues and I was in."

"So you shipped out, just like that?" Leslie asked.

"Yeah. Two days later I was out on the high seas on my way to Bombay."

"India?" she asked.

She was impressed. At least, I responded as if she were. "Yep, all the way to India. First we made stops in Hong Kong and Japan, and then we went on to India. God, what a country that is."

"What do you mean? All the people and the poverty?"

"Yeah, but it's more than that. Bombay's an incredibly busy city, day and night. People are always hustling, everywhere. Sure, there are the beggars and the whores, but there's a lot more than that.

There are a lot of rich people in India, too. I'd see all these very well-dressed businessmen in their expensive suits hurrying all over town. I've never been to New York, but I bet it's similar to Bombay. I mean, there aren't oxen and women in saris on the streets of New York, the way there are in Bombay, but I have a feeling things are similar."

Leslie laughed. "Not many oxen, but there are plenty of women in saris and everything else you can imagine." She momentarily rested her head on my shoulder, and I could smell her fresh, fine hair. There was nothing I wanted more than to hold her and kiss her and maybe make love to her, but the time wasn't right.

At one moment when I brushed her hair with my lips, she said, "Tell me about the whores in Bombay. Did you sleep with any of them?" She pulled away as she asked and opened two more cans of Coors. Her question sounded frivolous, but I should have noticed it was serious.

I didn't notice, though, probably because I was embarrassed. "There's really not much to say about the whores," I said.

"Come on," Leslie said, laughing again. "How many did you sleep with?" She handed me a beer and playfully punched me in the ribs.

"Just one," I said. "It wasn't very exciting, though." I wanted to get to another topic, but she wouldn't let me.

Still laughing, she said, "Why? What was wrong with it?"

By "it," she meant the sex, and I could feel my ears turning red. "I don't know," I said.

"Come on," she teased. "You can do better than that."

I forced a laugh and said, "Well, if you want the truth, there were several things wrong with it. I went to this whorehouse, this brothel, with two other guys who'd been there before, and, I don't know, I guess I was more excited by the idea of it all than I was by anything else."

"What do you mean?"

"I'm not sure. The whole thing was kind of depressing."

"How?"

"I don't know. There were all these women with hardly anything on, just standing around, looking bored, and waiting for some sailor to go off to bed with them."

Leslie tossed her head in an almost defiant way and said, "They wouldn't have been there if it hadn't been for all you horny sailors." She laughed again and said, "You haven't told me what was wrong with it."

"The truth is, it was my first time."

"You mean you were a virgin?" There was sympathy as well as humor in her tone.

"Yeah, I was a virgin."

"That should have been a great experience for you, then."

I couldn't tell if she was curious about my virginity and my first real sex experience because she was a virgin herself or because she was much more knowledgeable about the ways of sex than I was. I was still too embarrassed and sorry I had brought up the subject of whores to think of anything but my own dilemma.

Somehow, I managed to say, "I guess it would have been a good experience if it hadn't been for two things." I paused, waiting for her to ask what the two things were, but she remained silent, so I finally said, "First, there were a lot of very good-looking women, actually girls, there and I was trying to make my way to one who was especially beautiful. She couldn't have been more than fifteen or sixteen, and I don't know, she just didn't look like a prostitute."

"What does a prostitute look like?"

"I don't know. Lots of makeup, kind of cheap-looking, I guess."

"Like in the movies?"

I shrugged. "Yeah, I guess so."

"So tell me about your little whore."

Something about the way she emphasized "your little whore" bothered me, but I went on with my story. "I never got to her. I was walking toward her when another woman, another whore, stopped me and gave me a drink. She was very ugly and fat. I didn't know what to do. Like I said, I wasn't experienced, and, well, she just started talking and laughing, and I somehow ended up going to bed with her."

"That's too bad," Leslie said. She leaned over and kissed me on the cheek.

"What do you mean?"

She said, "I mean your first experience should have been beautiful."

I shrugged again. "Well, what could I do?"

"So that was it? You made love and left?"

"I wouldn't exactly call it making love," I said.

She laughed. "You fucked and left?"

That question caught me off guard, even more than her other questions had. In 1963, when I was twenty-four and Leslie Summers was eighteen, the word "fuck" wasn't commonly used, at least not when a boy and girl were talking to each other. Her direct and natural use of it had an extraordinary impact on me. Some of this had to do with our ages and the fact that I was caught in the abyss of love, but I'm sure it also had to do with the times. In 1963, I think those of us who had begun to mature in the fifties were still recoiling from a bizarre and by then invisible cross of McCarthyite and post-Victorian morality. Boys and girls did talk about sex, and they had it, too, but they didn't, at least as far as I knew, sit around talking about whores and fucking. But that's what Leslie and I were talking about, and despite my discomfort then, I knew I was with an extraordinary girl, and I loved her that much more for it.

"Yeah," I said, "I fucked and left." I should have left it at that, but I didn't. Something—maybe it was the beer and my brave new use of the word "fuck"—caused me to say, "That wasn't exactly the end of it, though."

"How do you mean?" she asked.

Sorry I'd opened my mouth, I said, "A few weeks later, when I was back on ship, I discovered I had the clap."

I don't know what I expected her reaction to be, but it wasn't anything like what I got. She put her arms around my neck, pulled me toward her, and kissed me. It was a long, passionate kiss. When it ended, she said, "That was a terrible first experience." She kissed me again, lightly this time, and ran her fingers through my hair. Then she whispered, "When we make love, I promise it will be a lot better."

It was some time before Leslie Summers and I ever made love.

IV

Rob Dawson has been barred from the Duck & Dog. Pat is saying,
"By Jesus, Johnny, you should've seen the man. Never have I seen a
nut slip so completely off its screw before. It was as if Satan himself
had crept into the man's body and taken over. On Monday mornin'
it was, he came in, carryin' a wooden toolbox. God only knows
where he found it. It was an ancient thing and as filthy as it was
old. It was full of things, by Christ, it was. A rusty handsaw with a
broken handle, a hammer with a wooden handle and broken claw,
screwdrivers, pliers, half a wooden rule, you name it, and by God it
was there. So Rob, he puts this on the bar. Right here."

Pat slaps the bar top in front of me. "And damned if he doesn't
start spreadin' his conglomeration of tools all over the place, from
here to creation. I say to the man, 'What in Christ's name are you
doin'?' And he comes right back, sayin', 'I got me a job.' I try to
congratulate him and encourage him to put his tools away at the
same time, when he says, 'Buy the bar a round.' Christ, Johnny, it's
only ten o'clock in the mornin' and he and I are the only ones in
the entire place, so, thinkin' the man's jokin', I say, 'That's a big
order for this time a day.' God in heaven, I shouldn't've said it, for
he picks up his hammer and slams it down, right here on this very
spot."

Pat runs his fingers over a deep impression on the mahogany bar top. "I can't believe what my eyes are seein', but I tell him that isn't the proper thing to do in a public establishment such as this, and he says, God strike me dead if I'm not tellin' the truth, he says, 'Public establishment, my ass! This is my home, and I'll have that round now.' Well, what could I do but take pity on the poor man. It was clear he needed a drink, and by Jesus I was feelin' the urge myself. So he sat there, nippin' at the tail of the dog that bit him, and I said, 'What's the new job you got?' Christ, you'd think I'd called him the son of a whore, the way he came back at me. 'What kind of job you think I got?' he yells out. 'You were here, you heard, just as clear as I did. You heard John Noble say I could come to work for him.' "

I'm listening to Pat as he brings me into his story about Rob Dawson, and I feel as though I have drifted into space and am looking back at the earth and slowly focusing in, first on the small Catskill mountain town of Woodstock, New York, then on the spire of the Dutch Reformed church on the village green, and then on the Duck & Dog, and finally on the bar where Pat is talking to a man who is me.

Rob, it seems from Pat's story, has taken it upon himself to be my soul and conscience. Before Pat finally had to kick him out of the Duck & Dog, Rob told another story about me. God knows where he gets his material, but from Pat's description, the story is largely accurate. It takes place before the Easton suicide story. Leslie has left me and taken off with Audrey, our young daughter. Rob hasn't told the story exactly as it happened, but he's close enough with his conclusion, in which I end up losing my child.

And now Pat's telling me Rob is off on what he called a global search to reunite me with my long-lost daughter.

V _____

Leslie Summers was the smartest and most creative person I ever knew. I have referred to her as a natural liar, which is accurate, but I should explain that her fabrications went far beyond the boundaries of "little stories" or "white lies." They were works of art, and as I realized years later, they were necessary for her survival. When she decided on a story, she treated it the way I treat wood. She carefully selected it and prepared it. Once it was seasoned in her mind, she trimmed every loose end precisely and carefully joined all the pieces. Then she planed, sanded and finished her story to perfection. I'm a skilled carpenter, but I could never build a house as well as Leslie could construct stories.

Of course, I'm making this analogy twenty-five years after I first fell in love with Leslie. In late 1963, I didn't know anything about carpentry, and I knew very little about Leslie Summers.

A few days after I had told the story about losing my virginity with the whore in Bombay, Leslie and I met after class for what I thought was going to be a quick coffee date. We were holding hands and walking across campus toward the Hill, when I noticed her hand was perspiring. That seemed odd, because it was a cold day and snow was falling. "You all right?" I asked.

She stopped and said, "No."

28

"Are you sick?"

"I'm not sick. It's something else." She began nervously searching through her purse. As she did this, I was reminded of the bag lady on the post-office steps in Denver. I think I was afraid Leslie was going to change, as she had in my first hallucination. Something momentarily caused me to believe she was going to become that pathetic old woman.

Leslie took a package of Pall Malls from her purse. Her hands were trembling as she tapped a cigarette from the pack. My hands were trembling, too, as I lit it.

She took a long, greedy drag on the cigarette, and her nostrils flared as she exhaled the smoke. "There's something I have to tell you."

Tiny flecks of snow were glistening from her hair, and she seemed thinner than she had been a few days earlier. She was also pale, not just because her tan had faded, and she suddenly seemed very fragile.

She looked up at me and said, "I was afraid to tell you why I had to go back to New York. I was going to lie and say my mother had died. That's what I told my instructors and the dean's office. But I'm not going to lie to you." She took another deep drag on her cigarette.

"Can we go somewhere, somewhere private?" she asked. "I have a lot to tell you."

"We can go to my apartment. Yanish is down in Denver today with some new girlfriend."

"Good," she said.

We held hands but didn't speak as we walked the three blocks to my apartment on Pleasant Street.

I wasn't prepared for what Leslie told me when we got to the apartment. She chain-smoked Pall Malls and paced around the tiny combination kitchen–living room. Occasionally she'd stop pacing and would pick up some object and examine it. As she did this, she would nervously bite at her lower lip. She seemed to be weighing thoughts, as though she were silently composing a poem, looking for a cadence.

"I had a baby last summer," she said.

My reaction was multidimensional. Her words, or at least the meaning behind them, seemed to be coming from different angles. "I had a baby last summer." She might as well have said, "I had cancer last summer." That's the way I heard her.

I first felt sympathy for Leslie, but then the words began to take shape in my mind. She'd had a baby. A child. Leslie Summers had gotten pregnant and given birth to a baby.

I think I avoided her eyes as I stumbled over her words. I say this because there's a void in my mind when I think of the time Leslie Summers told me she'd had a baby. When I think of this exact moment, I can't close my eyes and bring her image to mind. I can, however, hear her voice, and I can detect fear and uncertainty in her enunciation.

The words echoed in my head. "I had a baby last summer." Where was the baby? How did Leslie Summers get pregnant? Who was the father?

"Father" was the word that finally stuck. I don't know if Leslie said it then or if I invented it. I began to feel both rage and jealousy. Something, some little switch, tripped in my brain, and any sympathy I had felt for Leslie was suddenly turned inward. I was feeling sorry for myself. Somewhere the word "rape" appeared. Leslie was talking, but I wasn't hearing *her*. Her voice was only background noise as I envisioned myself as the victim, as the one who had been raped.

"His name was Juan Lanzo Ernesto," I finally heard her say.

I stared blankly at her. Whose name was Juan Lanzo Ernesto? I wondered. Nothing was making sense.

"I was raped by a boy named Juan Lanzo Ernesto," she said.

"Oh, Jesus." I put my arms around her. It was as though I was trying to shield her. Our faces were touching, and I kissed her repeatedly on the forehead.

"I'm sorry," I finally said. I don't know if I was saying I was sorry she'd been raped and had a baby or if I meant I was sorry for my reaction, or my lack of reaction.

"There's nothing to be sorry about," she said.

There was everything to be sorry about, but I couldn't express it.

"The baby's dead now," she said. "That's why I had to go home."

"Dead?" I released my hold on her.

"It's for the best," she said.

She sat down at the small kitchen table, and I sat across from her.

"How did the baby die?" I asked, realizing I couldn't even grasp the fact of its birth.

"The doctor called it crib death." She lit another cigarette.

There was something then, something about the way she smoked and looked at me, that caused me to understand there was more to the story than she was telling me.

It seems incredible to me now to realize how Leslie Summers was always able to stay one step ahead of me, how she consistently planted one thought, or emotion, and then diverted me onto something else. Strategy was instinctive with her.

There was passion in Leslie's account of her baby's birth and death, but it was all too fast, although I didn't realize it then. "Birth," "death," and "rape" were fired so rapidly that I didn't have a chance to get my bearings. Whenever I tried to back off and put the pieces together, she would throw another obstacle in my way.

There was a grimace on her face when she began telling me about Juan Lanzo Ernesto.

"I felt sorry for him," she said.

Sorry! I didn't want to hear about him. At that moment, I wanted her to go away. I was the tragic victim then, and I didn't want to know about the sordid details of Leslie's past. I had enough trouble with my own demons, and I didn't want her to provide me with more.

"I felt very sorry for Juan Lanzo Ernesto." Still, the grimace was on her face.

I didn't want to hear his name. Having grown up in Colorado, I assumed he was a Mexican. My own built-in racism told me that. I didn't know about Puerto Ricans in New York, not yet, but Leslie wasn't going to allow me that ignorance for long. She was making it possible for me to fear and hate an entirely different culture. I didn't want to feel that way, but I couldn't help it then. I wondered, momentarily, if I'd feel the same way if Juan had happened to be white and from Boston, and I immediately knew the answer was no. Suddenly, I didn't mind hearing his name. Leslie was giving me a chance to feel superior, to feel hatred.

"Juan was incredibly good-looking and he disrespected everything."

"How did you meet him?" I was angry with myself as soon as I asked. I didn't want to know how he had raped her. I didn't want to know about her child, *their* child. I wanted to stop everything we were talking about. I wanted to delete it from our experience and begin again. I wanted to begin my life with Leslie Summers at that moment. I didn't want a past for either of us, but there I was, asking the question. I'm an idiot, I thought.

She curled her lips, and I imagined that same sudden insolence was what had attracted Juan.

"You're not going to believe this," she said, "but I met him at a Yankees game. No kidding."

The sarcasm was gone now.

"I had gone to the stupid game with several girls from Wharton, this private school I went to, and since I was the only one who didn't know anything about baseball and because I didn't care, I was always the one who went to get sodas and hot dogs for everyone else. I was buying a tray, you know, those cardboard containers of stuff, when I saw three Puerto Rican guys staring at me. They were just standing there, staring, and I was really getting uptight. I mean, here I was, this thoroughbred WASP, looking like a perfect preppy, being stared down by these Puerto Rican Bronx hoods. One guy, Juan, was flashing his white teeth, and I almost expected him to unzip his pants, it was so obvious what he had in mind.

But, no, he just grinned and played with a silver cross that was hanging around his neck."

Leslie was an entirely different person as she told me this story. She was absolutely unaware of the agony I was going through as I listened. At least I thought she was unaware. It was as if she had slipped into a time warp, as if there had been no mention of her baby's birth and death. I was fascinated.

"I couldn't help but stare at him, and his eyes caught me every time. It was the first time I had ever really been turned on by a guy, and I was off guard. I was embarrassed by what I was thinking, by what I was feeling, but then something kind of brought me to my senses and I realized I was being a stupid adolescent."

She paused and glanced at me. Apparently my expression didn't show what I was feeling, because she went on with the story. "So I ignored him. But then, as I was carrying this tray of stuff, Christ, I tripped. Hot dogs and Cokes were flying everywhere, and I fell into some jerk's lap. I started to apologize as I tried to get up, but the idiot hadn't even noticed me. I was dying. Then I felt someone's arms slip around my waist and pull me up. When I was on my feet, I turned around, and there he was. The same Puerto Rican hood with the cross.

"I tried to back away, but I couldn't. He was built like, God, I don't know, Superman. First I was afraid, but then he said something. I didn't know what, my head was still spinning, but it was gentle, even sweet. I glanced around, looking for the other guys, but they were gone. So I looked back at him. He had me this time. I mean his eyes did. Finally, he asked if I was all right, and I said yes. He said good and started to walk away. I don't know what I'd thought he'd do, but it wasn't this. So, like a real jerk, I went after him. He was so indifferent I wanted to kill him. He glared at me with these intense Latin eyes, and I realized I was falling into the weak, helpless little girl role. 'I just want to thank you,' I said. 'You're welcome,' he said. Then he started to walk off again. So, what did I do? I said I'd like to know his name. 'Juan Lanzo Ernesto,' he said. He said it with a fierce sense of pride. I wanted him to say more, to talk to me, but he wouldn't. He wasn't about to humble himself in front of a little gringo chickie. So I stupidly opened my purse and pulled out a pen and a scrap of paper and wrote my name and phone number. He took the paper, flashed me another cocky grin and walked away. 'Maybe I'll call you someday,' he said. Then he was gone—and I was a vegetable."

I was listening, trying to identify with Juan, but knowing I couldn't. I felt even more jealousy as she continued to talk. I was in the position she had been in with him. She had me where she wanted me, and I felt helpless and small. I don't know why, but I asked, "Did he call you the next day?"

She frowned. It was almost a pout, one that I would see frequently as I got to know Leslie Summers. "No, the clever bastard. He waited a week. I was going absolutely crazy. I felt like a sex-crazed idiot. I was this seventeen-year-old, overly protected, rich white girl, and my juices were flowing uncontrollably because of some good-looking Puerto Rican hood I had met at a stupid baseball game."

This was the first mention she had ever made about being rich. It didn't exactly surprise me, but it did stick in my mind. I didn't say anything. Instead, like a fool, I fantasized about being like this Puerto Rican god she was describing, wishing desperately that I could do something to make her juices flow, the way he had. I'm not sure, but I think I was wondering if she was telling me all this, in such detail, because of what I had told her about the whores in Bombay. I wondered if she was somehow trying to get even with me, trying to settle the score.

Leslie lit another cigarette and offered me one. I took it and noticed my hand was shaking as I lit it and listened to her.

"Of course, I couldn't tell anyone about him. I couldn't even tell Mary Beth, my best friend, what I was going through." She laughed. "I mean, can you imagine the talk at a preppy girls' school if I'd let on that I was soaking my panties over a Puerto Rican guy?"

She paused for a reaction, which I'm sure she saw on my face. It must have been the same as it was when she said, "So you fucked and left?" Leslie's directness was startling to me, and it was also very arousing. I wanted to stop her then. I wanted to push her to the floor and make love—no, fuck her. But she put me off effortlessly.

"So, anyway, when I was about to get him out of my mind, out of my pants, there was a phone call. Of course, it was Juan. I was almost prepared for him, but not quite. I expected him to ask me out, and I couldn't wait to tell him I didn't go out with assholes I met at baseball games, but he didn't give me a chance. He just wanted to know how I was. I told him fine, and he just said good and started to hang up. So what did I do. God, I can't believe how stupid I was. I asked him out."

Leslie abruptly stopped talking and looked at her watch. I smoked and waited for her to tell me about her date with Juan, but she didn't. She looked confused for a moment, as though trying to remember something, but, as usual, I missed what was going through her mind. "I have to go now," she said, glancing back at her watch.

I looked at the clock above the sink. It was only six-fifteen. "Don't worry about dinner," I said. "I'll spring for a hamburger."

"No, it's not that." She stood up and gathered her books. Then she said, "John, I don't want to hurt your feelings, but I have to meet a guy. I said I'd meet him at six-thirty."

I felt as if I had been shot. It was impossible for me to understand how she could have told me all these things, these intimate things about her baby, death, rape and Juan, and then simply stand up and say, "I have to meet a guy." She caught my expression immediately, but not without gentleness. "Look, John, I don't mean to be rude, but I've had this date for several days, and I can't get out of it now." She leaned down and kissed me lightly on the lips. "I don't want to hurt you." She backed toward the door and said, "Don't let me hurt you."

I felt numb, hollow, unable to speak, the way I do in nightmares, but I finally managed to lie: "I don't hurt so easily."

She saw through me then, as she would for the next four years, and said, "This guy I'm having coffee with is some football jock who's in one of my classes. You already know how I feel about sports. My regard for football is as high as it is for the Yankees."

"You don't have to explain anything to me," I said with artificial courage.

She brushed a wisp of hair from her right eye and winked. "How about meeting me tomorrow after class?"

"I'm not finished until five," I said defensively. I wanted to shout at her and say, "What about your baby? What about all this shit you've been telling me? What about me? What about the fact that I'm in fucking love with you?" Of course, I didn't say these things.

"Five's fine," she said with an intonation that made it clear that she knew I'd cut classes for the rest of my life to be with her. "I'm out of class early tomorrow, but I like to study in the Memorial Center music room. Why don't you meet me there?"

"Okay," I said. "I'll be there a little after five." I went to the door with her and watched as she walked, under the streetlights and through the light snow, down Pleasant Street.

It was only after she had disappeared that I realized she had been lying about the music room. I studied there all the time and I had never seen her there. This was the first time I caught her in a direct lie.

I went to bed with my clothes on that night and wrestled with my demons.

VI _____

I'm in my pickup in the A&P parking lot, planning to go inside the market to buy the morning *Times* and a carton of glazed doughnuts for Mike and Jack, when I see a strange, gnomelike character creeping out from behind a large garbage Dumpster. It's Rob Dawson. I want to pull out of the lot and avoid a confrontation, but it's too late. It was too late when I pulled in, because as I soon learn, Rob Dawson knows I'm a creature of habit. He has been waiting for me.

He approaches the truck, and I see he's carrying a cracked, time-worn, red patent-leather belt. He's obviously excited as he waves the belt across the windshield, and I see he's missing most of his upper teeth. I hadn't noticed it before, and I wonder if it's because they've just been knocked out or if I had never paid attention. Two weeks ago when we were in the Duck & Dog, when he was telling my story, he laughed a lot. It was dark at the bar, as it always is, but I think I would have noticed if his teeth had been missing.

I roll the window down, and he almost hits me in the face with the belt buckle. "I been lookin' everywhere for you, John. Then I 'membered your truck's here most every mornin'." He's pleased with himself, almost to the point of being delirious, when he chuckles—actually, it's more like a cackle—and says, "I found it. Found the belt."

He offers it to me through the open window, but I can only stare at it and at him. The belt, even with its cracks and age, is colorful in contrast with Rob's grayness and toothlessness.

"I found the belt for you, John."

I touch it lightly, wondering if it's something we talked about during a drunk I can't remember. It can't be the belt he's excited about. That doesn't make sense. I realize it's a child's belt, a little girl's, and it makes me think of the belts every girl in my elementary school wore when I was a kid in the mid-forties.

As I take it, he says, "It's Shirley Temple's belt."

"Huh?" I can't imagine what he thinks I could possibly want with a Shirley Temple belt, or why he thinks I would even know such things existed.

"Goddammit," he yells, "it was Shirley Temple's belt."

It's cold out, very cold, so I say, "Come on around to the other side and get in."

"Take the belt," he insists.

I do and he backs away from the pickup.

"You take care of that belt," he says, urgently. "I nearly got killed gettin' it for you."

"Come on, Rob, get in the truck. Get in and tell me about the belt."

We both see a patrol car coming toward us on Mill Hill Road. Rob turns abruptly and runs back toward the Dumpster. "That's Shirley Temple's belt," I hear him shout one more time. He stops and turns toward me again. "Just you keep it. You keep it and you'll find that kid of yours."

"Wait!" I yell after him. "What are you talking about?" But he's gone.

Rob Dawson is more than a drunk. He's crazy, but there's something about his madness that makes me take him seriously. I look at the belt and turn it in my hands, and I remember when I saw it last.

When Audrey was two, one of her playmates was Myrna Dawson. She always wore the belt and was very proud of the fact that her daddy had gotten it for her when he was in the circus. I didn't know Rob Dawson then, but I did know his daughter, and now as I stare at the belt, I remember Myrna Dawson hung herself last Christmas.

Rob Dawson might as well be speaking in tongues, and for all I know, he is, but I somehow understand he knows more about my daughter than I do. I'm curious and afraid.

VII _____

Leslie Summers was in the music room the next afternoon, and I was surprised. I had dwelled all day on her lie about frequently studying there. I had thought about it on the way to my job in Denver that morning, and I had let it grow and fester during the morning hours. It wasn't that "little lies" normally bothered me. I was used to them, just as I was capable of them. But Leslie's lie had been different, or so it seemed.

Some of this, the way I felt about it, undoubtedly had to do with the fact that I loved her and wanted absolute honesty in our relationship. I had, after all, been honest with her. I thought so, anyway, until I began to realize, that morning in my office, that I had left voids in the things I had told her. The things I had said had been truthful, but there were—and this realization hit hard—all those things I hadn't said. They were the lies. I had told her about the surface things, about my dead father, about my mother and brother, about being in the Merchant Marine, and I had even gone so far as to admit that I had gotten the clap from an ugly whore in India. But I hadn't told her anything about me. I hadn't told her about my demons, about my hallucinations when I was looking for her, I hadn't told her I loved her. I hadn't told Leslie Summers any of the really important things about me.

I was a liar by omission. That was the conclusion I had reached before I got back to Boulder that afternoon. I had caught Leslie in one little lie, and I had come close to risking everything by confronting her with it. Guilt enveloped me when I thought about this. Leslie knew virtually nothing about me, and I knew more about her than I knew about anyone else in the world. Or so it seemed when I took inventory of the "truths" that had passed between us. She owed me nothing, yet she had told me about her baby's birth and death, she had told me (some) about Juan Lanzo Ernesto, who had raped her, she had even told the truth about her date with the football player. Had I been in her place, I knew I would have hidden these things.

It was because of these musings on my dishonesty that I was surprised when I found Leslie Summers waiting for me in the music room. I was ashamed and felt she would have seen through me as I had seen through myself. I wouldn't have blamed her if she hadn't shown up.

She was sitting on the floor next to the Steinway piano, reading a letter, when I saw her. She glanced up and saw me as I approached her. Quickly, she slipped the letter into a book, gathered her other books and stood up.

"Boy, am I glad you're here," she said. "I'm starved."

"Hi. Me, too. I mean, I'm glad I'm here," I said, reaching for her books.

I felt another twinge of guilt. I had automatically reached for her books out of what I thought was good manners, but I realized I was hoping for a glimpse at the letter, which was sticking out from the book she had slipped it into. Was it from a boyfriend in New York? I wondered. From Juan?

"I'll take you up on that offer you made to spring for a hamburger last night," she said.

"You've got a deal." Already, I felt better. Simply being with her again was lifting the weight of the day's thoughts. "Anywhere special?" I asked.

"Yeah, let's go to the Sink." She brushed the ever-menacing

wisp of hair from her face and laughed. "It's got a chaotic feeling that matches my mood today."

I held the music-room door open for her and said, "You've had a rough day?"

"No, not really. Just chaotic."

"What's that mean?"

"Nothing, really." She tried to avoid the question with another laugh, but then thought better of it. She shifted her books and took my free hand in hers. "If you want the truth, Mr. John Noble, my day has been chaotic because I've been thinking about you."

She began taking long strides along the Memorial Center hallway, swinging our arms as we walked.

"Well, I guess I'm flattered to know you've been thinking about me," I said, giving her hand a squeeze, "but I have to admit I'm a little nervous about the chaotic bit."

"Don't be," she said, with a teasing quality in her voice. "It was good chaos. At least, now it's good."

We walked out into the cold, dry Colorado air. Four or five inches of snow had accumulated since the day before, and our boots crunched loudly as we walked toward the Sink, which was on the Hill.

I liked the Sink. It was a noisy 3.2 beer bar and hamburger joint which had been popular with CU students for decades. The front of the place was well lighted, with a few booths, a long bar and a charcoal pit, and was where the more mature, or the more serious, students usually sat, drinking Cokes, eating hamburgers, and discussing Hegel, Kant and whatever else was important to them. The rear of the Sink was at least four times larger than the front, and it was a sort of catacombs with several small rooms. The lights were dim and the crowd was always noisy. It was packed with initial-carved pine tables and benches, and the jukebox was continually blasting. There were crude drawings of generations of students and professors on the walls and ceiling, and there were translucent glass blocks which served as windows.

The corners of the various rooms were always darkest and usually it was difficult to find a table in them, because boys and girls who were seriously in love or who were seriously falling out of love got to them first, and they stayed there.

Chaotic and noisy as it was, I liked the back of the Sink for the sense of comradeship it generated. Virtually everyone who went there went for a good, fun-loving drinking time or for an intimate, darkened, in-the-corner time. I also liked it because of the contrast it held for me. My grandmother, my father's mother, had been a student at CU, maybe fifty years earlier, and had spent a lot of time in the Sink, too. Only then it had been called the Sunken Gardens and had been an ice-cream parlor. Whenever I talked to her, I liked to tease her by telling her how her Sunken Gardens had sunk to the bottom since she had been there.

Leslie and I were fortunate that first time we went to the Sink together. We found an empty table in one of the dark corners.

We made small talk, which I can't remember now, as we ate our hamburgers and drank the first pitcher of beer. But then, as the beer and holding hands began taking effect, our talk took on a more serious nature. I had intentionally avoided asking Leslie about her date with the football player the night before, and that turned out to be good strategy, because she brought it up.

"I'm really glad I went out with the jock last night," she said. There was something mischievous in her face and voice.

I first felt offended, but only for an instant, because she said, "I was glad because he made me realize how lucky I am to know you, John."

"That's flattering," I replied. "At least I think it is."

"It is," she said, squeezing my hand. "He was your standard, let's-get-it-on-baby jerk. Like most of the boys I've met around here. That's why I'm so fond of you. You're not like that."

I wasn't sure I wasn't like that, but I was glad she thought so.

I think she was getting a little high, and I know I was, as we began our second pitcher of beer. She dropped the previous night's date quickly and said, "I know I left abruptly last night."

"You didn't have a choice," I said. I had already forgotten how I felt when she had told me about the date, and forgotten about my musings on my dishonesty.

"I want to tell you more about Juan," she said, giving my hand another gentle squeeze.

"You don't have to." I don't know if I meant I didn't want to hear any more or that I didn't expect her to feel obligated to tell me more.

I'm not sure if I'm making this up now, but I think I remember hearing the Beatles' new song, "I Want to Hold Your Hand," on the jukebox as we talked, as Leslie talked, that night.

"I know I don't have to," she said, "but I want to. I want you to know everything about me so you can decide if you really care for me or not. So you can decide if you care for the real me, not just the person you think I am."

"Care for you," I almost blurted out. I wanted to shout, "I'm in love with you, whoever you are!" But I didn't. Instead, I felt even more guilt because of my own dishonesty, because I had revealed so little of myself. It seemed to me then that I was asking her to accept me on good faith while I was at the same time insisting that she prove her worth to me. That wasn't the way it was, but it was what I was thinking then as she told me more about Juan Lanzo Ernesto.

"After I had asked Juan to go out that first time he called, I thought of every excuse you can imagine so I could get away from Wharton and meet him in the city. I knew how to get around the headmistress and Mrs. Crawford, our housemother. Anyone who's been in prep school knows how to do that, but my real problem had to do with the other girls, especially my best friend, Mary Beth. I couldn't use the same old stories about my mother's sixth miscarriage or about my dumb brother, Scott, who broke his arm in football practice, or about my best friend from the old school who had been killed in an accident. I had used all these excuses, and so had every other girl in the school. I was a wreck, trying to think of something. I almost told Mary Beth what was going on, just so she could help me come up with the best of all possible stories. She was a master at bullshitting people. She was so good that I'm convinced she'll end up doing something like writing speeches for the president.

"Anyway, I thought about getting Mary Beth to help me, but I knew I couldn't. Talented as she was, she also had the biggest mouth at Wharton, and I wasn't about to pick up the rep for asking guys out, especially Puerto Rican hoods from the Bronx. Of course, I thought about lying to Mary Beth, telling her about this super stud from Harvard or somewhere that I'd met, but I knew I couldn't pull it off, because she'd bug me with so many questions that I'd get mixed up and blow it. I didn't have a lot of time, since I'd made the date for Saturday and had only three days to get my act together.

"I finally decided on a simple lie, one that would sound simple at a place like Wharton, anyway. I told Mary Beth and the other girls that I was going to L.A. for the weekend. Not for any particular reason, just to get away and see what happened. That way I wouldn't have to describe some fictitious guy and explain my great romantic encounters when I got back. All I'd have to say was that I had bombed out, that I hadn't met any great guys.

"The whole thing was kind of dumb, but it worked. Once I had started the story, all the girls were encouraging me, and all I had to do with Mrs. Crawford and the headmistress was use the normal excuses.

"I had planned to take the train down to Grand Central on Saturday afternoon, meet Juan there, and go out on our date. But then I thought it would look better if I went on Friday, so everyone would think I was spending the whole weekend in L.A. It wouldn't be a problem, I knew, because Daddy has an apartment on the Upper East Side. I mean, the family lives in Westchester, but Daddy works in the city and has this great apartment for when he works late. He stays there a lot during the week, but on Friday nights he always takes the six-ten martini express back to Croton to spend weekends with the family.

"So I schlepped down to Grand Central on the train, carrying this big suitcase with everything I'd need in Southern California. When I got there, about four that afternoon, I put the suitcase in a locker and wandered around East Side boutiques, waiting until I thought it would be safe to go to Daddy's apartment.

"Anyway, I was wandering around in Bloomingdale's, killing time, when I decided I'd get a new dress, something stunning and sexy. That would show this Puerto Rican creep what class was. My father may not be Dr. Spock's idea of the perfect parent, but I'll say one thing for him. He provided his wife and little darlings with plenty of credit cards, and that's a redeeming quality in anyone.

"So I bought this slinky dress. It was so suggestive it even turned me on, and I could just imagine what it was going to do to my Latin stud, but I didn't care. I felt great in it, and after all, this was for my big trip to L.A., which is how I was going to explain it to Mary Beth and the other girls."

Leslie paused, and even in the darkness of our corner, I saw the pensive look on her face. She pulled her hand away from mine and refilled our glasses with beer. I noticed a slight slur in her voice when she asked, "Do you believe in dreams, John?"

The question sounded oddly out of place. "You mean do I believe there are meanings behind them?"

"Yes and no," she said. She searched through her purse for cigarettes, but couldn't find any. I offered her a Marlboro, which she took. She briefly examined it and neatly snapped the filter off. I lit it and she said, "I hate artificiality."

She took a deep drag on the cigarette and blew the smoke in my face. There was something defiant about the way she did it, and I was annoyed. She picked up the filter from the table and held it toward me. "This kind of artificiality," she said. "If you're going to smoke, smoke."

I was still trying to make sense of her question about dreams, and although I realized she was a little drunk, I couldn't understand why she was now talking about smoking. I wondered if I was drunker than I thought.

She dropped the filter back onto the table and laughed. It was a quick and artificial laugh, one that seemed to contradict what she'd just said about artificiality. "Filters are like condoms," she said.

I was perplexed.

"They get in the way. They take away from the pleasure. If you're going to enjoy something, enjoy it all the way."

I shrugged, not knowing how to respond.

She laughed again. "I'm making a point," she said. This time her laugh was genuine. "But I admit I'm obscuring it. When I asked if you believed in dreams, I didn't want the filtered response you gave me. But that was unfair. I shouldn't have expected you to be on the same wavelength I'm on."

"Hey, wait a minute," I said, trying to lighten the mood, "you're doing it again."

"Doing what?" She brushed her hair from her eyes.

"Confusing the hell out of me."

"I know." She giggled in a teasing, schoolgirlish way. "By dreams, I mean do you think things can get better? Don't you sometimes have little pictures in your head, pictures of things which are the way you'd like them to be but which seem unobtainable?"

"Well, yes, I guess I do, but I'm still lost." I didn't know if she was just drunk or if she really did have a point to make.

"I'm talking about dreams of something better. Unfiltered, uncluttered dreams. Not the kind you have at night, but the kind you carry around all the time. Don't you have dreams like those?"

"Of course I do, but I still don't know why you're asking me." I'm not sure, but I think this was the first time I was directly angry with Leslie Summers. Angry when I was with her. She seemed to be toying with me.

"I'm asking because I have dreams about you, about us. Don't you understand I think I'm falling in love with you?"

Her aim was perfect. I blanked out all my confusion and said, "I'm falling in love with you, too."

"I know that, silly." She held my hand again and gently kissed it. "That's why I'm talking about these little dreams. I don't want to put neat little frames around them and just put them on my dresser where I can stare at them. I want them to be alive and three-dimensional. That's why I'm telling you about Juan."

"What?"

"Don't interrupt me now. I've been watching you, and I know it's not pleasant for you to hear me talking about some boy I knew, about a boy who made me pregnant, but if I don't tell you this, your dreams aren't going to be real, and neither are mine. If you're going to be in love with me, it's like I said a little while ago, I want you to know who I am, not who you think I am."

"I think I know who you are," I said, knowing immediately I shouldn't have said it.

"You don't know a fucking thing about me." She didn't say it angrily. It was matter-of-factly, but still it startled me. "It's fine for me to be a dream, but don't ever turn me into an illusion."

"I don't think I'm doing that," I said. I wish I could have appreciated her warning then, but I couldn't. My head was cluttered with the beer and her frankness.

"I want to finish telling you about Juan," she said, "but you've got to stop sitting here feeling sorry for yourself while I tell you."

"I didn't know I was feeling sorry for myself," I said, realizing as I said it that I had been.

"I've got to tell you the whole story or you'll never know me. You'll just have your little picture. It will be a dream that can't come true." She crushed her cigarette out and said, "Promise you'll listen to me without getting angry and without feeling sorry for yourself?"

"I'll do the best I can." I felt helpless.

She laughed. This time it was cheerful. "Okay, here goes.

"I guess it was about six o'clock after I bought the slinky dress. I decided it was safe to go to my father's apartment then. I took a cab up to East Eighty-first and had fantasies about the great night I was going to have by myself. I was going to take an outrageous bubble bath, drink champagne, listen to classical music, fix my hair, experiment with makeup and even lie nude under the sunlamp for my California tan. I was going to wear a sexy negligee, too. It wasn't that I planned for anyone to see me in it. It was just that I wanted to wear it and lie around, feeling sexy. When I got out of the cab, I went into a little boutique on Third. I bought the negligee and I also bought some silk bikini panties.

"I got to the apartment building and knew the first thing I had to do was get around the doorman. I couldn't just say 'Hi, George' and go on up to the apartment, because he would mention it to Daddy. So I hung around outside the building, feeling like a criminal as I waited for something to distract George. As I was about to lose hope, a huge, ostentatious silver Rolls pulled up to the entrance, and some blond bubblehead, who was so decked out with fur that she looked like a mink with spiked heels, started to get out. She was loaded with packages and even had a dumb-looking miniature poodle on a leash. Things couldn't have been better for me. George was about to kill himself, taking her stuff, helping her out, hanging on to the dog, thinking about the tip. I knew he'd have to escort her to her apartment or to the apartment of the rich slob she was shacking up with.

"The moment George, the bubblehead and the poodle got on the elevator, I tried the right key the first time and didn't even have to wait for an elevator. Luck was with me.

"But the whole charade fell to pieces."

She paused and I asked, "What happened?"

"This is embarrassing, but it's part of the story about what happened with Juan." She took another of my Marlboros and snapped the filter off. As I lit it, she said, "I got to the apartment, unlocked the door and walked in, and then I heard the goddam stereo playing—something dumb and schmaltzy like Johnny

Mathis—and I realized I'd had it. I started to slowly close the door and back away when I heard Daddy yell, 'Hi, honey.' I knew damn good and well I wasn't the honey he thought he was talking to, and I felt cornered. There was no place for me to go. Then I saw him. He was suddenly standing there, naked except for these high black rubber boots, a rubber vest and crotchless rubber underwear. He was holding two martinis. I didn't know who was more surprised and scared, Daddy or me. I had never seen a man with an erection before, and I certainly hadn't planned on the first one being my own father. Needless to say, the erection didn't last long. All we could do was stand there and feel sick and ashamed.

"Finally, he grabbed me and pulled me inside. Then he slammed the door and yelled, 'Sit over there!' What could I do? I dropped my packages on the floor and sat on the couch while he went to the bedroom. I'm not sure what I was thinking, but I felt like a moron, because never in my entire, naive life had I imagined my own father sleeping around with other women, and I certainly couldn't have imagined him as a freaky sex pervert who was into rubber.

"It was weird, but instead of hating him, I felt sorry for him. I don't know why, but I could only feel pity, and I was praying he'd feel the same way about me.

"Thank God he did. Not exactly pity. What he clearly felt when he came back into the living room, wearing slippers and a bathrobe, was shame. He had to know I was up to something, but more than that, he felt terrible because of the way I had caught him. There wasn't a lot we could do except stand there and feel awful.

"After a while, he said, 'I need another drink.' I didn't know what he'd done with the martinis he'd had when he came to the door, but I could understand why he wanted another. 'I'd like one, too,' I said, and he didn't question me. If anything, he seemed relieved.

"We both drank, and I felt the glow immediately. He poured us each another and said we were going to have a visitor soon. He told me to stay where I was while he got rid of her. Just then we heard a key in the lock and he flew to the door, and I heard some dumb chick squeal, 'Oh, no!'

"Daddy seemed to take forever, but finally he came back to where I was sitting and said, 'Well, I can't lie my way out of this. You've got me.' He was trying to sound almost humorous, but there was a hesitant tone in his voice, and I knew he was trying to size me up, trying to determine if he'd blown his whole life, wondering if I hated his guts and was going to run home and tell my mother everything.

"I was surprised at my own reaction. I knew I wasn't exactly innocent myself. I hadn't come there to deck myself out in rubber and play kinky sex games with my Puerto Rican lover, but I thought of the dress and other sexy things, and I realized there wasn't all that much difference between Daddy and me at that moment. Our motives, or at least our situations, were essentially the same. I got up from the couch and put my arms around him. And I started crying like a baby.

"Somehow, we got through this. He told me how he and my mother hadn't slept together regularly for five years, he talked about the pressures of his business, which is advertising, and he went on about his loneliness. I don't know why, but I understood, and I promised I wouldn't say anything to my mother or anyone else.

"As weird as it might seem, that turned out to be a great night. I had never really known my father before, but now I did. We drank and stayed up till about four in the morning. I was drunk and confused, but I didn't feel hurt. Even the next day, I felt all right about things. There were still questions in my mind, but I felt I had made a new friend."

As it turned out much later, this was a profound understatement.

"Daddy had to go back to Westchester. He said he'd told my mother he had business which was going to keep him over that Friday night, but he had promised to be home in time for a cocktail party that evening. He asked if I wanted to go back with him and said we could make up some story to tell my mother, but I said no. Then I told him I had a secret, too. At first, he seemed slightly shocked, in a fatherly way, but that changed quickly. He knew, just as I did, that our relationship would never be the same, that we were friends now.

"When I told him about Juan, I didn't get the lecture about virginity or scummy Puerto Ricans, as I would have under different circumstances. He did, however, tell me to be discreet with Juan or with any relationship I ever had, but he didn't lecture. He told me in a man-to-man way, as though I were his son instead of his daughter.

"And that was it. He went home and I stayed in the apartment and prepared for my date with Juan. Even after all the crazy things that had happened, I felt like an adult for the first time in my life. Juan Lanzo Ernesto was going to be in for a surprise. He wasn't going out with some dumb little chickie. He was going to have his hands full with a woman."

I didn't realize how long we had been at the Sink, and I was surprised when the lights flashed on and off for the midnight beer call.

"I had no idea it was so late," I said. I felt awkward, because Leslie's dorm closing hour was eleven. "You're going to get into trouble."

"No, I'm not," she said, winking at me.

"Don't they ground you or something when you're late?"

She stood up and put her jacket on. "Yeah, they do, but I'm covered." There was something sly and seductive in her voice. She was clearly drunker than I was, but she still knew what she was doing.

I stood up and put my jacket on, too. "What do you mean, you're covered?"

She put her arms around me and said, "I checked out for the night before I left this morning."

"You had this planned?"

She kissed me. "Yes."

I couldn't think of anything I'd rather do than spend the night with her, but there was a problem. Yanish and I shared a bedroom, which was actually only a sleeping alcove, separated from the living room by a curtain, and he was home.

"I know what you're thinking," she said, pulling away from me and buttoning her jacket, "but I've taken care of that, too."

"I don't know what you mean."

She grinned sheepishly and said, "I rented a room for us at the Skyways Motel on Twenty-eighth Street."

"You're serious?"

She took my hand and led me toward the front of the Sink. "Of course I'm serious."

I faked a laugh and said, "You really set me up."

"Yeah, I did."

We went outside, where it was snowing hard.

VIII _____

"Mother of Christ, this is a peculiar little town," Pat's saying to Hervey Shultis when I sit down at the bar.

"Peculiar," says Hervey, who's a sheriff's deputy as well as an off-duty regular at the Duck & Dog. "My family's been here going on three hundred years now, and you can bet your ass I've heard some pretty good stories, but this is the first goddam grave robbery I've come across." He grins and shakes his head. "Lou and I couldn't believe our frigging eyes when we got up there to the cemetery."

Pat winks at me and pours my customary bourbon and water. "Reckon you've heard all the latest, Johnny," he says, placing the glass in front of me.

"Dumb sonsabitches," Hervey mutters.

"Guess I haven't," I say. I've had an especially rough day, dealing first with Rob and his mysterious red belt and then with a New York City woman I'm building a weekend house for, and I'm not sure I'm in the mood for Woodstock chatter.

But Hervey and Pat change that. Hervey says, "Goddam if it doesn't happen every winter about this time, soon's it starts to get cold. Those fuckers find some way to get arrested just so they can have a warm bunk and three squares a day. You'd think the county was running a hotel for them."

"By Jesus, it's the truth," says Pat, laughing and slapping the bar.

"Go on, Hervey, tell Johnny here what they did. Tell him the way you told me."

Hervey picks at his teeth with the corner of a matchbook cover and assumes a serious expression. He's about my age and size, but he has a well-established beer belly and a deep receding hairline. He looks as all-American redneck as any man could, but he has been blessed with both a sense of humor and some compassion.

"So who's been robbing graves?" I ask, offhandedly, expecting to hear a standard exaggerated account of Hervey's day on patrol. There's nothing he loves more than making his job sound like an adventure novel.

He can't help but grin when he says, "You know that old son of a bitch Rob Dawson, of course?"

"How could I not know him and live here?" I say, realizing I should have guessed who Hervey and Pat were discussing.

"You're gonna love this, Johnny," Pat says.

Hervey glances at Pat, as though to tell him to shut up, and then he says, "Lou Hoffman and I were making our last morning rounds yesterday, right, when we got the damnedest call. Old lady Peters, you know, who lives behind the cemetery, well, she called in and reported some suspicious activity in the graveyard. Hell, nobody took her seriously. She's always calling, reporting something suspicious, especially there in the cemetery. Beats my ass, but I think she's just worried as hell about winding up there herself soon and wants to make sure it's safe. So, anyway, we get the call and have to check it out, just routinely, you know. So Lou and I drive up there and we don't see anything, but then we get to the back, where all the new graves are, and I'll be fucked if we don't see a fresh mound of dirt, but there's no one around. We both start to feel a little creepy as we approach, and then we see something moving behind a large maple. Christ, you could have said boo and both Lou and I would have dropped our loads."

Pat interrupts and says, "Get on with it, man. Tell Johnny what you found."

Hervey says, "You want to tell him or you want me to?"

Pat sighs impatiently.

"So we get out of the car, with our hands on our guns, and we hear, 'Don't shoot, don't shoot, man.' Then, Christ, if we don't see Lucky, you know, Lucky Ambrosio, come out from behind the tree. He's decked out as usual in his patched blue jeans, bandanna turban or headdress or whatever you call it, and junk jewelry, and he says, 'We ain't doin' nuthin' wrong, man.' Then he glances around with those beady little eyes of his, like he's on speed, and says, 'Come on, man. Hey, Rob, don't pull this shit.' Then I'll be a son of a bitch, old Rob Dawson comes slinking out from the hole they've just dug, and he's holding a goddam tin box, about the size of a shoe box, and a frigging kid's belt. So, what the fuck, Lou and I don't know what to think when Rob says, 'They're mine. Buried 'em with Myrna.' Then like a frigging bat out of hell, he darts across the cemetery. Lou, he takes off after the dumb son of a bitch. I'm standing there, wondering what the hell's going on, when I see Lou catch up with Rob. Christ, he tackles him like it's a Super Bowl play, and they both go flying to the ground, and I hear Lou yell, 'Oh, shit!' Lucky and I run up to them, and Rob's down with his face smashed into someone's tombstone. He sits up, spitting blood and teeth everywhere. I grab Lucky's turban and hold it to Rob's mouth, but Rob, he just pushes my hand away and somehow manages to say, 'Leave me alone.' He's still holding this red kid's belt, and he starts to swing it at me. So I back off."

I feel chills shooting through my body. I start to ask about the tin box, but Hervey beats me to it.

"So Rob's sitting there, now he has Lucky's filthy bandanna in his mouth, clutching this belt to his skinny little chest. I look around and see Lucky picking up all these papers and old letters and things that fell out of the box when Rob hit the ground. Lou, he kind of comes to his senses and starts helping Lucky. Rob, he stands up, madder than hell, but he can't say anything with the bandanna in his mouth. I start to ask what's going on, and Rob takes off again. I'll be fucked if I know how he did it, after knocking all his front teeth out, but he just split. Lou started after him again, but I said, 'Let him go. He's easy enough to find.' Anyway, we pick up all the letters and things and stuff them back into that tin box, and we take Lucky back to the squad car. Then we go to Town Hall and call Justice Blankenship. It's not even seven in the morning yet, and she's not exactly excited about our call. When we tell her what's happened and who we got, she just says, 'Let them both go. Damned if I'm going to give those bums a free ride this winter.' So that's what we did."

"What about the box?" I ask.

"Screw the tin box," Hervey says. "Lucky, he said it's important to Rob, so we let him keep it. Christ, he took it from his own daughter's grave. What can you do?"

I'm no longer hearing everything Hervey's saying. He's laughing with Pat again, and saying something about how Justice Blankenship had the town quietly cover the grave. I want to find Rob Dawson and Lucky Ambrosio.

IX _____

Madness and dreaming fascinate me. I'm not qualified to discuss either professionally, but personally, I have come to the conclusion that the quality of our dreams determines the degree of our madness. We're all capable of madness, but I think most of us maintain a functioning sense of sanity as we plod through our lives. Our dreams fluctuate and sometimes lead us toward dangerous confrontations with madness, but on the whole, I think there's a balance that allows for what the world at large perceives as normalcy. I believe it is the high quality of my dreams that has allowed me to survive my experiences with Leslie Summers. I have refined these thoughts over the past twenty-five years; however, I was first aware of them that snowy November night in Boulder when Leslie took me to the Skyways Motel.

Leslie Summers had a unique and peculiar way of paralleling her life with her fabrications. It took me years to understand this, but she was somehow able to simultaneously invent and act out her own life. She didn't trust her fate; she consciously created it.

When we got to the motel, we struggled out of our wet boots and jackets. Then she began unbuttoning my shirt and ran her fingers through the hair on my chest. I pressed my body against hers, but she pulled away and said, "Let's not rush this. Let's love each other slowly and gently."

"Okay," I lied. I put my arms around her and tried to kiss her on the lips, but she turned her face and pulled away again.

"Very slowly," she said.

I could only repeat, "Very slowly."

I watched transfixed as she began unbuttoning her blouse. She did it slowly and deliberately. As she removed it, she said, "Well, aren't you going to take your clothes off?"

I suddenly felt feverish and knew my face was betraying me as it turned redder and redder. Leslie giggled and began removing her skirt. I somehow managed to get my unbuttoned shirt off, but I fumbled with the button and zipper on my blue jeans. As anxious as I was to get my pants off, I was also shyly aware of my erection.

Leslie was wearing a slip, which she left on as she helped me with my pants. I started to take my underwear off, but she said, "No, leave them on."

I was confused, but I complied. She kissed me lightly on the cheek and then took my hand and led me to the bed. I watched helplessly as she turned the covers down. She smoothed the bottom sheet with her hand and then got in bed. I got in next to her and she switched the light off.

We cuddled silently in the dark, but whenever I touched her intimately, she would move my hand. I could respect her wish about not rushing into lovemaking, but I was confused, because I could not understand what we were doing almost naked in bed together if she didn't want to make love. I was also torn between my respect and what I can only crudely call a severe case of lover's nuts. I was in a great deal of pain and was about to make a stupid joke about taking a cold shower if we didn't get something going when she said, "I know how you feel."

"You do?" I said, trying to distract myself.

"Of course I do," she said seriously. "I feel the same way."

I almost said, "You couldn't possibly feel the way I do," but an instant of good sense stopped me.

"I want to make love with you, too, John." She kissed me. "But I'm not ready. Not yet."

"I'm willing to wait a couple of minutes."

She didn't laugh. "Seriously, I can't think of anything better than making love with you, but it has to be right, not like it was that night with Juan. Do you understand?"

I didn't understand, but I said, "Yes," and hated myself for it.

"Can't we just lie here and talk?" She squeezed me.

"Of course we can." I kissed her hair.

"I have to finish telling you about Juan," she said. "To love you the way I want to, I have to purge myself of Juan, and I don't think I can do it if I don't talk about it. Do you understand?"

"I think so."

"I don't want to hurt you, John. I seem to hurt people a lot. I don't want to, but I do. I hurt Juan terribly. He had nothing going for him, absolutely nothing. I came into his life and gave him some hope, but then I blew it up in his face. I destroyed the last bit of pride he had."

I wanted to ask how she could talk this way, feel this way, about someone who had raped her. But I didn't, because she began crying. "I'm sorry I'm being so insensitive," I said.

"You're not being insensitive. Just hold me for a minute."

We lay there, holding each other. Finally, she pulled away and sat up in the bed. I heard her searching through her purse. She blew her nose. Then she flicked her lighter and I saw her hands were trembling as she lit a cigarette.

Her tone of voice changed dramatically as she began telling me more about Juan Lanzo Ernesto. "I spent most of the afternoon doing the things I had planned to do the night before. I tried on the dress, sexy panties and negligee, I fixed my hair, experimented with makeup, all that sort of thing. I felt about as feminine and attractive as I ever had, but I also felt stupid. There was no getting around the fact that I was an inexperienced seventeen-year-old. Who was I kidding when I thought I was going to impress some street punk with my fancy clothes. I kept looking at myself in the mirror, and the more I did, the more I felt like a little girl playing grown-up. I was having mixed feelings about this date, and I finally realized there was no point in adding to them, in adding to the confusion I already felt—about myself, and I guess about Daddy, too.

"I finally decided to wear my regular skirt and blouse. I didn't want to appear to be something I wasn't, and I didn't give a damn if I impressed him or not. So I put the new things away in the Bloomingdale's bag and dressed as my normal, preppy self. Instead of playing the prima donna role and taking a taxi, I took the subway back to Grand Central, where I'd told him to meet me.

"I got to Grand Central about ten minutes before we were supposed to meet, and waited under the clock, as I'd said I would. I expected him to be late, just so he could show me who was boss, so I was surprised when he showed up a few minutes early, too. We just stared at each other, and I had to admit to myself that it was romantic. At that moment, neither of us was trying to pull anything off on the other. He was wearing an immaculate black suit and a conservative blue tie. He didn't look anything like the insolent hood I'd met at the baseball game. Even the cross was missing. The only things that were the same were those dark, sexy eyes and his teeth when he smiled. Any pretensions I'd had about my own superiority immediately vanished."

Leslie put her cigarette out and leaned over and kissed my cheek. "Am I boring you?"

"You're driving me a little crazy," I said, "but I don't think you could ever bore me." I wanted to turn the light back on so I could at least see her wonderful body, but I thought better of it and rested my hand on her thigh.

"We went out to dinner. I had suggested a little restaurant I knew in the East Sixties, thinking he wouldn't know much about restaurants in Manhattan, but he knew more than I'd guessed. He suggested we go to the Oyster Bar in the Plaza Hotel. That was high-class, even for me, if you know what I mean. The Oyster Bar is terribly swanky and very expensive, and I wouldn't have imagined that Juan would ever know about it, much less be able to afford to take me there.

"Needless to say, this preconception was wrong, as many others proved to be. Not only did he know about the Plaza and the Oyster Bar, but he also knew everyone there. The maître d' greeted us warmly, as though we were visiting royalty. I was astounded. The waiter, André, greeted Juan as though he were a movie star. They talked for a few seconds. André left and came back with drinks and elegant appetizers. I was paralyzed and couldn't do a thing except watch and listen as André made suggestions and Juan made selections.

"I had been so far off, at least I thought so then, with my images of Juan that I felt, once again, that I was the most naive and unsophisticated child in the world. Here I was going to be the gracious, condescending lady, going out with this low-life creature for the sense of adventure, like the bored housewives I've read about who like to seduce truck drivers and construction-worker types for the sake of satisfying their so-called animal desires.

"While we ate, the people who worked there were as solicitous as they could be. I had no idea what I had gotten into, and I felt like an ass. To make things worse, Juan was a perfect gentleman, not at all what I had expected. I was sure it had to be clear to him that I felt out of place. I got as drunk as I could without falling on my face, and the liquor made me feel a little more comfortable.

"After dinner, I figured he was going to make the big move and try to get me up to a lavish room in the Plaza and put the make on me. But it wasn't that way at all. We went outside. It was one of those chilly, but not cold, New York fall nights. Central Park was across the street from the hotel, and there were several horse-drawn carriages there. I felt like I was walking from one movie set to another. He asked if I wanted to ride through the park. It wasn't exactly as though all this was terribly unusual. I mean, I've always lived a rather pampered life. But on this night with Juan, everything seemed out of context. My discomfort had nothing to do with the experiences I was having. It had to do with my expectations."

Leslie ran her fingers across my chest again. That instantly aroused me, and I pulled her closer, but she stiffened. "We rode through Central Park in absolute silence. He chose not to speak, and I was unable to. He had his arm around me, and I nestled up against him. My head was spinning. Part of it had to do with the liquor, but most of it had to do with the circumstances of the evening. I was a little girl, falling in love, and I was struggling to somehow transform myself into an adult. Of course, I was furious with myself for not wearing the new dress.

"After the ride in the carriage, he asked, 'Would you like to go to a quiet little bar I know for a drink?'

"I said, 'No. Why don't we just take a walk and maybe go to my apartment.'

"He grinned and gave me a sly little wink, which I clearly understood. 'Not my apartment, exactly,' I said. 'It's my father's, but he's not there on weekends.'

"He took my arm and began leading me across the park. 'We can't walk through Central Park at night,' I said. 'It's too dangerous.'

"He brushed off my remark with a laugh and said, 'I can take care of us.'

"The way he said it made me know it was true, but I didn't understand why. There was a piece missing, but it was going to be a while before I'd understand what it was.

"It was one of those perfect New York nights. The sky was clear, the moon was almost full, and the air was crisp as we meandered through the park. We talked some, but mostly we just held hands and felt good about being with each other. I was infinitely more comfortable than I had been in the Oyster Bar, and I was thinking about what would happen once we got to the apartment. I have to admit my thoughts weren't terribly virtuous. If I was going to lose my virginity, I wanted to lose it that night with Juan.

"What a dummy I was! I lost my virginity, all right, but it wasn't as I had planned, and Juan wasn't who I had thought he was."

Leslie's sudden anger sounded forced as I lay there in the dark with her. I'm not sure what it was, but I had a feeling that I wasn't hearing the entire truth. One thing that struck me was that she hadn't mentioned any changes in Juan's speech. She couldn't have helped but notice the difference between the language of a street hood and the Juan she had just described. I felt a little guilty doubting her this way and thought maybe I was reading too much into this, but still I had a strange feeling that she was making up at least one of the two Juans she had described. But I couldn't understand why. There didn't seem to be any reason for her to lie, unless, I finally reasoned, she was doing it to hide something she couldn't bear to face.

I think Leslie sensed there was something wrong, too. I think she realized I was doubting her then. She slid back down on the bed and hugged me. "I'm sorry if this is confusing," she said.

"I think I'm following you."

"I mean, this was such a traumatic time in my life, and I know I'm not making it very clear."

We pressed our bodies together, and I didn't care if she was telling the truth or not. All I wanted to do then was make love with her, and under normal circumstances, I think I would have forced the issue, but there were seldom normal circumstances with Leslie Summers. I edged a hand to her breast and she pulled away from me and continued with her story.

"When we got to the apartment, he was an entirely different person. Not right away, but it didn't take long."

I was angry then, not only because of the rejection I felt, but also because of the way she was insisting on telling the story. Her attitude had changed just enough to make me want to tell her I didn't want to hear any more. She wasn't simply telling me about this night with Juan. She was rubbing it in. I started to say something, but she wouldn't let me.

"I'm putting all the blame on Juan," she said, sitting up again and lighting another cigarette, "and that's not fair. He turned out to be scum, but I was, too. I encouraged him."

I wanted to say, "Encourage me, too," but I didn't.

"When we got there, I fixed martinis, the way Daddy had fixed them the night before. I was on my own turf, more or less, and I could tell he was impressed, just by the way he walked through the apartment and looked at things. At the shelves of books, at paintings and prints, at the furniture, at all the things that showed my father was wealthy and a man of taste."

She feigned a laugh, but at least it was intentional, and I realized she was deliberately letting me know that she knew I was thinking about his rubber sex toys.

"Anyway, because of the way Juan was looking at things, I knew he was pulling off some kind of charade himself. He was doing what I had planned to do. He was like a child staring at toys in a store window. It was nothing he said. It was the way he examined things with a naive curiosity that gave him away, and I suddenly realized I was on top after all.

"We drank several martinis and talked about nothing in particular. We sat on the couch and stared out at the sea of lighted apartment buildings and joked about how we'd like to have binoculars or a telescope so we could spy on people and maybe catch them making love. It was this kind of talk that led to other things. We made out some, but there was nothing heavy at first. I knew Juan was full of shit, that he had put one over on me earlier, and although I didn't understand exactly how he'd done it, I was flattered in a perverse sort of way. I guess it was because I was important enough to him to make him want to impress me with a phony background. I couldn't help but feel proud of myself for knowing this and not letting on to him. The charade was clearly two-sided, but I had the upper hand.

"Anyway, between talking about spying on people making love and the martinis and the idiotic mood music I had put on the stereo, I decided I'd give this Puerto Rican phony something he'd remember. I went into Daddy's bedroom and took my clothes off. Then I put the bikini panties and sexy negligee on. Sure, I knew I was asking for trouble, but I figured I could handle it.

"You should have seen the ridiculous expression on his face when he saw me. I curled up next to him on the couch, realizing we were in for some heavy necking and maybe more, but I didn't care. I did want to have sex with him, at least I thought I did, but I wasn't sure I wanted to go all the way. The turn-on that had been there earlier in the evening wasn't as strong as it had been, but still there was an attraction. Street hood or not, he was a very good-looking guy.

"We fooled around on the couch and fell to the floor. He was trying to kick his shoes off and undo his belt buckle while kissing me and touching my breasts. I giggled at his clumsiness, and he got angry. This was the first time—no, the second; the first time was at Yankee Stadium—I had seen this fierce sense of independence, of pride, in his face. And now, even in the dim light, I could see it. Furious with me for laughing, he pushed away and stood up. He took all his clothes off. I was scared, but I was also impressed. He was beautiful, even more so than I had imagined. When he came back to me, I had stopped laughing, and knew there was only one thing on his mind. It showed in his eyes. I wanted to scream and run away from him, but I also wanted him. I don't mean I wanted to fuck my virginity away—I still wasn't certain about that—but I did want to have sex with him. I wanted to feel his body against mine, I wanted to drive him crazy."

I slowly began to realize Leslie had set up a situation with me that was parallel to the one she and Juan had been in that night, and now she was going to tell me again that she had been raped. I couldn't help but wonder what she expected. Was she provoking me intentionally, or was she testing me? I felt trapped. Either way, I ran the risk of doing the wrong thing.

It was impossible then for me to know how deep Leslie's hatred of men was. And even if I had been able to recognize this, it would have been equally impossible for me to understand why the hatred and fear existed. I lay there and resigned myself to whatever fate had in store for me. It seemed clear that I was going to have very little to do with it.

"I felt his knee slide along my legs, and I also felt the warm dampness of my own body. Before I knew what was happening, his hand was between my legs. I didn't know whether to scream or encourage him. I didn't have to think about it for long, though, because he suddenly stopped. He looked almost wounded, as though he had been surprised by a sudden shot. He seemed embarrassed when he removed his hand, and for the first time since all this had begun, he spoke. 'I'm sorry,' he said, almost bashfully. 'You're a virgin, aren't you?' I found his apology very attractive. I could have stopped everything then, but I wasn't content to do that. I said, 'I'll be a virgin forever if you're going to feel so bad.' He looked confused, but that didn't last long. He tore my new panties off. Then he pulled the negligee over my head, and we were both naked. I knew nothing was going to stop us.

"But something did."

Leslie stopped talking, as though waiting for me to ask what had happened. I didn't ask, though, not because I didn't want to hear, but because I was thinking of doing the same thing Juan had. I couldn't help but feel that was what she wanted me to do, that that was the ultimate point of her story.

But I was wrong. As I timidly put my hand on her thigh beneath the slip, she said, "At the very last moment, I chickened out. I said, 'No! We can't. I might get pregnant.' "

I took that as a cue and removed my hand. Leslie turned away from me and got out of the bed. She switched the night-table light on and began looking for cigarettes in my shirt pocket. She found one, broke the filter off, and after lighting it, nervously inhaled the smoke and then exhaled through flared nostrils. She sat on the edge of the bed with her back to me and said in a controlled voice, "I honestly don't know if I was really worried about getting pregnant or if it was that I was afraid of giving up my sacred virginity."

I felt tense and uncomfortable as I stared at her back and watched smoke rising around her head. I felt I was the one being raped at that moment. I was very much aware of the fact that Juan's violation of Leslie Summers could hardly have been categorized as rape. It was a strange sensation, but I was in absolute sympathy with him.

"It was too late," she finally said. "There was nothing I could do."

She stood up again and snuffed the cigarette out. I saw a momentary hint of hatred in her eyes as her face hardened. I didn't know how to react. I felt minuscule and stupid, wondering, Why can't I think of anything to say? Why am I frozen here, frozen and helpless?

She lay back on the bed and cuddled up next to me. "I'm sorry," she said, kissing my forehead.

"For what?" I heard myself asking. My own voice sounded like a stranger's.

I think I expected her to say she was sorry for exaggerating, for leading me to believe she had been an innocent rape victim, but I was wrong again, for she said, "I'm sorry I've burdened you with my seamy past."

"You haven't burdened me with anything," I said. "I want to know everything about you."

She forced a little laugh. "You're not going to believe this, but I knew then that I was pregnant. It's weird, but women have a way of knowing these things."

She was right. I didn't believe her. I understood that I was naive about a lot of things, especially where Leslie Summers was concerned, but I also knew it was unlikely that she would have gotten pregnant after just that one time. I rationalized my conflicting thoughts and decided she had her reasons for telling me all these things. Maybe this was her way of not hurting me. Maybe she called it a rape to make me feel better, to let me know I was going to be the first person she would willingly make love with.

Even now, a quarter century later, I find it hard to believe I could have been so dense. Just as I began to get comfortable with the thought of becoming her first true lover, she hit again:

"I didn't see Juan on a regular basis after that night at Daddy's apartment. I still had to go to school, and I wasn't about to let him come to Wharton. Of course, when I could get down to the city, I did, and we made love every time. No, we didn't make love. We fucked, just the way you fucked your whore in India."

I simply could not understand why she was telling me this. I wondered if this was a lie, too, and then I reversed my logic and wondered if there had in fact ever been a lie. Why would she try to make me believe she had been raped and then go on to say she had slept with Juan every chance she got? My mind began closing in on me. I couldn't think clearly. It was as if I had been drugged.

In this numbing confusion, I heard Leslie laugh. It was a deliberate, self-assured laugh, as she said, "I had to find out who Juan really was. I knew he wasn't the sort who hung out at places like the Plaza. I knew he was basically the street punk I'd met at the baseball game, but I still didn't know what his game was." She forced another laugh. "I'll give him credit for one thing. He was smarter than I'd thought." There was a contemptuous tone to her voice when she said, "It didn't take long to break him, though."

That remark startled me more than anything else she had said.

"He was real lowlife, after all. It was easy for him to pull off the Plaza trick. You want to know who he was? He was a goddam busboy in the Oyster Bar. That was how he pulled off his little trick. It was a snap for him to get his friends to go along with the game."

I wanted to believe she was knocking Juan because she thought it would make me feel better. But my sympathies were with him. I was angry with her, but I had no choice in this matter. Even with my misgivings, I was hopelessly in love with Leslie Summers.

I slept fitfully that night in the Skyways Motel. I would drift off, only to be awakened by Leslie's breathing or by a twitch in her body. A few times I placed my hand lightly on her hip and marveled that I was sleeping in the same bed with her. Other times I felt angry about Leslie's "rape" story and my inability to understand it or her reasons for telling me the way she had.

But mostly, as I lay there with her, I could only think of the lust

I felt. I cuddled up next to her and thought of trite little things such as how we fit together like spoons in a drawer. I could smell her fine, clean hair and skin, and I tried to convince myself that I could, if I was very gentle, make love to her without waking her. But then I felt revulsion toward myself, knowing that even if it were possible, it would be the cruelest and most dishonest rape of all.

I did, eventually, make love with Leslie Summers that night, but I did it within the safety of my own dreams.

X ————————————————————

Jack and Mike hiked up to the top of Overlook Mountain with me this morning. This has become a ritual with us. Every December, a few days before Christmas, we take this hike and cut a tree. Kay doesn't go with us, because she's not particularly outdoorsy. Also, she's a few years older than I am and is a little overweight and says she doesn't have the stamina she once had. Her real reason for not going, aside from simply not liking mountain hikes, is that she sees this as a special day for the boys and me. It's a plain old-fashioned father-and-sons day, and one that has indeed become very special in our family.

This annual hike provides more than comradeship between the boys and me, and it's also more than an outing. It has become a kind of religious pilgrimage. Not religious in any traditional sense, but religious in terms of our family. It seems to reaffirm our sense of unity. By this I mean family unity as well as unity with something greater than we as individuals are.

From the top of Overlook Mountain, we can see across the Hudson Valley to the hills of Connecticut, to the Berkshires in Massachusetts, to the Green Mountains of Vermont, and we can, of course, see all the surrounding Catskill peaks and valleys. We can also see the small village of Woodstock, which is probably the most exciting view of all, certainly for Jack and Mike, because this is where they have lived all their lives, and this view of their town in its entirety must give them a proprietary feeling.

I may be exaggerating this, but I have seen the faces of my sons as they have gazed down at their town, and I know there's something special going through their minds as they look at this microcosm of nature, architecture, and humanity.

Although the ultimate purpose of our annual pilgrimage is to cut a tree, take it home and decorate it for the holidays, there is more. About a mile and a half into our hike, we come upon a small handcrafted church, called the Church on the Mount, which sits back in the woods as though it has always been there, almost as though it grew naturally, along with the surrounding white pine, hemlock, rock oak, birch and red maple trees. I know this church well, because it is where Kay and I were married sixteen years ago. We selected it not for religious reasons, but for its aesthetic interest. It was built, single-handedly, in the twenties by a man named John Henderson, who later became known in Woodstock as Father Jack. I met him when Kay and I were married, when he was ninety-two. He was late for the ceremony, because he was up on the steep cedar-shake roof replacing broken shingles. He shouted an apology down to us, and then after he had married us, he told us that his first responsibility was to the "House of Man." Any other priest or minister would have obviously called it the House of God, but Father Jack didn't talk that way. He had built it out of the native lumber I love so much and had maintained it over the years, not for an evasive and abstract God, but for people who needed a place where they could celebrate life or grieve because of its disappointments.

I don't know if Father Jack was really an ordained minister or priest. There has been a great deal of speculation in Woodstock about this over the years. I have heard that he was really a Bavarian prince named Karl Hanau who left his homeland in shame after the First World War, and I have also heard he was a bandit named Black Jack Henderson, who in the early part of this century became notorious for robbing trains in the Midwest. I question both stories, but I like them, because I liked the man and I get pleasure from the local color and controversy he's still able to provide for Woodstockers, even though he has been dead for fifteen years.

Farther up the mountain, maybe half a mile, there is another religious shrine. It is a Buddhist monastery, and although it might seem out of place to those unfamiliar with this area, it fits as beautifully and perfectly in the Catskills as Father Jack's church does, as it would on any mountainside in Japan, where I was a few times as a young Merchant Marine. The monastery is very large and in a clearing, but the graceful Oriental architecture and the surrounding mountain peaks give it a humbling ambience. It is not at all ostentatious in this setting, as are so many ornate and architecturally "correct" temples of worship I have seen throughout this country and the rest of the world. Like Father Jack's simple church, there is nothing pretentious about the monastery. It belongs where it is.

At the top of the mountain, two and a half miles above the monastery, there is the greatest temple of all. At least to Jack, Mike and me it's the greatest. It's the remains of an old hotel, the Overlook Mountain House, that was built in 1871 and destroyed by a fire in the 1920s. Because it was constructed of native bluestone, concrete, Italian marble and iron, most of the superstructure is still standing, and it doesn't take much imagination to know that this was once an elegant hotel. Mike and Jack and I have spent countless hours up there, sitting on the thick, solid walls, gazing at 360-degree panoramic views, and making up stories about the people we could imagine coming to this hotel over a hundred years ago.

I imagine the building in terms of its architecture and decor. I see marble arches and high pounded-tin ceilings, mahogany chair rails, blue and purple velvet draperies, white linen, crystal goblets—things that suggest opulence and royalty, at least in my mind. I see fancy horse-drawn carriages arriving with aristocratic New Yorkers and heads of state from all over the world. And I see complicated assignations in the corners of the towers that were once there.

Jack, my ten-year-old, sees Cinderella-like ladies and handsome young princes living there all the time with unicorns and other mythical beasts. And he sees happy children who will always be children and never have to worry about growing up, and who will be able to eat as many sweets as they want without having to worry about going to the dentist.

Mike, my fourteen-year-old, has a more contemporary vision. He sees the hotel as a sort of elaborate nineteenth-century discotheque, where teenagers can get away from boring adults.

It is there, near the ruins of the old hotel, that we always find our tree. We try to find trees that are being overshadowed by larger and older trees and that have very little chance of survival. We see no point in killing anything that has a chance at a long and healthy life. I feel this way when selectively cutting lumber for building projects. It's for this reason that we usually end up with reasonably ugly trees. They are never full and symmetrical like those grown on Christmas-tree farms. They are almost always scrawny and uneven. We like them this way, because they present a challenge when it comes to decorating them. This is where Kay's genius comes in. She knows instinctively how to make the best out of the worst.

Every year we name our tree. Last year we named it Fred, because it made us think of Fred, the man who hauls our garbage away. Fred is a genuinely sweet man, but he's also very ugly. The year before, our tree's name was Zelda. Jack named her and explained that Zelda was a scrawny witch in one of his picture books.

The tree we found this morning wouldn't win any horticulture contests, but it is more attractive than those we've had in the past. We chose it not because it was threatened by surrounding trees, but because some thoughtless hiker had banded it; he or she had cut a strip of bark from its circumference, which means death to any tree.

I know now that Jack and Mike have been listening to some of the late-night conversations Kay and I have had about Rob Dawson and my daughter, because they suggested we call this year's tree Audrey.

XI _____

I had planned not to see Leslie Summers again after that night at the Skyways Motel. My reasons were simple: As much as I loved and wanted her, I was afraid of what she could do to me. I wasn't especially sophisticated in the ways of love, but neither was I so naive that I didn't know she had been less than honest and fair with me when she had told me about Juan. Also, I was angry. Part of the anger had to do with her comment about "breaking" Juan. The more I thought about it the next day, the angrier I became. It was the whole idea of one human being even thinking in terms of breaking another. It rang of slavery. When I thought of Leslie in this context, the next day and in days to come, she was very unattractive to me.

Another reason for my anger had to do with the more personal aspects of that night. She'd had no right to tease me sexually as she had. But since she had, I thought later, I should have forced myself on her. She was asking for it. Of course, as compelling as this reasoning seemed, when I thought about it I knew I wasn't the sort of person who raped girls, regardless of the circumstances.

I did manage to avoid Leslie for over a week. She called several times. I was polite on the surface, but there was a coldness, too, and it was intentional. I did not want to see her, at least until I'd had a chance to sort things out in my mind.

Of course, my reserved behavior was the most effective ploy I could have dreamed up. I didn't mean it as a ploy, and that undoubtedly made it all the more effective.

It was on a Friday, a little over a week after I had last seen Leslie, when I came home from class and found a note from Yanish on the kitchen table. It read, "I'm in Denver for the weekend. Have a great time. —Yan."

The note was odd for two reasons. First, Yanish was almost always in Denver or somewhere on weekends, and second, he had never bothered to leave a note before.

I took a long shower and wondered what Yanish was up to, but then my mind drifted to other things, including Leslie Summers. I was, in a strange way, proud of myself for staying away from her, but I was also lonely, and I knew my loneliness wasn't for female companionship in general. It didn't matter what I told myself, I missed Leslie Summers. I didn't understand then what makes one person love another, nor do I understand it now, but I did know learning not to love Leslie was going to require more than just a conscious decision. A decision, like a New Year's resolution, could easily be broken or reversed.

When I got out of the shower, I called a girl I knew in Denver. Carissa Clark and I had been neighbors and friends in high school, and while we had never had a romantic relationship, we went out together sometimes. Over the years, I had nursed her through several unpleasant relationships, and now I thought I would talk to her about my problem. When she answered the phone, I forced cheerfulness and said, "Hey, is this the beautiful, sexy Carissa Clark of Brentwood Street?" There was silence, so I said, "Carissa, it's me, you know, old John Noble, formerly the Brentwood stud. How 'bout let's gettin' it on and goin' to the movies tonight?" She laughed and said something about being in the middle of another tragic love affair. Then she said that depending on how things went with her date that night, she might be free for a Saturday-night movie. I laughed too, and said I'd check my calendar and get back to her the next day.

I felt a heaviness coming on after talking with Carissa, because I was still thinking about Leslie. Carissa would at least have helped me get my mind off Leslie.

My depression wasn't to last for long, though. After I hung up, I went into the sleeping alcove that passed as a bedroom in our apartment, and I discovered who had asked Yanish to leave the note.

Leslie Summers was in my bed. She giggled and said, "Ah, so you're the Brentwood stud. I've been waiting for you." She turned the blanket down and revealed her nude body. She patted the mattress and, still giggling, said, "Let's see if you're as good as your rep."

I don't remember exactly what my first reaction was, but I know it was quickly followed by a combination of lust and love.

"Well, let's see what you've got, stud."

I sat on the side of the bed. I wanted to say something like "Is this another of your little games where we get to peek but not touch?" But that isn't what I said. It was more like "You certainly have a way of being in the right place at the right time."

She pulled me down next to her and said, "Well, baby, I checked my calendar and realized I'm free tonight."

I choked out a laugh and said, "I see eavesdropping is one of your specialties."

She began kissing my neck playfully and pulling on the towel I had wrapped around me. Then she whispered, "I have more than one specialty."

"I bet you do."

She yanked the towel off me and said, "I can see you have a specialty of your own."

My embarrassment and surprise faded quickly when she rolled over on top of me.

We made love throughout the night and well into the morning hours. At first, our lovemaking was frantic, but later it became slow and gentle, and eventually we drifted into a sleep free of dreams.

* * *

I woke first, late the next morning, and I could only stare at the beautiful girl sleeping next to me. The anger, fear and confusion I had felt had vanished, and there was no question in my mind about the love I had for Leslie Summers. I thought back to that day on Flagstaff Mountain when she had said, "When we make love, I promise it will be a lot better." She had lived up to her word.

I must have watched her breathing, slowly and evenly, for more than an hour before she woke and put her arms around my neck and pulled me on top of her. "I love you," she said. "I love you more than anything in the world." She pressed hard against me and kissed my lips.

"Oh, God, I love you, too," I whispered. "You don't know how much I love you."

"If it's half as much as I love you, I know. I want to stay here with you forever, John."

I entered her again, but we didn't exactly make love. We stared at each other and cried, and then we licked each other's tears.

For the next several weeks Leslie and I were apart only on weeknights when she had to stay at the dorm and when we had to be in class and when I was at work in Denver. Yanish, as always, was accommodating on weekends, and I prayed to all the gods and saints I could conjure up that his current relationship would last.

I know we talked a lot during these weeks, but I don't remember much of what we talked about. We made love to the point of exhaustion, and I know we talked of being together forever, but I cannot recreate any of our conversations. I know that at one point Leslie attempted to apologize for that first night we'd slept together at the Skyways Motel, but that seemed such a distant and foreign part of our past that I asked her not to mention it ever again, and I remember her sense of relief when I made that request.

The Christmas holidays and school vacation came and brought with them (from my point of view) both a sense of impending loneliness and one of relief. Relief only because of the time it would provide for the tremendous amount of work I had to do in order to catch up with and pass the courses I was taking. I had never been a great student. Until the time I met Leslie Summers, I had maintained a low B average, but only because I had worked hard. By the Christmas break, I was failing two subjects and barely passing the other three. Leslie, on the other hand, had a 4.0 average.

It was (or so I believed then) a combination of Leslie's good sense and my fear of failure, along with my poverty, that kept me from going back to New York with her for the holidays. I had broached the subject several times, but she had gently dissuaded me by explaining that it would be difficult for her parents to accept not just me, but anyone she brought home. It hadn't been that long, after all, she had said, since she had been in trouble. There wasn't much I could say to that. She had also made a point of not giving me her phone number, for the same reason. She said she wanted to do everything she could to keep things right with her parents.

I had prepared myself for a dreary farewell, but putting her on the plane at Denver's Stapleton Airport was much easier than I had anticipated, because Leslie had said, "Look at it this way—the sooner I leave, the sooner I'll be back."

"You certainly have a way of making things sound better than they are. I'd hate it if you were my executioner."

She kissed me before boarding the plane and said, "You be a good boy while I'm gone or I'll see that I am your executioner."

"How could I not be good when I have you to think about?"

She laughed and replied, "I'm talking about your grades, silly. You work hard while I'm gone so we'll have time to play when I get back."

That was all the motivation I needed, and I did manage to catch up with my schoolwork over the vacation. It was also during this holiday when Leslie was in New York that I bought an engagement ring with the intention of asking her to marry me when she returned.

* * *

She was scheduled to return on a Thursday evening in mid-January. Early that afternoon I was nervous and excited, not only in anticipation of being with her again, but also because I had carefully planned how I was going to give her the engagement ring.

I went overboard, so to speak, with my preparations, but it seemed important then. I had put a bottle of French champagne in an ice bucket next to my bed—our bed—and I had covered the top of the bed with fresh red rose petals. I hadn't worked the details out precisely, because mood and circumstance had a lot to do with my overall plan, but the general idea went something like this. Assuming she would feel as passionate as I knew I would, I was going to slowly take off her clothes and mine and carry her to the bedroom, where I was going to place her in the middle of the bed of rose petals. We were going to take turns sipping the champagne from one glass, and when it was gone, I was going to begin making love to her. As I did, I was going to slip the ring onto her finger.

But things didn't work out that way. Late in the afternoon, an hour or so before I was going to leave for the airport, the phone rang. It was Leslie, and she was crying as she spoke.

"What's wrong?" I asked. "You miss the plane?"

"Oh, John, I'm so sorry." Her sobbing was loud, and it was difficult for me to understand her.

My entire body began to tremble when I asked again, "What's wrong? Why aren't you on the plane?"

She blew her nose. "John, I'm not coming back. I . . . I can't."

"What in God's name are you talking about?" I felt tears welling up in my eyes.

There was a long pause. But then she said, "I'm pregnant again."

I felt sick to my stomach, and my head began to throb. "Are you sure? I mean, have you been to a doctor?"

"Yes, I'm sure. I'm pregnant all right."

I reached into my pocket for the ring. I stared at it and said,

"Leslie, it's not like it was before. I mean, it's not the way it was with Juan. I love you. I want to marry you."

She cried even harder and couldn't speak for several minutes. However, she was eventually able to say, "I've decided to have an abortion."

"No!" I heard myself shouting. "Don't do that. Get on the next plane and come out here. We'll figure out what to do then."

"It's no good, John. I have to do it my way."

"Leslie, I'm in love with you. I love you more than anything in the world. Please, God, for both our sakes, come back."

There was another long pause.

"Leslie, can you hear me?"

"John, I can't talk much longer."

"Please don't hang up." I was pleading with her. "Leslie, you've got to come back. Let's get married and have the baby." I broke down and began crying then.

"John, I can't come back. It's too late. I can't ever come back."

"But you can. It's my baby, too. Just come back and we'll work things out. I swear we will."

"That's the problem," she said. Her voice sounded weak.

"What's the problem?"

"I'm not sure it is your baby."

"Leslie!" I screamed.

"I'm sorry, John. I'm very sorry."

"Leslie, I love you!"

Her voice was even fainter. "You don't want to love me."

"Leslie, don't talk that way. Don't ever talk that way."

"Sorry . . . I . . . sorry."

"Leslie!"

It was too late. She hung up.

XII _____

It's two days before Christmas, and I'm in the Duck & Dog, having my usual after-work drink. Hervey Shultis comes in and sits next to me. He's in uniform, but he removes his badge and tie, which is his way of announcing he's off duty and ready for a few drinks.

"How's it going, Hervey?" I say.

He regards me in a vaguely humorous, all-knowing way and hands me a copy of today's *Woodstock Herald*, our weekly news and gossip source. "You seen this?"

"Not yet. Why?"

He puts his glasses on. They're wire-framed, tinted prescription glasses, the kind pilots and rural sheriff's deputies wear on television. He takes the paper back from me and opens it to the Letters to the Editor section. "You're going to love this," he says. "You're going to fucking love it."

"Come on, stop being so mysterious," I say, taking the paper back from him.

He points to a block of type and says, "The dumb circus monkey's up to his old tricks again." He yells across the bar to Pat, "How 'bout a round? Make Johnny's a double—he's going to need it."

"I already have a drink," I say. Then I see the signature to the letter Hervey has pointed out.

"You're going to need another one," Hervey says. "Go ahead, read it."

To the Editor:

I, Rob Dawson, want to apologize to certain Woodstock people for the way I've been acting lately, and for the way I have bummed money and liquor. I was once a circus trapeze artist, and I have also tried to make my living as a painter, but I have come into a situation of poverty and drunkenness which I can't control. Since my wife left me several years ago and my daughter Myrna died last Christmas, I do not have much personal hope anymore, but I have one good thing left in me and I want to do it this Xmas for the one person who lowered himself to offer me a job.

This person knows who he is and if he wants to know about Myrna's little friend and Shirley Temple's belt, he can find me at Fr. Jack's when it gets dark on Xmas Eve.

Merry Xmas to all,
Rob Dawson

P.S. I don't know if you can print this, but if you can please ask "my friend" to bring a bottle of whiskey or at least a six-pack.

"Shit," I mutter.

Hervey laughs and slaps me on the back. "I figured this'd get a rise out of you. What's the old burnout up to this time?"

My scalp is perspiring, the way it does when I eat hot peppers or Chinese mustard. "I don't know," I say. "I mean, he's been bugging me since I offered him the job a few weeks ago."

Hervey laughs again. Then he shouts at Pat, "Where's that round?"

Pat yells back, "For Christ sake, man, can't ya see you're not the only one here?"

Hervey slaps me on the back again and says, "No kidding, what's this all about? This Shirley Temple's belt, it's got to be that one Lou and I saw him take out of Myrna's grave, you know, when we found Rob and Lucky there in the cemetery."

"Yeah, I know," I say, finishing my drink and wishing Pat would hurry with that round. "You know how screwed-up Rob is."

"Christ, who doesn't."

"He stopped me last week, I guess after you and Lou found them there. He gave me this belt and said it once belonged to Shirley Temple, that he'd gotten it when he was in the circus. Christ, I didn't even remember he'd been in the circus."

"He is the circus," Hervey says. "He's all three rings. But why'd he give you the belt?"

I shake my head. "I don't know. He said something about it helping me find my daughter."

Hervey scratches his head and squints his eyes. "What daughter you talking about? You got a little secret life going?"

The way he says it annoys me, but I don't say anything.

"Where's the kid now?"

"I don't know. I haven't seen her since she was almost three, back in '67."

"So how's Rob know about her?"

"Beats me," I say. I don't want to get into a long-drawn-out discussion with Hervey.

"Come on, you don't have to bullshit me. Why you figure he wants to meet up at the old church?"

"I honestly don't know."

"Here you go, gents," Pat says, placing drinks before us and taking my empty glass. The bar's filling, so Pat can't spend much time chatting with us about Rob Dawson and his letter, and I'm thankful for that.

"Really, what's going on?" Hervey asks. "I mean, unofficially." He taps the badge in his shirt pocket, showing he's not asking as a cop.

"I don't know," I say, truthfully. "Like I said, he gave me the belt and said it has something to do with my daughter, that it will help me find her. Of course, I didn't take him seriously. I mean, how do you take someone like Rob Dawson seriously?"

Hervey grunts a laugh. "Yeah, I know what you mean." He downs his drink in one gulp, and seeing Pat is still busy with other customers, he reaches over the bar, grabs a bottle of Old Crow from the rack and refills his glass. He starts to fill mine, but I move it away. He looks disappointed as he replaces the bottle. Pat sees him, but only frowns and shrugs. "So what are you going to do? You going to meet him at the old church?"

"You think I'm crazy?"

"Everyone else in this weird little town is. Why not you?"

"You've got a point," I say, hoping he'll drop Rob Dawson and the letter.

Of course, he's not about to. "Tell you what," he says, placing a hand on my shoulder in a fatherly sort of way. "I think you ought to go up there, you know, to the church, tomorrow night."

"What for?" I ask.

"I'm curious about this letter, that's all. Simple curiosity."

"Listen, Hervey," I say, standing up, "I've got to get home and help Kay and the boys decorate the tree."

He squints and says, "So, you going or not?"

I shrug and say, "I don't know," but even as I say it, I realize I probably will meet Rob tomorrow night at Father Jack's church.

As I leave, Hervey shouts, "Good luck and Merry Christmas."

XIII _____

When I was six, after my father was killed in 1945, I apparently committed my first truly violent act. I don't know if I'm actually recalling what happened or if I'm simply remembering my mother's account of what I did that day.

The victim of my murderous act was a stray cat who had the misfortune to wander into our backyard a few days after we learned my father's plane had been shot down. I apparently lured this cat into the artificial warmth and safety of my grasp and somehow managed to get it close to the top of a large cottonwood tree in our yard. I must be remembering this, or possibly I'm remembering only what my mother said I said then, but I tricked the cat into supposing it was safe high in this tree with me, probably by petting it. It was purring loudly, I seem to remember, as I removed it from the cradle of my arms and held it out away from the crotch of branches I was sitting in. Far below us was a dark green picket fence which separated our yard from the neighbors'; however, as I stared down at it, it became a solid and high black barricade, a wall. My demons were not merely laughing. They were jostling me, trying to lodge me from my safe perch in the tree, trying to force me out of it.

I remember standing up in the tree, with the cat outstretched in my hands (that is, I think I remember), and I remember the sudden hissing and squealing of my demons. Something tore at the flesh on my arms and hands and there was blood. I was screaming, "Daddy, don't die, don't die!" and the hissing and squealing became louder and even more furious with me.

There was a momentary silence, and then the afternoon sky lit up with thousands of little bursts of light. Daggers of light were flying everywhere around me and there were menacing and insistent popping noises.

Then everything was black and quiet until I heard my mother shouting, "Johnny! Johnny, climb down!"

I stared down, and the Germans on the other side of the wall were Mr. and Mrs. Jensen, our neighbors, who were picking up the body of the cat, which had been killed from the fall and burned on the poorly insulated power lines that stretched from their house to the utility pole in the alley, far beneath my perch in the cottonwood.

I climbed down, crying but denying even to myself that I was responsible for the cat's death. My mother led me back inside the house, where she held me in her arms until I slipped into a dark and peaceful sleep where there were no demons, where there was no Germany.

My second act of murder occurred in a hallucination that January afternoon in 1964 after Leslie Summers called and told me she was pregnant again and didn't know if I was the father. What I can only describe as a black hood of jealousy floated in that day and somehow slipped itself over my head. My peripheral vision was gone and sound was dulled, but I could see everything directly in front of me. My vision was clearer than it had ever been, and I could see beyond the walls of the apartment, beyond the distance that separated me from Leslie Summers and her *other lover*, Juan Lanzo Ernesto. They were the new demons of my life, standing before me, laughing and daring me to come after them. I could see a silver cross hanging from Juan's neck, swinging in a brilliant light, almost hypnotizing me. His teeth and Leslie's were glistening with the moisture of their passion as they laughed and teased me into a chase. Leslie's laughter became louder, it became a screeching, hissing, taunting "Catch me if you can. Catch me if you can." She began running through a meadow of goldenrod, brilliant in what was now the summer Colorado sun. I blinked, still blinded peripherally by the black hood, and upon opening my eyes, I saw she was naked. I tried to run, but something made me heavy and clumsy, and I could move only in slow, plodding steps. My vision narrowed even more and I saw her holding another's hand as they ran out of Boulder and up Sunshine Canyon toward the snow-capped Continental Divide, laughing, caring about nothing other than their passion. I somehow lost my feeling of heaviness and clumsiness and began running after them, and I became part of them as we rolled and tumbled among the wild mountain flowers. As I was about to consummate my passion, I was struck by a deafening blast of severed power lines and laughter. As I floated back to the meadow, I saw Leslie Summers eagerly copulating with Juan Lanzo Ernesto, whom I had just murdered.

These are the things I remember. What I don't remember is how, that evening after Leslie's call, I ended up on Curtis Street in Denver's skid-row district. I vaguely recall taking the keys from the ignition of my '49 Chevy and walking toward the newspaper office where I worked part-time. I stood in the doorway of the decaying two-story brick-and-frame building and stared in the near-darkness at my desk and the old swivel chair I had spent so many hours in, and I shivered as frigid gusts of wind whirled powdery snow into miniature tornados. I could feel the tears beginning to freeze on my cheeks as I said goodbye to Helen Ferguson, my boss, who wasn't there, but who I believed would somehow hear my farewell. I turned, slowly but with certainty, and walked across the street to Mule's Café, a little diner where I had usually had my morning coffee.

Even now, recalling this strange, almost mystical part of my past from the safety of a quarter century, I can see Mule, tall and slight, in white trousers and shirt, standing over the grill, flipping eggs and pancakes for the drunks and derelicts who had no other place to go for food or warmth.

I sipped coffee at the counter and waited in a stupor of silence and anguish for Eunice Williams to come in.

Eunice was around forty-five, and tall with broad hips that were out of proportion to her otherwise slim body. Her skin was the color of coffee with a moderate amount of milk in it, and she had curly red hair and a patch of ebony freckles across her face that made her striking. I knew her not as a prostitute, but as I knew many of the street people in this area of Denver, only because I happened to work for an eccentric woman who saw no point in moving her newspaper office to another neighborhood just because this one, where the Rocky Mountain Tribune had been for over half a century, was going through hard times.

I didn't know Eunice or Mule or any of the other Curtis Street people intimately, but in the nearly two years I had worked for Helen Ferguson at the newspaper, I had learned to know them well enough not to be intimidated by them. I had gotten to know Eunice best the summer before, not by design, but because of chance. I had gone by myself to the horse races one afternoon and had won around fifty dollars, a considerable amount of money for me in 1963, and as I was heading out toward the parking lot, happily whistling because of my good fortune, I happened to see Eunice leaning against an iron pillar beneath the grandstand. I could see she was distressed, so I went up to her and asked what was wrong.

She was holding one shoe with its high heel broken off. She regarded me with a frown, the kind that showed she didn't recognize me. I said, "John Noble. I work for that little paper on Curtis Street."

Her frown spread into a wide grin and she said, "Yeah, that's who you are. I knew I knowed you from somewhere."

I thought she was going to hug me, but she didn't. "I just

happened to see you," I said, "and wondered if anything was wrong." I glanced at the broken shoe and said, "Guess there is."

Still grinning, she said, "Oh, guess I jus' went an' did it." She laughed. "I'm so dumb some o' the time. Like always, I was gonna get myself rich with the horses, but what I gone an' done is gamble away all my money and break my shoe on top o' everything."

I laughed, too, and held the money I'd just won out to her and said, "I might be able to help a little bit." Then I felt embarrassed, realizing she might think I was trying to buy her services.

"Oh, no, honey, I can't take yer money. I know you work too hard for what you got."

"How do you know that?" I asked, surprised.

"Oh, I know these things. That's my business, knowin'." She patted me on the shoulder and said, "I can always get me some more money, but what I need now, honey, is a ride. You give ol' Eunice a ride back to town?"

"Of course I will."

As we drove back toward Curtis Street, she told me she had a boy about my age, but he had run away when he was sixteen. That, she said, was how she had come to notice me. I made her think not of her son, but of who she'd like him to be, except for my color, she added, laughing.

That was how I came to know Eunice Williams, and it was because she was the sort of person she was that I found myself waiting for her that blustery January evening in Mule's Café. Of all the people I knew in the world then, she was the one I knew who wouldn't, if she had it, hesitate to loan me the five hundred dollars I felt I needed in order to go to New York and find Leslie Summers.

I was right. When Eunice came into the café and after I had told her not everything but that I had to go to New York and find my girl, who was pregnant, she said, "Honey, I don't have that kind o' cash on me, but you jus' sit tight here an' I'll go out an' see what I can scare up."

Within twenty minutes, she was back with the full five hundred. "Listen," I said, after hugging and thanking her, "I got a little better than a thousand in my account, what I've saved for school, but there was no place to cash a check tonight."

I started to write out a check, but she tore it out of the book and shredded it. "Now, what banker you think's gonna cash a five-hundred-dollar check for Eunice Williams?" she said, laughing. "You jus' go on an' find that girl o' yours an' do the right thing. There's gonna be plenty o' time for you to pay me back."

XIV _____

Kay and I talked last night after Mike and Jack went to bed, and we agreed that it's important for me to meet Rob Dawson in Father Jack's Church on the Mount this evening. Kay doesn't think anything concrete will come of this; however, she knows me well enough to understand that I will have to find out for myself. She sees Rob simply as one of Woodstock's more interesting and colorful crazies, but she doesn't put much stock in his claim that he can help me find my daughter. And even if she did, I'm not convinced she thinks it's wise for me to go off on a search for a daughter I haven't seen in over twenty years. In short, Kay's attitude is a sympathetic but conservative "leave things as they are."

But there's the flip side of the issue, which Kay understands, too, and it is this understanding which reinforces our marriage and my love for her. She knows, I think even more than I do, that there's a restlessness within me that, once I have seized upon an idea, will not leave me alone until I have pursued it to its limits. Kay knows it's important for me to find my daughter and try to get to know her. She's sympathetic, but she has asked me not to let Rob's fantasies and my imagination do anything foolish.

I don't blame Kay for her concern, because I know, too, that I am capable of slipping into a past that is still trying to tempt me. Through Kay and our years together, I have learned emotional caution and moderation, but still there is that ghost of my younger self which refuses to give up its hold on me, which I think means there is something about me that says my life will not be whole until Audrey and I meet face to face.

These are the thoughts I'm having as I walk along Camelot Road toward Father Jack's church high up on Overlook Mountain. It won't be dusk for another hour or so, and it wouldn't take more than half an hour for me to walk to the church, but I'm walking slowly, dallying intentionally. Whether Rob has any real information or not is almost beside the point. I would, of course, love it if he were to give me a slip of paper with Audrey's address and phone number on it, but that's not all I'm looking for. I'm looking, to be sure, for my daughter, but more than that I'm looking for something which may help to make sense of all that happened so long ago and continues to haunt me. I'm looking for my sake as well as for the sakes of those I love.

Camelot Road is appropriately named, not because it leads to an Arthurian paradise, but because along its way there are so many once-utopian buildings. The buildings themselves, most of which are in an irreversible state of disrepair, are not utopian, but what they stood for (and still stand for) is. These are houses, studios, barns and even privies of the first idealistic artists and craftspeople who came to Woodstock in the early part of this century in search of something better, of a life that offered more than everyday rewards of trade and commerce. They were attracted, I'm sure, by one another and the sheer beauty of this Catskill Mountain community, in much the same way Leslie and I were twenty-odd years ago.

I am pausing now on the road and gazing down at a large gambrel-roofed barnlike house. It is imposing because of its size, compared with the more modest houses on Camelot, yet it blends into the mountainside with its weathered gray-brown clapboard siding and its gray slate roof. It looks as though it has been here, nestled in this forest of pines, hemlock, oaks, maples, birch and mountain laurel, for as long as or longer than the other Camelot dwellings, but I know better, for it was I, along with Leslie and an old friend, Will Paulson, who built the house during the last months of Leslie's pregnancy and the first months of Audrey's life.

The house, still and silent now, is owned by a Wall Street financial analyst and his wife, who use it on weekends and for two or three weeks during the summer months. But I remember when it was bustling with life and energy. I remember every detail of how it came to be, of how it was our Camelot.

As I stand here on this cold, overcast day before Christmas, staring at this house and remembering the dreams it once held for Leslie and me and our daughter, I'm tempted to warm myself with a few nips from the bottle of Old Crow in my backpack which I have brought for Rob Dawson, but I decide against it, knowing the liquor will bring on even more melancholy than I'm feeling now. I start to walk away, but I can't. There's something compelling about this moment, something that is urging me to stay on. It's an illusion, I know (though I wouldn't have realized this years ago), but I see a warm glow of fire flickering through the old secondhand double-hung windows in the house, and listening carefully, I hear a young child squealing, and a young mother laughing. The sun is breaking through the hazy clouds and mist and I can hear the rhythmic tapping of a carpenter's hammer and the buzzing of a circular saw. Peering down through imagined or remembered shafts of light, I can see the faintest hints of a house recently framed. And even farther, still in my mind's eye, I see an old barn in Stone Ridge, about twenty miles south of Woodstock, standing deserted, unused and in the early stages of decay, in a farmer's field, and drifting even farther, I see an apprehensive young man and a pregnant young woman (actually, a girl) talking to an old farmer and his wife, both of whom are smiling broadly at the questing eagerness of these two *children* who would, if it's at all possible, like to have the old barn and tear it down so they can reconstruct it on the acre of land they have up the road in Woodstock. And I feel the sense of energy and purpose they had when they began razing the huge building that had been given to them by the farmer and his wife.

There is no confusion in my mind as I stare not at the dark and deserted house down the hill but at the little pictures or waking dreams Leslie used to speak of, the ones that depicted things the way we hoped they would be, but that seemed impossible. The dreams of something better.

It's strange, almost in a mystical or religious sense, standing here now and realizing I'm consciously dreaming of a better past. And dreaming—still backward—of loving hands (our hands) which carefully marked every timber in this house, of hands which carefully penciled charts, showing where every chestnut post and every hemlock crossbeam should go to recreate the idiosyncrasies of the original building on its original site. Of hands, which after hours of toil and care touched each other. Of hands, which in the darkness of night and the comfort of bed touched the ever-swelling belly of Leslie Summers, the mother of the child within.

These are my little pictures now, my dreams of a more perfect past.

I have other pictures, too, of myself as a young man, standing outside the great, intimidating Fifth Avenue doors of the elegant Plaza Hotel on that cold January afternoon in 1964, testing myself, willing myself to work up the courage to go inside, to find the Oyster Bar, where Leslie had told me Juan Lanzo Ernesto worked.

I'm told Juan Lanzo Ernesto no longer works at the Oyster Bar. And upon questioning André, the waiter who was Juan's friend, I learn Juan was hurt by a girl he had loved, by a girl who had mothered his baby and who had left him. I learn Juan went back to Puerto Rico shortly after the baby's birth, that he is studying at the university there, trying to improve himself so that he can one day prove himself to Leslie Summers, this girl he loves.

Then I am on a plane, flying to an island, looking for a boy who is my enemy, my rival, so I can ask him to tell me where Leslie Summers is, force him if necessary. There is an address which André has given me. It is in Río Piedras, where the University of Puerto Rico is. I am sick from the sudden reversal of climate. Both temperature and humidity are torturing me as I wander, as though in a trance, looking for a bus, the Number 1 bus to Río Piedras, seeing every number but one, and asking someone and learning of *públicos*, private taxis, and being driven to an address (God knows this is the twentieth century!) on James Bond Street, to an apartment where Juan Lanzo Ernesto lived, but where he no longer lives.

And now wandering aimlessly on a San Juan beach where tourists' glass-and-steel monoliths rise grotesquely above pastel hovels, I face the warm, blue-green Atlantic, wondering why I am here, wondering if I can swim out into this beauty into the safety of exhaustion and drowning, but not wanting this, either, yet testing fate and feeling a sudden burning in my hand and arm, and not learning until later that I have been stung by a Portuguese man-of-war, and waking up in a hospital, with friendly white walls, dark-skinned nuns and crucifixes, with voices telling me in Spanish and English that I will be okay.

And then, feverish, I leave the hospital, find the Number 1 bus this time, go to the university, and after many lies, learn Juan Lanzo Ernesto is no longer in school, that he is back with his family in Mayagüez, a small city on the west coast of Puerto Rico.

Now, burning with fever, heat, humidity and anticipation, I am on yet another bus, with old men and women and children who seem old, too, people with baskets and gunnysacks, with chickens and sandwiches, eating and talking quietly with humility. Even with this, I am lost in my own confining thoughts of self-pity, envying these people who know at least where they are going, silently invoking a faceless God to let Juan Lanzo Ernesto be my friend, not my adversary.

I stare out the window as the bus moves inland toward the

mountains and away from the sea. Everything is so lush and overgrown that I can hardly see the mountains we're traveling through. Sometimes, though, there are powerline breaks in the trees and I can see the ocean again. From this distance, it's gentle as it slaps the shore. I have a sudden urge to abandon my search for Juan (actually, for Leslie) and to get off the bus now and go down to the water, thinking I'll erase my past and begin over here. I see small huts constructed of tin, tar paper, cardboard, scrap lumber, palm fronds and mud. Poor, listless people, filthy children in rags and skeletal dogs and cats are milling around these huts, and I'm thinking of the poverty I saw in India, and of plucky Eunice Williams and the other street people in Denver. There is something I love about these people, believing I can simply stop my life and start over with them. I invent a beautiful Puerto Rican wife whom I will love even more than I love Leslie. We will swim naked in the sea. At night the sand will still be warm from the day and we will make it hot again with our passion.

But I don't get off the bus. I have to go on to Mayagüez and find Juan. The huts with their people and dogs and cats are depressing me now, so I look beyond them to the sea again, where I see fishing boats and imagine yet another life for myself. I would like to be in the rain and wind and sun with the men on these boats. I would like to be a friend to them and to their families. I would like to be a part of them.

The bus dips back toward the sea and passes through tiny villages where people are staring at us and envying us (I think) for going somewhere. They would like to be going, too (or so my feverish brain tells me), and I feel sorry for them because they cannot. The bus passes through a village called Aguadilla, and I see young boys laughing and swimming, and I think again about getting off.

It is two o'clock in the afternoon when we stop in front of a dismal white stucco building which is the Mayagüez bus station. All the other passengers are suddenly animated and chattering noisily, happy to be at their destination. I want to be happy, too, but I am overwhelmed by depression as I step off the bus and gaze around this desolate town. I can hardly breathe as the dust and heat attack my lungs, and as the realization of what I'm doing sinks in. For an instant, I no longer care about Juan Lanzo Ernesto or Leslie Summers. I want only to be back in Colorado. I want to be a child again, safe in my mother's arms.

Both my fears and my emotional condition must show, because the bus driver puts his hand on my arm and in halting English asks, "Are you okay, señor?"

"Yes, sí," I say. Then I ask, "When is the next bus back to San Juan?"

He looks both puzzled and concerned when he answers, "Six in the p.m."

"Thank you." I feel good about that. The bus trip back will take four hours, which will give me time to get to San Juan's Aeropuerto Internacional for the eleven-thirty flight to New York.

I walk away from the station and see a hotel sign two blocks away. I decide to go there and ask if I can leave my backpack while I look for Juan at the address I was given at the university. I'm feeling weak and dizzy when I go into the lobby. The desk clerk says something in Spanish which I don't understand. I say, "I just want to check my pack for a few hours."

He stares blankly at me.

"I'll pay you a dollar, just for leaving my pack here." I hold it up for him to see.

Still, he doesn't understand. He holds up four fingers and manages to say, "Four dollar and cold-air room."

I understand and decide an air-conditioned room will be worth the cost, even if I use it for only a short while.

I pay him the four dollars and he shows me to my room. It is actually cold and I feel my fever and depression diminishing. Nothing has ever felt so good as this small air-conditioned room. The clerk shows me the shower and an icebox, where there is a bottle of cold water.

There's a double bed in the room, and the cold air is directed toward it. I decide to lie down for a few minutes, to relax and think about what I'm going to say to Juan when I find him. But I fall asleep immediately, and I dream.

I am in a strange town, walking alone on a narrow street that is stone-silent except for the occasional sounds of cars in the distance. A boy and a girl, perhaps a few years younger than I, pass by, and they're laughing. I want to be with them, but they go on and I feel lonelier than I ever have. And now, through the trickery of dreams, I don't know if I'm awake or not, but I think I am when I see another figure approaching me. I start to walk on by when I hear a voice say, "John." It's a familiar voice, and then I see a face, which is familiar, too, yet something prevents me from recognizing it entirely, but I pretend and say, "Hi." This person is a girl, and she's glad to see me. I try to focus on her face and concentrate on her voice, but I can't, and I think I'm drunk. She says, "Do you have a room?" I say, "Yes," and she puts her arm in mine and we walk to the hotel. She takes her clothes off and says she will fuck me for a dollar, and I say, "Fine." As I take my clothes off, she asks, "What are you doing here?" I say, "I don't know." Still, I'm trying to recognize her, but I can't. She laughs and says, "I don't know what I'm doing here either." She tells me she has been in London, but didn't like it there because it was so cold and lonely. She puts her arms around me and says, "I need the dollar." I'm confused, but she says, "I want to love you anyway, but I need the dollar for an abortion." Now I know. I can see her clearly. It's Leslie Summers. I back away from her, but she laughs again and says, "Be happy," and suddenly I am. We fall onto the bed, and I hear a knock at the door. I start to get up, then I see the desk clerk standing next to us. He's frowning severely as he says, in clear English, "No visitors." I turn to look at Leslie, but she's no longer on the bed. The clerk sits next to me and places his hand on my penis. I'm terrified and try to get up, but I can't. He grins and all his teeth fall out onto the floor. I want to pick them up, but I still can't move. His laugh turns into a deep, animal-like groan, and he says, "This is an island for people who have no place to go." I hear a pinging sound. First it's gentle, but then it gets louder and louder, and I realize it's raining.

I wake with a start. It is raining and it's dark outside. I go to the window and crank open the metal blinds. I have never seen rain come down with such force. It is louder even than the air conditioner. I stand there, listening and remembering my dream, feeling sick again from my fever and from knowing I have missed the bus back to San Juan.

I dress quickly and go downstairs to the lobby, and when I go outside, I realize it has stopped raining and I'm surprised to see that in such a short time the clouds are already beginning to clear. Outside people who were sheltered in shops begin to pour onto the street, and I feel surrounded by a friendly flood of humanity. I am glad sleep has prevented me from catching the bus, and I feel up to the task of finding Juan Lanzo Ernesto, but first I want to eat.

It is hot again as I walk toward the town square, which is near the little bus station. There's a café with an advertisement for pizza on the window. This sounds good, so I go inside and learn they have almost anything I could want, except pizza. I laugh and order a grilled ham-and-cheese sandwich and a beer, India, *la cerveza de Puerto Rico,* the menu reads. The waitress is nice and laughs, too, when I say something about the pizza sign. She tries to explain in Spanish, but I can't understand her. She is young and not very pretty, but I like her because of her laugh. I take from my pocket a piece of paper which has Juan Lanzo Ernesto's name and address on it. "Do you know where the Calle Guido is?" I ask.

"Calle Guido, *sí,*" she says. She starts to explain where it is in Spanish, but stops and giggles when she realizes I don't understand a word.

I say, "I'm looking for Juan Lanzo Ernesto on the Calle Guido, number 44."

Her smile drops into a frown when she asks, "Juan Lanzo Ernesto?"

"*Sí,*" I say, and I hold the paper out to her.

She looks at it and seems to be tracing his name with her fingers. "Juan . . . Lanzo . . . Ernesto," she says slowly. I can see from her face and nervous tracing of his name that she knows him, that he means something to her. There are no tears in her eyes, but I know they're close.

"I'm sorry," I say, and she seems to understand.

She hands the paper back to me and says, "Calle Guido." She takes my hand and leads me toward the door. She points across the square toward the bus station and says something that I still can't understand. She goes to the cash register and picks up a pencil and pad of checks and comes back to me. Then she makes a sketch of the square and the streets across from it. She marks the bus station and sketches a road behind it. The road is straight for what I judge to be three or four blocks, then there is a bridge over a river or stream and the road curves to the left. After the curve, she pencils in two buildings. One she labels "Coca-Cola" and the other she marks with a picture of a truck. She draws a large X over the truck, which I understand to mean it's broken. Next she draws another road to the left of the truck picture. She writes "Calle Guido" and draws in four or five houses, one of which she labels "44." She hands me the map and I say, "*Gracias.*" She smiles and goes back behind the counter.

I finish my sandwich and beer and wonder about her relationship with Juan. From her reaction, I guess she was once his lover or would like to be. It strikes me as strange that I know two girls from different parts of the world who have somehow been intimately involved with this young man I am looking for. I want to talk to this girl about him, but I can't, of course.

When I pay my check, I thank the girl again and impulsively take her hand and kiss it. She looks very sad when she smiles and says, "*Gracias.*"

I go outside and walk across the street to the square. At one end there is a large white structure which looks like an official town building. At first I think it's built of marble or granite, but when I look closer, I see it's stucco, only more polished than the other stucco buildings I have seen. There is a small pool with a fountain in front of the building, and several young boys and girls are wading in it. I see one small boy trying to climb up on the statue of some military hero in the center of the pool. He slips on its wet surface and falls into the water beneath it. The other children laugh at him, and I find myself laughing, too. On the steps of this official building several old men are playing cards and dominoes. I watch for a few moments and am mesmerized by the sharp slapping sounds of the dominoes as the men slam them down on the concrete steps. Whenever someone makes a good play, there is a lot of noisy and good-natured laughter and chatter, and something about this and the laughing children in the pool makes me feel good, even happy. I'm very nervous about going to the Calle Guido, but these people, who seem so content with the simplest of occupations, cheer me up. As with the people I saw from the bus, I want to somehow get to know these children and these old men.

On the other end of the square there is an imposing Catholic church, and it appears to be made of genuine marble. On opposite corners of the square there are black-and-white television sets mounted on pedestals, and people are crowded around them. I think about watching, too, but decide against it. It's getting late, and I want to try to find Juan tonight.

I walk away from the square and approach the bus station. There I pause and look at the map the girl drew for me, and I walk along the first road which leads to the bridge. Only a half block or so from the square the buildings become small and shabby. There are frame houses and shops, several of which have been boarded up, and a little farther along the road, there are shacks similar to those I saw from the bus. Ill-fed and flea-infested dogs sniff and bark weakly at me, but I'm not afraid of them, because they don't look strong enough to pose a threat.

There are rows and rows of broken-down houses and shacks. On many of the porches there are old women sitting in straight wooden chairs, staring silently out at the street. On one porch I see a parrot standing on a wooden railing. I stop and impulsively say, "Hello." The parrot cocks its head and stares at me. It doesn't say anything, but something about the way it stares makes me think it is able to speak, but too bored to bother. I'm reminded of the silent old women.

The farther I walk, the shabbier the houses become. They are as bad as anything I ever saw or smelled in the slums of Bombay. Most of the yards are littered with rubbish and decaying cars and trucks. Children are playing in these yards, seeming not to notice the filth. I feel sorry for the kids and wonder if Juan Lanzo Ernesto lives in a shack like these.

I cross the bridge and follow the street to the left, and I notice the houses on this side of the stream are in better shape. They all seem to be freshly painted and have neatly kept lawns. There are several bars and a pool hall, but they are neat and clean, too. A few people are on the street, and they don't seem to be as miserable and bored as the old women and the parrot were.

I look again at the map the girl drew for me and follow it to a storefront with a large Coca-Cola sign on its window. Across the street I see a garage, where two men are working on a large truck. I turn left and look up to see "Calle Guido" on a sign. My hands are trembling as I look at the sketch of the house labeled 44. I walk slowly. There are a few people on this street, too, but they ignore me. The houses here are modest, but they're the nicest I've seen in Mayagüez. I can see people through the windows and open doors, and it occurs to me that this could be any town in any country in the world.

Now I'm standing in front of number 44. Lights are on inside, but I don't see anyone moving about. I almost hope no one is home, but then I hear a baby cry and I see a woman walk across the living room. I walk slowly toward the porch, and the baby's crying gets louder. A man's voice calls out something in Spanish. My entire body is trembling, and I'm sweating, aware of my fever again. I stand in front of the screened door and try to knock, but my hand is frozen. I want to turn around and run, but someone suddenly appears at the door and flicks the porch light on. I'm temporarily blinded and can't clearly see the man who is speaking to me in Spanish. I blink and say, "Excuse me. Is this the Ernesto residence?"

"Yes," the man replies in English.

"I'm looking for Juan Ernesto," I say, aware that my voice is quivering.

The screened door opens. The man steps outside and says, "I am Juan Lanzo Ernesto."

I can only stare at him. He doesn't look at all like the picture I had imagined from Leslie's description. He's maybe five-six or -seven and slight, although muscular. His face is very fine, even delicate, and his dark eyes are large and appealing in a dreamy sort of way. He looks very young and is prettier than he is handsome. His hair is black, thick, straight and neatly groomed.

I finally manage to say, "My name's John Noble. You don't know me, but . . ."

"John Noble, from Boulder, Colorado," he astonishes me by saying. "Yes, I know you. I have heard about you."

He speaks English with no trace of an accent, and I feel a moment's guilt for doubting Leslie when she failed to mention the speech characteristics I'd assumed he'd have. He sounds as American as anyone I have ever known.

"Leslie Summers has told you about me?"

He surprises me when, smiling broadly, he grasps my hand. "Oh, yes, Leslie has told me about you." His handshake is firm and sincere, and I immediately feel comfortable with him. "Come inside," he says. "I want you to meet Leslie's son."

XV _____

It's snowing lightly as I resume walking up Camelot Road toward Father Jack's church and my meeting with Rob Dawson. In February and March, I usually complain about the cold and the snow in this part of the country and I talk about moving south, but I like this weather early in the winter. It seems to cleanse, not only the landscape, but also my head. I like to take deep, cool breaths and feel the snowflakes as they fall on my face and hands.

I have been dreading this meeting with Rob since last night, when Hervey showed me that pathetic letter in the *Woodstock Herald*, but now I feel better about it, and walking slowly and alone as I am, I realize something is causing me to believe, or hope deeply, that Rob really will know something which will help me find Audrey. Maybe it's the holiday spirit, that good feeling Kay, the boys and I always have this time of year, or maybe it's simply the snow and the sharp, cold air, but I feel optimistic now, even giddy with a sense of anticipation.

It's dusk, and the snow is beginning to fall faster. I can just make out the outline of the church's steep gable roofline and modest bell tower.

Now the dark cedar-shake facade of the small church is visible. I walk on and am suddenly startled when I hear the church bell ringing. No one has used this building as a church since Father Jack's death, but the bell is clearly ringing now.

Of course, it doesn't take me long to realize Rob Dawson is probably the one who's ringing in my arrival. I'm amused, thinking he's celebrating not my presence, but the imminent arrival of the Old Crow.

I take a flashlight from my backpack as I walk around to the front of the church and am relieved when I find the heavy, handcrafted oak door unlocked. Inside, I stare over the seven or eight rows of pews at the altar with its crude but attractively carved saints, Virgin and Christ Child, and I'm surprised to see candles flickering in the otherwise darkened building.

The bell is still ringing, but it sounds muted from the inside. I shout, "Rob! Hey, Rob, come on down." I turn the flashlight on and aim the beam upward.

I jump when I feel a bony hand on my arm and see Rob Dawson hunched over next to me. I shine the light on his face. He looks more ridiculous than usual. He's wearing a heavy black-and-red-checked coat and a red stocking cap with a large white wool ball on top of it. His dark, sunken face is almost lost in the folds of the coat's collar and the cap, which is pulled down to his bushy black eyebrows. His eyes are beady and birdlike, his nose resembles a beak, and his mouth is drawn in because of the absence of so many teeth.

"John, somethin' weird's happenin'." His voice is unsteady.

"Who's ringing the bell?" I ask. I continue to aim the flashlight upward, but I can't see the bell tower, which is over the back of the church behind the altar.

"That's what I mean," Rob says, tightening his grip on my arm and tugging. "I thought you was ringin' it. I mean, you know, like as a joke on me." He pulls on my arm again and tries to lead me toward the door.

I stand fast and say, "That's strange. I thought the same thing. I thought you were ringing it."

The bell is ringing more furiously now, and Rob's still tugging at my arm. "Listen," I say, breaking away from him, "it's probably someone we know, someone who read your letter and is trying to trick us." I think of Hervey Shultis. Maybe this is why he urged me to come up here, so he could scare the hell out of us. This is the sort of practical joke he would like. "Hervey!" I yell. "Is that you?"

Rob huddles up next to me, as a frightened and dependent child would. I can't help but feel sorry for him. Sorry and protective as I put my arm around his frail shoulders.

"Hervey!" I yell again.

The bell stops ringing, and Rob and I hear a vaguely familiar voice shout, "Hey, Rob, Merry Christmas, man."

We hear scrambling in the tower above. Then we hear someone climbing down the ladder behind the altar. I flash the light in that direction, and Rob laughs when we see Lucky Ambrosio appear from behind the carved Virgin, holding a six-pack of Black Label beer.

"Hey, Lucky," Rob says, "what you doin' here?"

Lucky shields his eyes with his free arm and says, "Man, you're blindin' me. Move the light."

I move the flashlight as he walks toward us. In the dim candle-light, he looks more bizarre than ever. He's wearing red galoshes and multicolored wool leg warmers over his jeans. They're held up with a black woman's garter belt strapped around the outside of his pants. His worn blue denim jacket is covered with colorful patches and peace symbols from the sixties and seventies, and his head-dress, held on with a gold brocade band, is a kaleidoscope of tie-dyed colors. His face would look almost angelic, framed as it is, were it not for the circles of red rouge around his eyes and the junk jewelry hanging from the hem of his headdress. This seems more like Halloween than Christmas Eve.

"How's it going, Lucky?" I ask, holding the flashlight so he can see my face and Rob's.

"I'll be fucked," Lucky says, now standing in front of us. He looks at Rob, as though I'm not here, and says, "I sure as hell didn't expect him to show up." He hands the six-pack to Rob.

"What's this for, Lucky?" Rob asks.

Lucky sighs and regards me suspiciously. "It's your goddam Christmas present. I didn't think anyone else would bring you one." He slides down into a pew and says, "Man, I sure could use a joint."

"How about some bourbon?" I ask, trying not to laugh at the ridiculousness of the three of us here in Father Jack's church on Christmas Eve. I can't for the life of me understand why I'm here, but I'm glad I am. Leslie Summers once told me I was destined to have a mediocre life, and moments like this give me pleasure because they seem to contradict her pronouncement.

"Hey, John," Rob says, almost apologetically, "you really brought a bottle? I mean, you read my letter and brought a bottle for me?"

I reach inside the pack and say, "Sure—it's Christmastime, isn't it?"

"Man," Lucky says, standing up, "for someone straight, you're okay."

"Don't talk that way to John," Rob says, placing the six-pack on a pew.

"Hey, man, I didn't mean nuthin'. Just like always, flappin' my big mouth."

I unscrew the bottle's cap and, handing the bourbon to Lucky, I say, "It's all right."

Lucky takes an eager swig. He wipes his lips with the hem of his headdress and hands the bottle to Rob. "Yeah, you're okay, man," he says to me.

Rob stares at me as he drinks. Then he hands me the bottle and, pointing toward the altar, says, "I lit them candles, you know, just in case you came, thinkin' it would make it, you know, kind of holy, bein' Christmas and all." He sniffs slightly and adds, "Guess I was thinkin' some 'bout Myrna, too. It was a year ago tonight."

"The candles look great," I say, feeling a knot in my stomach. I walk toward the lighted altar, and they follow me. I can't help but think anyone watching us through the windows would think we were a strange Christmas procession.

"Hey, man," Lucky says, "you ain't drinkin'." I try to hand the bottle back to him, but he says, "No way. You first. I don't drink alone."

I grin and say, "Rob's drinking with you."

He pushes the bottle away. "That's not what I mean." He sounds disgusted with me. "I mean, for Christ's sake, it's Christmas and you're too straight to drink with bums like Rob and me."

I laugh out loud at the idea of drinking on Christmas Eve for Christ's sake and say, "Nope, I'm not that straight." I take a swig and immediately feel the liquor go to my head.

"Hey, yeah, that's more like it," Lucky says, almost cackling with his little victory. He takes another drink and holds the bottle toward Rob.

Rob doesn't take it, though. He's reaching in the pockets of his coat. He can't seem to find whatever he's looking for and mutters, "I know it's here."

"What you lookin' for, man?" Lucky asks impatiently.

"Somethin' I brought for John," Rob says, reaching inside the coat's breast pocket.

Lucky takes another drink and passes the bottle back to me. I am lifting it toward my lips when Rob gleefully says, "Found it. Here it is, John." He holds his hand out to me.

I lower the bottle and ask, "What is it?" I look closely and see it's a crinkled, time-worn snapshot. It looks like the school pictures Jack and Mike bring home every year.

Rob grabs the bottle from me and drinks again before handing the photograph to me. "Take a good look, John." There's something somber about his tone, and I think I know who the picture is going to be of.

I hold the photograph under the flashlight's beam and feel my hands quiver as I look at the face of a thirteen- or fourteen-year-old girl with long, straight hair and very dark and intense eyes. It could be Leslie Summers a long time ago, but it's not. The smile is mine and Leslie's, and it's the one I saw on a three-year-old's face over twenty years ago. The last time I saw this face it belonged to a baby, and now I see it belonging to a near-woman. I stare at this photograph of Audrey, and I can't help but feel sorry for myself as I think of all I have missed. All the things I have taken for granted and even failed to notice as Jack and Mike have grown are suddenly very apparent to me as I look at this photograph of a stranger who is my daughter.

"Where'd you get this?" I ask, realizing it sounds like a demand.

Rob almost cowers, as if he's ashamed. "I thought you'd want it."

I hardly hear him as I turn the photograph over and see girlish handwriting:

Hi, Myrna, how about this! I look like a zombie. Hope your school picture turned out better.

Love,
Audrey 1978

My voice is unsteady again when I turn the photograph over and stare at the image of my daughter and ask Rob, "Is this what was in the tin box? Is this why you and Lucky dug up the grave?"

Rob says, "You were nice to me, and I wanted you to have it for Christmas. It was Myrna's, but she'd want you to have it. There's some old letters, too."

I want to ask about the letters and the red belt, but not yet. I put my arms around Rob and hold him as he cries. For some reason which I simply cannot explain, I think of a scene from *Moby Dick*, where the sailors are squeezing whale sperm in a vat. Melville, in describing this, was showing the profound sense of comradeship this particular job generated. I have experienced it a few times when mixing plaster. Sometimes lumps, or potatoes, as we call them, will form in a bad bag of plaster, and guys in my crew and I have to squeeze them out with our hands. And there is that sense of comradeship Melville described. It's something sensuous or sexual between men, but it's not overt homosexuality. This, at least, is the way I feel about it, and it's what I'm feeling now as I hold Rob Dawson. We have both lost daughters, but his loss is irrevocable.

XVI _____

When I met Juan Lanzo Ernesto on the porch of his mother's house in Mayagüez, Puerto Rico, on that warm, humid night in January of 1964, I hardly knew what I was doing there. There were blurs in my mind that said I was looking for someone I loved. Leslie Summers, of course. And there were other blurs that said I had to be where I was in order to find her. There was also something that said I had to prevent her from having an abortion. I didn't care that the child she was carrying might be someone else's. I cared about being with Leslie again, but I wanted the unborn child, too. I wanted anything that had to do with Leslie Summers, and there on the porch with Juan, I even wanted him, because he and I had Leslie in common.

And then there was the baby. Leslie's baby. The child she had said was dead. When Juan took me into the bedroom where the infant, Michael Lanzo Ernesto, was being rocked in Juan's mother's arms, I almost broke down. Not because of Leslie's lie, but because of the relief I felt for her. It didn't matter then that she had lied. She'd apparently had her reasons, and that was enough.

When Señora Ernesto handed the baby to me, I held him as though he were mine. I'm probably exaggerating, but this seven-month-old boy felt and smelled the way his mother had. I kissed his forehead, and a momentary lapse of logic allowed me to hold and kiss Leslie Summers again. I recall glancing at Juan and seeing an expression I had never seen before and have not seen since. It was one of consuming warmth and trust. At that moment, Juan Lanzo Ernesto and I were one in our mutual love for this child and his mother.

After I handed the baby back to Señora Ernesto, Juan said, "Shall we take a walk?"

I nodded. "Yes, I'd like that."

We went outside and slowly retraced my steps back toward the town square. Juan's voice was both passionate and controlled, and as we walked, I had a strange awareness of doppelgänger. I was walking along a dimly lit street in Mayagüez with Juan Lanzo Ernesto, listening as he talked about the girl we both loved, but I was also walking across the University of Colorado campus with Leslie Summers and listening to her. There were moments, instants, when I saw myself from both points of view. When I was walking with Juan, I saw myself holding hands with Leslie and walking with her. As I would try to touch what I saw, everything was reversed, and I was walking with Leslie and watching myself with Juan. Sometimes I was listening to Juan as he told me about Leslie, while at other times I was hearing Leslie as she told me about Juan. It was as if I were standing in front of a mirror. I was on both sides, but everything else was different.

Something, maybe it was the howling of a dog, finally brought me back to my time and place, and I was listening to Juan as he said, "We were in Leslie's apartment."

"Her father's fancy apartment on the Upper East Side?" I asked.

He laughed, a small, sympathetic laugh. "Leslie has a way of exaggerating." It wasn't an accusation; it was a statement of fact.

It took a few moments, but I realized Juan was telling me the story Leslie had told about their date and the subsequent rape. His was the same story, but it was also different, and it made me think of telephone, the party game children play, where one child whispers something to the person next to him, who in turn repeats it to his neighbor, and so on until it gets back, entirely altered, to the one who began the game. Juan was giving me his version, and I instinctively knew it was the one that was closer to the truth.

"I took her to dinner at the Oyster Bar in New York. I was able to do that because I worked there. Otherwise, I would never have been able to afford it."

"I know," I said, feeling sure of myself. "That's what she told me. Did you take a horse-drawn cab ride through Central Park, too?"

He glanced up at me. "So she told you in detail?"

"She didn't leave much out," I said. "At least I don't think she did."

"She told you about her father?" He stopped walking and reached into his pocket for a packet of cigarettes. He offered me one and lighted both his and mine. I noticed as he exhaled that he did it with flared nostrils, as I had seen Leslie do so many times.

"She told me she had, well, more or less caught her father in an embarrassing situation."

He laughed again. This time it was cynical. "Embarrassing," he said. "Embarrassing." He repeated the word as if he were examining it, as though it were an object rather than a word. "Embarrassing is an interesting way of putting it." We resumed our stride.

"What do you mean?" I asked. I was beginning to feel uncomfortable, not with Juan, but with the realization that he knew a lot more than I did.

"She didn't tell you the whole story, then?"

"Apparently not," I replied. "She said that the night before she was supposed to go out with you she walked in on her father, who was, I guess, waiting for his mistress, and caught him in some sort of weird rubber sex costume. Something like that."

We approached the bridge I had crossed earlier, and when we got to its center, Juan leaned against its painted tubular railing. He smoked in silence for a few seconds before saying, "What she told you is true, but you didn't hear the entire story."

I shrugged.

"Did she tell you about being raped?" he asked.

I felt shy and didn't want to repeat Leslie's accusation, so I said,

"Yes, but I knew she wasn't telling the story exactly as it happened." My words were coming out awkwardly, and I added, "I mean I knew you hadn't really raped her."

"Me, raped her?" Juan said incredulously. "She said I raped her?"

I was confused. "Yes."

He laughed again. It was a dangerous-sounding laugh. "I want you to see something," he said. He struck a match and tilted his head back. "Do you see this?" He ran his finger along a raised white scar on the underside of his chin. It was about two inches long and followed the jawbone. Judging from its whiteness and thickness, I could tell it had been a deep wound.

"Yes, I see it."

He flicked the match to the pavement and said, "I got it that night when I was with Leslie."

I didn't understand.

Juan put his hand on my shoulder in a brotherly way, and we began walking again. "Leslie *was* raped that night, but not by me."

I didn't believe him, yet I asked, "Then who did it?"

He sighed. "We went to her place, to her father's apartment, and got drunk."

"She told me that," I said.

"And we went to bed together."

"That isn't exactly the way she put it," I said.

Juan removed his hand from my shoulder. "No, I'm sure she didn't, as you say, put it that way."

"She said she intentionally provoked you, but then decided she didn't want to go all the way." I felt silly saying "all the way."

He shook his head. "My friend, you're missing what I'm trying to tell you. There was never any question about making love."

I impatiently said, "Look, I don't know what you're trying to say, but I wish you'd get it out."

He stopped again and faced me. For the first time since we had met, I noticed the silver cross Leslie had described, hanging from a chain around his neck. "Her father caught us," he said.

"What do you mean, caught?"

"He came back to the apartment when Leslie and I were in bed. He surprised us and cut me with a beer-can opener, what you call a church key. Then, after I left, he had sex with his own daughter. She told me he raped her. Now you must surely understand who Michael's father is."

I felt solid and stupid. Instead of taking in what Juan was telling me, I wanted to run away from him, away from Puerto Rico, but, as if caught in a terrifying dream, I couldn't move.

I don't know how long we stood there in silence before I finally heard him say, "Now you know."

There was something almost perverse about the way I said, "Tell me again." I believed him, but I wanted to hear him repeat the details.

Juan seemed to understand, for he said, "Leslie's father raped her. He is the father of her child."

"But why do you have the baby?" Nothing was making sense. "Why did she say he was dead?"

Juan began walking again, and I followed after him. "As far as Leslie is concerned, Michael is dead."

"That's not true," I insisted. "She told me about him. She went back to New York in October. For his funeral." My voice trailed off.

"That's what she told you. It was easier to tell you that."

I ignored this and asked again, "Why do you have the baby?"

"If I didn't have him, he would be dead." He put his hands in his pockets and hunched over as he walked. "And because I love Leslie."

"You love her?"

"As much as you do."

"Does she know this?"

"Of course."

"What are you going to do about it?" I asked.

He startled me by replying, "The same thing you're doing. I will continue to love her."

We approached the town square, which was crowded with people watching the television sets in the opposing corners. I wanted to ask more, but I couldn't form words around my thoughts. I wanted to feel anger toward Leslie for the lies she had told, but I couldn't. Her lies, I reasoned, hadn't been malicious. They had been necessary. Necessary for her survival. How, I wondered, could I have failed to see what she had been going through? When she told me about that night when she walked in on her father, how could I have missed what she was trying to tell me? I wanted to know more, but I also wanted to change the subject, and I foolishly asked Juan about the girl in the café who had drawn the map for me.

He looked surprised when I mentioned her, but he said, "We were going to be married once, when we were very young. A long time ago."

"But then you fell in love with Leslie?"

He nodded. "I went to New York to make money for our marriage, and . . . you know the rest."

I was shocked as I stared at Juan and thought of the heaps of human rubble Leslie had managed to leave behind.

I'm recalling things now, but I don't know for certain where reality is separated from the fiction allowed by time and my imagination. After Juan told me about the rape, I willed a sort of protective shield around myself. I somehow refused to let the things he had told me sink in. I knew he was still talking as we sat on a bench in the Mayagüez town square, but I allowed myself to hear and absorb only tiny bits as I looked at the people who were standing in opposite corners of the square, watching the public television sets.

I remember nervously laughing during dramatic scenes in *The Untouchables* as Eliot Ness and Italian gangsters shouted at one another in Spanish, which I couldn't understand. I also remember jolts of English as Juan talked.

I saw a man and woman walk into the square with five little girls. They all sat on the bench next to the one Juan and I were sitting on and silently watched television. They were wearing what I imagined were their best clothes, and I found myself enjoying them. It seemed clear that they were poor and that this was a special night of entertainment for them, but it was even clearer that they were a family, that there was a closeness between them that didn't require money or luxuries, and I imagined one day having this same sort of unity with Leslie and our children. I could still hear Juan in the background, but his words were only so much noise then, noise without meaning to me, as I invented a family which consisted of Leslie, me, the baby Michael, the child Leslie was now carrying. I stared at the man and his wife and their five little girls as they stood up during a commercial break between programs and began walking toward the church opposite the official building where I had earlier watched the old men playing dominoes and the children wading in the pool. This family had been waiting for Mass to begin, and I realized I wanted to go into the church with them.

I stood up and, glancing back, saw a look of both surprise and understanding on Juan's face as I followed the family to the church. Inside, it occurred to me that this was the first time I had ever been in a Catholic church, and I felt good and secure sitting in a pew and being surrounded by hundreds of devout people. The priest began a prayer, which I couldn't understand, but which nevertheless held meaning for me as I bowed my head and closed my eyes and tried to see the same God I was sure all the other people could see.

But my God was not the same. With my eyes closed, I saw Leslie, who faded quickly into an image of Juan Lanzo Ernesto, holding the small child who had been fathered by his grandfather. When the prayer was over and I opened my eyes, I tried to will the God of these other people into my mind, but He would not come. I watched as these people stood up and went to the altar for communion. I wanted to go, too, but I felt guilty. This was their church, their God, not mine. I watched as four men began passing baskets around, and I felt sick as I heard small coins being dropped into them. These people, virtually all of whom were clearly poor, had no business giving what little they had to this God who I thought had done so little for them on this island, for people who had no other place to go.

I went back outside to the bench in the square where Juan was still sitting, lost in his own thoughts. I sat next to him, and he asked, "Did you find God in there?" I shook my head, and he smiled. "You're going back to New York to be with Leslie?"

"I'm going to try to find her," I replied. "She's pregnant again."

I was startled when he said, "I know."

"How?"

"She called." He looked away from me. "We're friends now."

"What did she tell you about me?" I asked.

"She said she was not going back to you or to Boulder."

"Did she tell you she's going to have an abortion?"

He avoided my eyes when he answered, "Yes."

"Did she tell you the child may not be mine?"

This time he looked at me, but he paused before saying, "You don't know Leslie Summers."

"What's that supposed to mean?" There was hostility in my voice.

"She's an illusion."

I tensed, remembering what Leslie had said—"It's fine for me to be a dream, but don't ever turn me into an illusion." I started to speak, but he put his hand on my shoulder, as he had earlier, and said, "I mean she is not what you think she is. She is not what she has told you she is."

I was growing impatient. "What is she, then?" I asked.

"She is someone who has had to invent a life in order to live."

"I don't care what she has invented, I'm in love with her, and that's something I haven't invented. As you know, I'm here because I want to find Leslie, and right now you're the only shot I have." I was surprised by my own firmness.

Juan stood up and began pacing. "I'll tell you where to find her," he said. "But I'll also give you some advice."

"I don't want advice," I said sharply. "An address will be enough."

With no emotion in his voice, he said, "It will be an address to hell, but I'll give it to you."

Juan wrote Leslie's New York address on a slip of paper and handed it to me. Then he began walking away. Before I could thank him, he stopped and said, "By the way, the child she's carrying is yours."

I hurried after him. "Do you know that for a fact?"

"Yes."

"But why did she . . . ?"

"Don't bother to ask why Leslie says things." He began to walk again, but stopped and said, "There's one more thing."

"Yes?"

"I have given you Leslie's address as a friend, as one who understands."

"I know."

"But I must warn you, again as a friend, that I will take Leslie away from you if I can."

"What does that mean?"

"Don't think that because Leslie is carrying your child I love her any less."

Juan disappeared into the dimly lit streets, and I wouldn't see him again for over three years.

Part Two _____

Searching

XVII _____

Of course, I went back to New York the day after Juan gave me Leslie's Seventy-fourth Street address on Manhattan's Upper West Side. I was distressed by the shabbiness of the neighborhood. To me then, most of New York City looked as dirty and run-down as Mayagüez had, only on a larger scale, probably because I was an innocent from Colorado, where even the poorest families usually kept their yards up and their houses painted. In Manhattan there were no houses or yards; there were only office and apartment buildings, littered asphalt streets, and an occasional scrawny tree, and it all looked dirty and uncared-for to me.

When I got to Leslie's building, a five-story brick row house that had long ago been painted pale green, I thought I understood what Juan had meant when he had said he was giving me an address to hell. It wasn't only that the building was filthy and tacky-looking; paint was peeling from it and several of the windows had been boarded over, and the boards on the ground level were covered with sloppy and obscene graffiti. There was also a stench that made me think of rotting fish. To get to the building's entrance, I had to walk down a few steps to a gray metal door with its lock ripped out. I pushed it open and stepped inside a dark foyer, where there was another locked door. Thankful that I had a lighter, I flicked it and held the flame up to a row of buttons on the wall. Only a few of the

125

buttons had names next to them, but Juan had given me Leslie's apartment number. I pressed the button next to the number eight and heard a buzzer and then a click. I pushed against the interior door, which opened immediately, and began walking up a gray metal staircase to the right of the door. I soon heard someone hurrying down the stairs. I recognized the footsteps on the noisy metal treads, not because of a good ear, which I certainly don't have, but because my senses were being guided by what I can only describe as my heart. I knew the person running toward me was Leslie Summers.

We met at what must have been the third floor and quite literally fell into each other's arms. I'm not certain how long we stood there, holding each other, kissing and crying, but it was long enough to attract the attention of a grumpy neighbor on the floor below, who opened her door and shouted, "Gwan! Show some respect fer the rest of us!" We laughed and walked, hand in hand, up the stairs to Leslie's apartment, which was surprisingly large and attractively furnished.

Once again, my memory is vague as I try to recall the details of our reunion. Leslie was wearing blue jeans, I'm certain of that because it was so unlike her, and she was also wearing a crisp white blouse with an Eton collar. Her skin was tanned, as it had been the first time I'd met her, and I recall thinking she, not I, looked as though she had just returned from a tropical island. Then we were in bed, making love as though no time had passed since we had last been together in Boulder.

I think the issue of her pregnancy came up that first day we were back together, but I know we didn't dwell on it. Nor did we talk about my trip to Puerto Rico and my meeting with Juan and Leslie's son. We made love, smoked occasional cigarettes and drank beer. That's the picture I have of that day.

In the few days that followed, we reaffirmed our love for each other, I talked her out of the abortion, and we decided to get married. I wanted to return to Boulder, have our wedding there and then go back to school, but Leslie had different ideas. She told me about a meadow in upstate New York above the town of Woodstock. It was called Magic Meadow, and she described it as the most beautiful spot she had ever seen. When she said she had dreamed since childhood of being married there, I was persuaded.

Six days after I arrived in New York from Puerto Rico, Leslie Summers and I were married in the snow-covered Magic Meadow by Woodstock's justice of the peace, and to my considerable surprise, we settled in Woodstock. That was Leslie's wedding present to me. Although we never talked directly about her family and the fact that her father had been the one who had raped her, she made it clear that she knew I was better informed about her past than I had been, and she said the cottage we moved into had been owned by her family. She didn't spell things out, but I was left with the impression that her father, out of guilt, had given it to her.

The cottage was small and dated back to the early part of the century and the beginning of the artist-colony days of Woodstock. It was constructed of exposed hemlock and chestnut timbers with mortise-and-tenon joints. These rich, gray-brown weathered posts and beams were set off by rough white plaster walls and ceilings, which gave the house a feeling of antiquity and intimacy. The floors were of random-width yellow-pine planks, which were pegged to the sturdy 4×8 joists. There was a massive bluestone fireplace, which, along with a wood-burning cast-iron kitchen range, provided us with heat. The outside of the small house was of rough-cut native pine siding which had long ago weathered to a rich yellow-brown, and the roof was of gray slate with downy moss growing over most of it. There was indoor plumbing of a sort, which is to say there was an old-fashioned hand pump next to the kitchen sink and the bathroom had a handsome hand-pounded copper tub that had to be filled by carrying buckets of water from the kitchen. There was also an old American Standard flush toilet, which similarly had to be flushed by pouring water into it.

Primitive as the cottage was, it was ours and we loved it, but we knew we would have to winterize it and add more space if we were going to raise a child there. It was a combination of this need, Leslie's brains, and my coincidental good fortune that not only gave us all the comfortable space we needed, but also launched my career as a carpenter.

A few weeks after we had settled in Woodstock, I was looking for a job—any kind of job, for we were short on money, especially after I cleared my account in Denver and repaid Eunice Williams—and happened to run into Will Paulson, an old high school friend, who was working for a construction company in the nearby town of Kingston. He helped me get my first job as a carpenter's helper, and on weekends he helped me winterize and add a room to the cottage.

Both Leslie and I took to the various aspects of carpentry naturally. I had done very little physical work, except when I was a cook's assistant in the Merchant Marine, and I realized I liked the strenuous work of framing a house as well as the intricacies of finish carpentry, and I also liked working outside in the Catskills air. Leslie liked the construction routine, too, not so much in a physical way but in an intellectual sense. She liked the design process as well as the engineering or architectural side of the business, load capabilities and maximum spans and that sort of thing. She was also very smart when it came to understanding the commercial value of real estate. She knew instinctively that most New Yorkers who came to Woodstock to buy weekend and summer houses were looking for the rustic qualities of the old but also wanted the conveniences of the new. It was this natural understanding of people and architecture that put us into a very satisfying and profitable business after only a few months in Woodstock. Leslie named our construction business New Old Houses. She did the designing, advertising, talking and selling, and Will and I did the building.

Our first house, after the renovation of the cottage, was the barn we were given by the farmer and his wife in Stone Ridge. Leslie had noticed the many old barns that were unused and neglected in our area of upstate New York, and she reasoned that we could get them for the price of our own labor in the razing of them. Neither Will nor I believed her, but this was just another instance of my misjudging her abilities.

Leslie's sense of drama and timing might very well have been envied by many an actor. She was seven months pregnant with Audrey when she decided we should check out the barn we had seen in Stone Ridge and commented on so often. The first thing she did, independent of me, was to become friendly with the proprietor of the hardware store in Stone Ridge. Even in late pregnancy and in financially tight times, Leslie had a knack for dressing well, in what I still regarded as New York chic, but when she went to Stone Ridge to discuss *business,* she dressed the part by wearing a plain and somewhat old-fashioned yellow gingham dress, what she called sensible shoes, and a kerchief on her head. In this costume she was more beautiful than ever, and I'm sure, even now, that it was her striking beauty, rather than her country affectations, that made her a hit with old Mr. Oosterveer, who owned the hardware store. He was, as I was later to discover for myself, a crusty and tight-lipped geezer who knew how to turn a dollar and didn't let anyone put anything over on him, but he had never before come across anyone quite so beguiling as Leslie Summers was. Two visits to his store and Leslie had not only the names of the farmer and his wife who owned the barn, but also a good part of their family history, as well as Mr. Oosterveer's endorsement for her scheme to "recycle" the barn on our land in Woodstock.

It was at this point that Leslie brought me into her plan. Of course, I knew what she was doing. That is, I knew she was trying to get the elderly couple to give us their barn so we could raze it and reconstruct it in Woodstock. But I didn't know how she was doing it until the Fourth of July in 1964, when we went calling.

I borrowed Will's beat-up International pickup and wore my standard work clothes, to which Leslie added a CASE baseball cap, for "authenticity," and she wore her pregnant-country-girl outfit, complete with a worn straw sun hat, and we set off for Stone

Ridge. She even brought a two-quart thermos of fresh lemonade and some homemade oatmeal cookies. I felt awkward and silly, but Leslie laughed and said, "That's perfect, exactly the way you should feel and act." She snuggled up to me as I drove and added, "Trust me and we'll be the happy owners of a two-hundred-year-old hand-hewn barn before the day's out."

I kissed her on the temple and said, "You even sound like a country girl." It was true. She had added just enough twang to her voice to sound like the real thing.

"Just you wait, honey, and you'll see what kind of gal you got yourself married to."

The farmer and his wife, Mr. and Mrs. Van Wagoner, received us as Leslie had said they would, with interested courtesy and without the suspicion that country people frequently reserve for strangers. Within minutes, as we sat on their front porch, drinking lemonade and munching cookies, the Van Wagoners were treating us almost as though we were their children, and Mrs. Van Wagoner was giving Leslie all the pre- and postnatal commonsense advice she could come up with.

When we—actually, Leslie—got to the subject of the barn and what we hoped to do with it, Mr. Van Wagoner was reluctant to discuss it. But that didn't last for long. To my surprise, and I think even to Leslie's, Mrs. Van Wagoner said, "Jerome, don't be a stubborn old fool. You know well's I do that the old barn is more a liability than anything else to us. Roof's beginnin' to leak, and we both know you're not about to go up there and fix it again."

"It's been on this farm a mighty long time . . ." began Mr. Van Wagoner.

"Pooh!" interrupted his wife, taking Leslie's hand in hers. " 'Nother year and the roof'll be gone. Then the top plates is gonna rot out, and what will we have? A big heap of unmanageable kindling, just like down at Ritter's place."

Mrs. Van Wagoner winked at Leslie, who lowered her head and smiled slightly. We both knew we had the barn then. But there were still formalities to go through.

Mr. Van Wagoner eyed me suspiciously when he stood up and walked toward the barn, which was only sixty or seventy feet from where we were. Leslie nodded for me to go with him, but before I had a chance, he said, "Well, don't know what I'm gonna do with the tractor if the barn's gone."

Mrs. Van Wagoner was quick to say, "I'll tell you what to do with it. What's it been, goin' on ten years now, since you last used it. Give it to these nice young folks, 'long with the barn."

The old farmer looked sadly at his wife and said, "Think we should get something for the barn. Lots of board feet here. Lumber's goin' for up to twelve cents a foot at the mills up in Wittenburg and Shandaken. And that's for pine and hemlock. Can't get chestnut at any price."

"What satisfaction you gonna get out of a few dollars?" demanded Mrs. Van Wagoner.

"Oh, we'll be happy to pay what we can," Leslie said.

"Nonsense," said Mrs. Van Wagoner. "We don't need the money, not for the barn and not for that old tractor." She walked over to her husband and said, "Now, Jerome, you know well as I do that you'll get about a hundred times more satisfaction out of seeing this barn go down and then grow back up as a fine home for this young couple and their baby. It's gonna be like giving away a little bit of history and giving it a new life."

As Leslie had predicted, we were the owners of this magnificent old barn by that afternoon. And we also had a tractor to help us raze and then reconstruct it.

I want to pass quickly but not entirely over the three and a half years of my marriage to Leslie Summers, not because they were fraught with unhappiness, but because they were, on the whole, the best years of my life. I was married to the brightest and most beautiful woman I had ever known, and by mid-1965 we had two crews working for us and were making quite a lot of money building old barns into houses for well-to-do New Yorkers, but the most significant event of our marriage occurred on August 24, 1964, at

11:27 A.M., when we became the parents of Audrey Summers Noble. I suppose all new parents feel they have done the most original and perfect thing when their first child is born, and I was no exception. The love I felt for my daughter and wife eludes description. It was there, clear and without question, and its very existence not only obscured my old demons but seemed to have utterly destroyed them.

Even now, over two decades later, I have to force myself to turn the corners of that shroud of happiness that so mesmerized me during those years to see the traces of gloom that were lurking, that led to the destruction of everything that seemed so perfect and permanent.

The first out-of-the-ordinary thing that happened after Audrey's birth was so ridiculous that I passed it off to drunkenness and Leslie's peculiar sense of humor. Leslie, Audrey, Will Paulson and I were celebrating the raising of the ridgepole of our new house, of the barn the Van Wagoners had given us. This is a traditional celebration in our part of the country; when the ridgepole, which is the highest part of the roof, is set in place, it's customary to nail a pine bough to it and then take the rest of the day off for a celebration, or topping-off party, as it's called. This is what we did. It started with a bottle of champagne that Leslie brought for the occasion. After nailing the pine bough to the ridgepole, I was to smash the bottle against the pole. Leslie had pointed out that the shell of the newly placed barn, with its gambrel roofline, resembled an inverted ark, and she thought we should "launch" our house for good luck. I agreed, but the bottle didn't. The glass was so heavy that it refused to shatter as I banged it against the relatively soft hemlock ridgepole. Never one to be a sore loser, I brought the bottle back down the ladder and the three of us drank its contents. When the champagne was gone, we went back to our cottage, and after putting Audrey down for a nap, we continued the celebration with a bottle of Scotch. After several drinks, Leslie began to tease me about the champagne bottle. "Even the Queen of England can shatter a bottle," she said.

"Against a steel hull," I replied, not taking her seriously.

I should have taken her seriously, though, because as Leslie, Will and I proceeded to get drunk, Leslie made several sharp remarks about my lack of manliness. To rub things in, she sat on the couch next to Will, who was considerably drunker than we were, and told him to take his shirt off and flex his muscles. There was certainly no contest. His arms made mine look like toothpicks. I suppose that had I not been drinking, I would have seen that Leslie was teasing, because she was drunk, too. But I didn't see that, and I became angry and jealous as she ran her hands over Will's arms and chest.

"What are you trying to do?" I asked.

Will was close to the pass-out stage, but that didn't stop Leslie from pulling him toward her and kissing him on the lips. She then glanced at me and said, "I'm kissing a man."

I lunged toward them, yanked a handful of her hair and pulled her off the couch. She felt limp, and I realized she was quite a lot drunker than I had thought. Feeling remorseful, I hugged her and said, "I didn't mean to hurt you."

She pulled away, and as a final jab, said, "You even fight like a woman." She turned and weaved toward our bedroom, but before she passed out, she shouted, "You want to be a woman, try having a baby like a woman."

I put that down to her condition and turned my attention to Audrey, who had been awakened by our fighting.

Audrey and I spent the rest of the afternoon and evening playing together in the yard. She had just learned to walk, and we played several games of chase, where I got on my hands and knees and she toddled across the lawn after me. Despite the pity I felt for myself, there was a great deal of fun and laughter whenever Audrey caught me.

When it began to get dark, Audrey and I sat on the old-fashioned slat swing on our front porch, and after a few minutes of swinging she was fast asleep. I put her to bed and threw a blanket over Will, who was still out on the couch. Then I went to our room and crawled into bed with Leslie. As I lay next to her, I felt guilty for my reaction to her teasing. I wanted to wake her and apologize, but thought better of it and soon drifted off to sleep.

During the night, I woke abruptly with a terrible pressure and burning in my bowels. I bolted for the bathroom, where I felt as though my insides were exploding. Hot fluids gushed from my body, and I was sure I was dying. The diarrhea lasted for several minutes, and when I finally thought there was a chance that I would survive, I heard Leslie laughing from the bedroom.

The night-light was on, and she was sitting on the edge of the bed, giggling. I was about to ask what was so funny when I saw the enema bottle on the floor. Outraged, I yelled, "Why in God's name did you do that?"

Still laughing, she said, "That's what it's like to have a baby."

"What the fuck are you talking about?" I picked the warm rubber bottle up.

She stood up and put her arms around me. "Sorry I teased you earlier," she said.

"Forget about earlier," I said, "what's this shit about the enema?"

This set her off again, and I was even able to see the humor in my question, but I didn't show it. "Why'd you do this?"

She stifled her laughter and replied, "Just so you could know what it's really like to be a woman."

"I don't follow you."

"A hot enema has to be close to having your water break when you're giving birth."

"You're sick," I said.

She pulled me to her again and said, "It was a joke. I didn't mean anything. I just wanted to see how you'd react to having your water break."

"You really are screwed up."

"Maybe." She laughed again and pushed me onto the bed.

Before I could say anything, she was on top of me and grinding against me. "You've got to learn to develop a sense of humor, sweetie."

"I've got a sense of humor," I protested.

"You have more than that now."

Of course, the argument was over.

Months went by before we had another fight. There were a few minor arguments, but neither of us attacked with the vehemence we had employed on the day of the ridgepole celebration, and time eased both my sense of humiliation and my concern.

There was another incident after we had moved into the barn we had reconstructed on Camelot Road. It was serious in that it could have killed me, but it was too subtle for me to be able to place absolute blame on Leslie. I had returned late one evening from Easton, New York, about a hundred miles north of Woodstock, where we had bought a house that had been built in 1776. We had bought it cheap, as a "handyman's special," and I was spending as much free time as possible fixing it up, partly as an investment, but also as a place for us to escape to on weekends.

When I walked inside, I heard Audrey playing upstairs in her bedroom with Myrna Dawson. They seemed to be playing hide-and-seek, because there was considerable shouting of "Found you!" followed by loud giggles. I laughed, listening to them. Leslie and Audrey had met Myrna at the town's recreation center early in the summer, and the two girls had been inseparable since. I didn't know Myrna's parents, but I knew her father had once been in the circus, because she bragged about him all the time, and Audrey sometimes chastised me for not doing exciting things like that.

I called out Leslie's name, but there was no response. I figured she was upstairs with the girls and had started to go up when I heard the downstairs shower running. I knocked on the door, but still there was no response. When I opened the door, Leslie was sitting on the edge of the tub, naked and staring at the spray of water. "What's wrong?" I asked.

"Everything," she replied, without turning to face me.

I knelt next to her and put my arm around her shoulders. She stiffened and said, "Please don't touch me."

"Hey, what's the matter?" I tried to kiss her.

"I said, don't touch me."

Her face was pale, and it was clear that something was seriously troubling her.

"What happened?" I asked.

She turned toward me and said, "My father called."

The mention of her father sent chills through me. I had tried to talk to her about him before, but without saying so she had always made it clear that he was not to be mentioned. That, of course, was understandable. "What did he want?" I asked.

She held her hands under the water and replied, "What do men always want?" Her tone was icy and clearly directed toward me.

The rhetorical question shocked me. Even with what I knew about her father, I couldn't let myself envision Leslie and him in sexual terms. Incest was a dirty word to me, but it didn't have a sense of reality. It was something my own psychology had blacked out, but as I stared at Leslie, it seemed to reach out and slap me. A vision of Juan Lanzo Ernesto's mother, holding the baby Michael toward me, appeared, and I stood transfixed as the infant transformed into a withered old man with a lascivious grin on his face. The shower water seemed to become the old man's gnarled hands, grasping her and pulling her toward him. I reached for her and tried to break his grasp. She shrieked, "What the fuck are you doing?"

Suddenly sobered, I realized I was holding Leslie's shoulders and had pulled her to her feet.

"Get your goddam hands off me!" she screamed.

I released my hold. "Sorry. I don't know what happened. When you mentioned your father, I . . . I don't know. Something happened."

"My father! Don't ever, ever mention him again!"

"But you're the one who said he called."

She began hitting me with both fists, and by the time I finally subdued her, she was crying. I held her and said, "It's all right."

"It's not all right," she insisted. "It's not all right." She held me and continued to cry.

When she finally calmed down, I wanted to ask again about her father, but I didn't. I merely asked, "Are you going to be okay?"

She looked up at me and said, "Yeah."

"You sure?"

She kissed me as if nothing had taken place and said, "Yep. Now I'd better take my shower."

Reluctantly, I left the bathroom, and she called after me, "Will you try to light the oven? I tried earlier, but couldn't get it going."

"Sure," I called back.

All I remember is a flash. When I came to my senses, I was on the floor and Leslie was standing over me. The hair on my arms was singed and my shirt was scorched. "What happened?" I asked.

"The oven blew," Leslie replied, with no emotion in her voice. "I must have left the gas on."

I'm not certain, but it must have been her tone of voice that made me think she had left the gas on intentionally. I was afraid. Afraid for myself. Afraid for our family.

In early July 1967, nearly two months before Audrey's third birthday, I received a phone call from my brother in Denver and learned our mother had died the night before of a heart attack. Although my brother didn't say it directly, it was clear that he at least partially blamed me for her death. After the funeral, he told me she had never forgiven me for dropping out of college and running off to marry Leslie in New York.

My mother's death and the guilt my brother placed on me left me feeling weak and awful; I was able to hold myself together only by thinking of my wife and daughter waiting for me back in Woodstock. A few days after the funeral, when the matters of my mother's small estate had been settled, I flew back to New York. At La Guardia I bought a stuffed rabbit for Audrey, which I was going to tell her was a gift from her grandmother. This wasn't entirely inaccurate, because I had inherited a little over eight thousand dollars.

Before leaving Denver, I converted my inheritance into traveler's checks. When I got home, I was going to suggest to Leslie that we spend the money on a vacation in Europe. I knew I could safely leave our construction business in Will Paulson's capable hands, and I thought it would be good for Leslie, Audrey and me to get away for a while.

What I didn't know was that Leslie had already thought about getting away. By the time I drove from the airport to Woodstock, it was nearly three in the morning. I took my shoes off when I stepped inside the house and went quietly to Audrey's room with the rabbit. I placed it on her pillow and leaned over to kiss her, only to realize she wasn't in the bed. Thinking she was probably sleeping with Leslie, I picked the rabbit up and went to our room. Even as I approached the bed in the darkness, I had a foreboding that my wife and daughter weren't there.

I switched the night-light on. The bed was empty and neatly made. On my pillow there was an envelope with my name written on it in Leslie's neat, girlish hand.

I dropped the rabbit, and my hands shook as I picked the envelope up. The note inside was short and vague.

John—I'm leaving. My timing is bad, but that can't be helped. It's better for me and it will be better for you, too. Don't try to find us. I'll be in touch.

Leslie

XVIII ———————————————

Lucky Ambrosio, Hervey Shultis and I are standing at the foot of a freshly dug grave in the Woodstock cemetery, listening to the Methodist minister's bored drone as he pretends to give dignity to a life that never commanded it. Lucky's head is bowed. His bandanna, or makeshift headdress, is no longer colorful. Sleet has clung to it and turned it white and stiff. Something about his stance and the headdress makes me think of Ingrid Bergman's movie portrayal of Joan of Arc. I couldn't have been more than ten when my mother took my brother and me to see the film, but I can still see Ingrid's face as flames began to consume her. I cried, and my mother thought I was crying for my father, thinking of the flames that had lapped at his body. I felt guilty as she tried to comfort me, because I was crying for Saint Joan, not my father.

I feel a hand on my shoulder. It's Hervey Shultis. He's staring blankly, not at the minister and not at the simple coffin hovering above this scar in the earth. He's staring at the frozen mound of dirt, which the sleet is turning white, and I know what he's thinking. The last time he was here, only a few weeks ago, there was another mound of dirt. Myrna Dawson's dirt from the grave next to this one.

Hervey's thinking what I'm thinking. I'm sure of it. First the daughter and now the father. But his thoughts—actually, my

139

thoughts—won't stop here. We're thinking of our own mortality. I want to shift my thoughts from Ingrid Bergman to the scorched remains in the box at our feet, but I can't, and I feel ashamed because I'm not grieving properly for Rob Dawson.

I'm staring at the mound of dirt. It's even whiter now, and it's solid with the cold. The builder in me is curious. I'm trying to imagine how the gravedigger's backhoe is going to be able to get these clumps of frozen earth back into the grave. I'm trying to kick my mind over to the minister's words, but I can't. I'm wondering how the machine was able to excavate this grave. I have been in the construction business most of my adult life, and I know it's impossible to excavate when the earth is as frozen as it is now. But people die in the winter, and they're buried when the earth is solid. Does God make exceptions for the dead? I know better, but I can't help thinking it. The gravediggers must have something that softens the earth, perhaps a salamander or some other portable heater. I've read that in Siberia the winter dead are stacked in icehouses to await spring burials, but that's not the case here.

> Some say the world will end in fire,
> Some say in ice.
> From what I've tasted of desire
> I hold with those who favor fire.

Now I'm hearing the minister's words. I asked him to read Robert Frost's poem "Fire and Ice." It seemed appropriate, but now it sounds absurd. I'm angry with myself and the preacher. Rob Dawson died in fire and now he's being buried in ice. That's the appropriate part. The absurd part is that he wouldn't have known the difference between Robert Frost and Jack Frost. I chose this for me, not for Rob. I chose the minister, too. Not for Rob, but for me. I don't know why I do these things.

> But if it had to perish twice . . .

I don't want to hear any more. The minister has no sense of cadence. He has no sense of the man he is awkwardly trying to lay to rest. I feel chills of responsibility. I think they're for Rob, but even as the thought passes through me, I know better. They're for me, but not in a responsible sense. In a selfish sense.

I realize I'm envious. Not of Rob because he's dead, but of Rob because he has managed to do the one thing I have been so incapable of. He is joining his daughter. There is nothing he wanted more, and now he's doing it. In moments their bodies will be side by side, but that's not the sort of joining I'm thinking of. I'm thinking, I guess, of their souls, or whatever it is that brings people together—dead people or living people. I don't want to think this way, but I can't help it. My life and thoughts seem as mediocre as Leslie Summers once said they were. I'm dealing with the embarrassment of my own foolishness and ignorance.

I'm staring beyond the ridiculous minister, beyond Lucky and Hervey, beyond the casket and mound of ice and dirt. I see swings and slides in the playground next to the cemetery, in the recreation field where Audrey and Myrna Dawson used to play together. It seems good, nice, that a playground and a cemetery have a common boundary. Nice for the dead, at least. I wonder about the children. But I have to stop this. What I'm really doing is resenting Rob Dawson because he is making me confront myself. He has led me to a precipice, to a moment I can no longer ignore. I resent him because he found his way by dying and left me behind to begin the search I have put off for so long.

My hands are in the pockets of my parka, and I feel the cold crispness of the patent-leather belt that supposedly belonged to Shirley Temple, and I feel the crinkled letters and photograph of my daughter. I finally understand what Rob Dawson was doing, what he is still doing. He's giving me a shot at dignity, at the same dignity I thought I was trying to give to him.

I look at Lucky again. He hasn't moved. He's crying, not with tears, but with his silence and stillness. He blames himself for Rob's death. I want to tell him it's not his fault. I want to confess, in much the same way I imagine Catholics confess their sins to priests. I want to do it for his sake, but for mine, too. I want to tell

Lucky I'm responsible for Rob's death. But that's not enough. Nothing is enough.

I'm crushing the belt now. I suddenly feel light. Not light-headed. Just light, as though I'm standing on the moon. Rob is talking to me. I don't hear his words, but I feel them.

You're the only one who ever was decent to me.

We're in the church. It's Christmas Eve—the night he died. I'm embarrassed by his sentimentality.

Rob knows what I'm thinking. "Cut the crap, Johnny. Take a look at that belt."

I hold the belt up and stare at it.

"Johnny, it's not the belt, it's what it means. It's the one thing in the world Myrna was proudest of. She and your little girl was always fightin' over it, you know. The way friends do. You find your girl, and this belt's gonna say lots more than all your fancy words. She's gonna remember."

"I don't know how."

"Bullshit. You show her that belt, and she's gonna love you."

I feel the belt tightening around my hand. Now my gaze is above the cemetery and beyond the playground. Overlook Mountain is covered with snow and sleet, and near its top I imagine I'm seeing the charred remains of Father Jack's church, where Rob died on Christmas morning, but I'm no longer blaming myself for providing the whiskey that led to the fire. Lucky says they drank the entire bottle and Rob insisted on having a religious service for Myrna, who'd died exactly a year earlier. One of the candles at the altar caught Rob's jacket, but he was too drunk to realize it. Lucky says he saw him burning, but he thought he was seeing the resurrection of Myrna.

Now I see myself in the remains of the church, standing on the altar where Hervey Shultis found Rob's body. I do understand the belt now. I do remember Myrna and Audrey playing with it. I remember Myrna's pride when she told us her father had been in the circus. I remember Audrey's awe and her disappointment because I had never done anything as exciting as that. And I know what Rob meant when he uncovered his daughter's grave and exhumed the belt, letters and photograph for me. I also know why he felt compelled that night in the Duck & Dog to tell me about my failed suicide attempt so long ago.

I feel weak as Rob's casket comes to rest. I pick up a chunk of frozen dirt from the mound above Myrna's grave and toss it into his, and I see everything around me with sharpened senses. I know this moment and everything about it will remain forever an indelible part of my experience. I am going to find Audrey, despite my fears and Kay's.

I wandered around our abandoned house for hours after reading and rereading Leslie's note, and while I don't have a clear recollection of what I was thinking, I know something was going on inside my mind as I searched every room and corner for traces or ghosts of my wife and daughter. There were moments of depression which were so stupefying that I felt I'd never be able to pull myself out of this emotional mire, yet even as I was yielding to this weight, there were other forces at work, forces which, had it not been for the experience of my mother's recent death, would have been alien to me. While one side of my psyche was searching for the artificial calm and safety of madness, the other side was mocking this with strength and purpose. Something was insisting that while I couldn't control my feelings, I could take a hold on my actions and emerge from these overwhelming circumstances of my life with a sense of resolve that would be unconquerable. This had happened when my mother died and again when my brother told me how disappointed she had been with me. My emotions had been so wobbly that I was convinced I'd die, but then something akin to a wondrous chemical seemed to release itself into my brain, and it gave me a strength I had never before known. I was able to get through the funeral and the formalities that went with it without a noticeable bruise. My focus was clear and straightforward, and I found it easy to avoid the distractions of grief.

There were moments in those early hours as I wandered around the house when I damned my mother, when I cursed her for abandoning me, yet even as I did this, the sweet spirit of resolve placed its hand in mine and brought on the contradictions of love and thanks for the armor and strength my mother's death had provided. When I emerged from my depression, I felt almost aloof to the situation that confronted me. There was, I knew, absolutely nothing powerful enough to prevent me from finding Audrey and taking her away from Leslie Summers. I wish I could say I was driven solely by paternal love, but that would be compromising the truth. Hatred and the need for revenge were the true forces behind my resolve.

It didn't matter then that I hadn't the slightest idea where I should begin looking for Leslie and my daughter. The solution, I reasoned, was almost mathematical. It was a syllogism of instinct and intellect. I knew they could be almost anywhere, but it was immediately apparent that Leslie would have anticipated my thoughts of checking the obvious places such as the apartment on West Seventy-fourth Street in New York or Juan Lanzo Ernesto's mother's house in Mayagüez, and while my first inclination was to tick these places off as improbable, a sort of inner voice told me that was exactly what Leslie would expect me to do. It was thus with the support of this inner voice that I began my search.

I recall with distinct clarity the moments, hours and days that followed my emergence from the shackles of depression and confusion. I had once dreaded the prospect of facing Leslie in a chess match, and now I was almost bullish in my eagerness to confront and destroy her.

After showering and shaving and changing into what I thought of as my grown-up clothes—a crisp white shirt, tie, sports jacket, slacks and black penny loafers—I repacked the shoulder bag I had taken to Denver with a change of clothing for myself and for Audrey. I then put my passport in my breast pocket, not because I thought I'd need it for international travel, but because it was a joint passport with a photograph of both Audrey and me, which I thought would be useful if I found her and had to prove to local authorities or anyone else that I was her father. I zipped the shoulder bag shut, but then opened it again and placed the stuffed rabbit I had bought for Audrey inside.

Even now, I can conjure up a precise image of myself then: walking out of the house, with the bag hanging from my shoulder, into the startling light and oppressive heat of this July morning, getting into my car and glancing around the circular shale drive-way, hoping this is all a ridiculous mistake and that Leslie's car will be there, but at the same time knowing it won't be, knowing this is real. Driving slowly on the rutted Camelot Road, hearing the tires of my sporty Volvo crushing the stone beneath them, hearing crows chattering menacingly at one another and at me, the intruder, seeing white birch trees standing in elegant contrast to the darker pine and hardwood trees, now noticing the abrupt change of sound as my tires leave the crushed stone and begin rolling over the warm asphalt of Overlook Mountain Road. Con-centrating on my own purpose, but being aware of the rest of the world, seeing houses, nestled in their wooded lots, seeing traces of color as my neighbors' dogs and children race across lawns and drives. Everything, sights and sounds, becoming a blur as the road straightens and my car begins to pick up speed.

I'm driving with a sense of purposefulness, ignoring its anti-thetical cousin, helplessness (or hopelessness), knowing full well, in a cold and analytical sense, what I'm looking for and rejecting the mockery of my ignorance. Noticing the white steeple of the Dutch Reformed church opposite the village green, seeing the hardware store, the grocery store, delicatessen, bus station, and funeral home as I brake for the stop sign at the town's center, seeing the morning regulars who have congregated on the stone benches around the village flag and war memorial to chatter away the day, wanting to call out to them, "Have you seen Leslie and Audrey, driving a white Chevy Nova?" but recognizing the futility of that, glancing to my left and seeing the ugly yet utilitarian brick facade and plate glass of the Woodstock Savings and Loan Association, and turning past the Duck & Dog, parking my car and going into the bank, where I'm startled into more loathing and determination upon learning Leslie has closed both our business and personal accounts, taking over fifteen thousand dollars. Invoking God to thank and bless my dead mother for the eight-thousand-dollar inheritance, knowing how crippled I'd be if Leslie had left me as penniless as she had intended to. Heading back to my car, looking up at Will Paulson's apartment above the Duck & Dog, thinking about going to talk to him about my troubles, but knowing he's probably at work on the house we're building, glancing around the parking lot for a lucky, heads-up coin, and weighing my next move.

The Methodist minister closes his Bible and covers it with a piece of clear plastic. Hervey Shultis and I turn to leave the grave, but Lucky Ambrosio stays where he is.

"Come on, Lucky," says Hervey. "Let's go for a drink at the old Duck."

Lucky won't take his eyes off his friend's coffin. "Naw, you go on. I'm stayin' here with Rob."

"Suit yourself," Hervey says, shrugging. "Let's go have a couple," he says to me.

We head toward my car, and I'm sorry Hervey didn't bring his. I want to be by myself. I want to consider my next move.

XIX _____

The Duck & Dog is crowded with people who have found the storm, which is rapidly turning into a blizzard, a good excuse for an afternoon of conversation and good cheer. The inevitable football game is on the television set at the end of the bar, and there's a crowd standing around Mick Murphy, who has two claims to fame. He's well versed in the works of George Santayana, which holds little meaning to the regulars, and he's Woodstock's bookie-in-residence. He will take bets on anything from horse races to football games to how fast a cockroach can get across the bar. Although he almost always comes out ahead in his gambling endeavors, he remains one of the most popular patrons of the Duck & Dog, probably because he offers more hope than anything else. When he gets drunk, he quotes from Santayana, and that's happening now as Hervey and I edge past him and the others who are listening, not for the philosophy, but for what they think may be reference to a hot tip. I manage to hear, "Philosophy is something reasoned and heavy; poetry something winged, flashing, inspired." Hervey mutters, "Bullshit," and clears a path to the far side of the bar, where we find two vacant stools. Pat, who has been watching our progress through the crowd, asks, "How'd it go?"

"It was a goddam shame," Hervey says. "How do you pay respects to a burned-out old circus boozer?"

Pat catches my eyes and I say, "Lucky's still there, blaming himself."

Pat knows I'm blaming myself, too, and he says, "Don't take it so hard, Johnny. I'm gonna miss that little devil myself, but . . . aw, shit, he's better off where he is."

Hervey's eyes widen in exaggerated mockery as he says, "Well, you going to get us a drink or give us a sermon?"

"By Jesus," Pat says, winking at me and embellishing his Irish brogue, "if it's a drink you're wantin', it's yer dear old mother's teat ye should be askin' for."

"Cut the crap," Hervey grumbles. "It's a cold bitch out there. Give me some of that top-shelf mother's brandy you got and a warm Guinness."

Pat sighs. "You know, from your many years of patronage of this fine establishment, that the Guinness is on tap and cold."

"So, the sooner you draw it, the sooner it'll warm up."

"By Christ Almighty, you've got a point there, I'll not argue it with you." Pat turns to me and says, "Johnny, what'll you have?"

"Just a Guinness," I say. "Cold's all right."

"You're an easy man to get along with, Johnny Noble," he says, turning to get our drinks.

"So what'd you think of that preacher?" Hervey asks. It sounds impersonal, but I know him well enough to understand that his tone doesn't mean he's uncaring. He's trying to lighten things.

"Not much. To tell the truth, I don't know why I asked him to perform the service in the first place."

He puts his hand on my shoulder, as he did at the graveyard, and says, "Hey, if you hadn't, no one would have. That was a fine thing you did, John. You were all the family old Rob had."

This embarrasses me, and I look away from him. I'm fond of most of the people here. This place has, over the years, become a sort of family for all of us. This was once Rob Dawson's home, too, even more than for the rest of us. I understand why Pat had to bar him, but I can't help wondering if he'd be alive now if he hadn't been kicked out. Maybe he'd have met me here instead of at Father Jack's church.

I have to stop thinking this way. Rob's dead and there's nothing I can do about it.

Pat brings our drinks and says, "On the house."

"Jesus, what got up your ass?" Hervey says.

Pat's too busy to banter with him, so he simply replies, "I just felt like being a decent fellow." He turns away, and I can sense Hervey's embarrassment.

There's yelling at the end of the bar as someone makes a touchdown, and I'm drifting back to the television sets in the Mayagüez town square and to Juan Lanzo Ernesto. I have wondered about him over the years, not with pity or hatred, but with a curiosity about fate's treatment of him because of what he did for his love of Leslie Summers.

"Hey, Johnny, loosen up," Hervey's saying. "Don't let Rob's death get you down."

"Yeah, right," I say absently.

"Look, that's the way things go. You did the right thing, what you could. That's what's important. Let's have a few drinks and put this behind us. Okay?"

"Sure." I like Hervey Shultis, but I don't want to be with him now.

"Bullshit!" he says. "Okay, don't loosen up. Hey, look, it's all right. I know how you're feeling. It's the same with me, but you know how I am. Always goofin' around, trying to make the bad things go away. Sometimes I wish I could be more like you, you know, just ride the waves till they smooth out."

His boyish honesty and eagerness to please are taking me out of my depression, and I'm grateful for that, but I can't shake my thoughts of Juan Lanzo Ernesto. I wonder if he's changed over all these years, or if, like Hervey, he has remained a boy.

My search for Leslie and our daughter took me to a world I had never before imagined. There was, I'm sure, a connection between this world and the one of my frightening childhood dreams, but in this one I didn't have the escape of awaking. I wasn't so naive that I hadn't seen through many of Leslie's lies and exaggerations, and I hadn't entirely dismissed Juan Lanzo Ernesto's comment—or warning—about her being an illusion and someone who'd had to invent a life in order to survive, but I hadn't taken this as seriously or literally as I should have. Blinded, first by love and then by hatred, I followed ignorance and my own sense of purpose to a world that was not only alien, but was becoming increasingly incomprehensible.

When I drove out of Woodstock on that July morning in 1967, I planned to go to the nearby town of Kingston to see Jeff Morgan, a lawyer who had helped Leslie and me with several real estate transactions. I was going to tell him what had happened, or what was happening, and ask him to help me; however, as I approached the traffic circle which had exits to Kingston as well as to the New York State Thruway, something from inside told me I was expecting Jeff to have godlike powers because he had a law degree. There appeared to me, not exactly a vision, but a sort of waking dream in which I was standing in a sterile courtroom with a high ceiling and institutional-green walls, dressed awkwardly and uncomfortably in a suit and tie. Opposite me was Leslie Summers, who was wearing a plain, yet suggestive, virginal white gown. And between us there was a doll, which I recognized as Audrey. Sitting above us was a stern-faced judge in a black robe who could not keep his eyes off Leslie. High above all of us was a gallery of spectators, all of whom were grotesque, Goyaesque men who were also staring at Leslie and making obscene gestures. I was holding the end of a rope which was wrapped around Audrey's tiny waist, and as I tugged on it and attempted to pull her toward me, I saw that Leslie was holding and pulling on the other end. I was momentarily confident that there was no contest, but then, out of the corner of my eye, I saw the judge raise his gavel. It came down in slow, silent motion, and as it did, all the spectators from the gallery leaped down to where Leslie was standing and grabbed hold of her section of rope.

I tugged on my end with all my strength until I heard Audrey scream, "Daddy, you're hurting me!"

The scream, more real than imagined, brought perspiration to my scalp and startled me back to my time and place, and I saw I had passed the Kingston exit and was approaching the thruway. Automatically, I braked and took a ticket from the uniformed man inside the toll booth. For miles there was only a blur of highway, trees, fields, road signs and other cars as I sped south toward New York City, where something akin to superstition and nervous logic told me I'd find my wife and daughter. I seemed to hear an inner voice that was saying if I got to the apartment on West Seventy-fourth Street, where I had been reunited with Leslie over three years before, I would find them there and catch Leslie off guard. I wasn't clear how I'd get inside and take Audrey from Leslie, but even as I worried myself about that, the layout of the apartment came back to my mind. It was a two-story apartment on the top floors of the building. The first floor consisted of a large living room and a bathroom, kitchen and bedroom, and there was a small terrace off the living room. The second floor was actually a horseshoe-shaped balcony over the living room with another bedroom at the rear, over the first-floor bedroom. As I drove and ran the locations and sizes of the rooms through my mind, my initial thought—or plan, by this stage—was somehow to get to the terrace and then quickly force my way into the apartment, even if it meant smashing the glass door that opened into the living room. But that idea quickly faded as I realized it would be virtually impossible to get to the high terrace from outside the building. I tried to visualize the buildings on either side and saw a much larger building on the left which had fire escapes all the way to its roof, and I knew I could climb up and drop down to the roof of her building. There was a skylight over the living room, from which I would be able to see what was going on inside and which, with only a screwdriver, I could remove from its frame. It would be approximately a seventeen-foot jump, but I knew I could reduce that to a much safer nine-foot drop if I silently removed the skylight and waited for the right moment, when Leslie was dis-tracted or in another room, and lowered myself to a hanging position before jumping.

I ran the plan through my mind over and over again as I drove down the thruway, and as I perfected both my means of entry and then escape with Audrey through the apartment's entrance and down the staircase to the street level, I lost all sight of what I'd do if they weren't there. That I had to leave up to fate and my intuition, both of which turned out to be shaky.

Even as I convinced myself that I could find them in the apartment on West Seventy-fourth Street and make my escape with Audrey, another memory worked its way into my brain after I crossed the Hudson River on the Tappan Zee Bridge and entered Westchester County. I headed south toward the city and happened to notice a sign for Hastings-on-Hudson. This at first meant nothing to me, but as I glanced at the sign a second time, I thought of Croton-on-Hudson and the girls' school where Leslie had said she had been a student when she met Juan Lanzo Ernesto. I pulled to the road's shoulder and fumbled through the glove compartment for a road map. Tracing the Hudson with my finger, I found the town of Ossining a few miles north of where I was, and then I spotted Croton-on-Hudson. Little shivers of satisfaction tingled through me as I shifted into first gear and pulled back onto the thruway and headed for the nearest exit.

When I got to the center of Croton-on-Hudson, I saw a cop parked at the side of what appeared to be the town's main street. I pulled behind him and got out of my car. As I approached his, I tried to retrieve the name of the school from my mind's recesses, but it wouldn't come. I was momentarily flustered, but when I said I was looking for a girls' school, a peculiar look crossed his face. It was the sort of look ordinary people sometimes have when they're in the presence of celebrities or the very rich. "Oh, sure, you mean Wharton, the Wharton School for Girls," he said, with exag-gerated courtesy.

"Yes, that's it," I replied. "Could you tell me how to get there?"

He glanced at my car in his rearview mirror, and I remember thinking he was trying to get a fix on me, to see if I was one of "them." Even though my Volvo was old, it was a handsome sports car in good condition and defied age and a basis for estimations of my status and wealth. Evidently he was satisfied, because he politely gave me precise directions to the school and offered to lead me there if I wanted him to.

"No, that's all right," I said. "I'm sure I can find it. Thanks anyway."

As I walked back to my car, he called out, "If you get lost, just come back here and I'll show you the way."

"Thanks, I sure will," I said. His courtesy pleased me, but it also made me a little nervous. I didn't have any evil intentions, insofar as the law was concerned, but still I couldn't help but feel a little guilty. I quickly passed that off, however, and headed toward the Wharton School for Girls, which was, according to the cop, located in a former private estate overlooking the Hudson River.

The school was even more impressive than the policeman had led me to believe. I had never questioned Leslie on her family's wealth, and while she had, when we first met, led me to understand that there was money in the family, I had never given it a lot of thought. I wasn't prepared then for the thoughts that assaulted me when I drove onto the grounds of the school. There must have been at least six or eight main buildings on the large compound which was on an embankment high above the Hudson, and there were numerous other buildings which were large, but small by comparison with the main structures. The predominant architecture was Doric Greek Revival, which was popular in the late eighteenth and early nineteenth centuries. A few of the buildings, both large and small, were newer and dated to the Victorian era. On their own, they would have been impressive, but next to the Greek Revival buildings with their heavy white fluted columns and bold, simple cornices, these late-nineteenth-century structures were poor cousins. The grounds were massive and elegantly manicured in a curious, almost British way. There were at least three topiaries on the vast estate-turned-girls'-school. One was made up entirely of shrubs that had been trimmed into the shapes of jungle animals. Another contained large exotic birds. And the third was made up of what appeared to be solid, sculpted geometric shapes. As I pulled into the driveway in front of the largest Greek Revival building and parked at a space marked "Visitors," I wondered why Leslie, with her imagination and her architectural interests, had never told me about these buildings and the gardens. I don't know if I, like the cop who had given me directions, felt both a sense of awe and inferiority then, or if I simply felt cheated. Cheated because after over three years of living with Leslie Summers, I was struck with the cold and intimidating realization that I knew nothing about her. There was a richness there that couldn't be denied or easily forgotten. The entire ambience of the place made me think of a time, years earlier, when, while on leave from the Merchant Marine in Germany, I had gone to Bavaria with a friend to see the wildly extravagant and ornate castles the crazy Bavarian king Ludwig II had built in the second half of the nineteenth century. As absurd as they were in their architectural excesses, they left me feeling not exactly breathless but weak with a sense of wonder and disbelief. They were fantasies that the mad king had transformed into reality.

As I walked into the main building, which I had rightly judged to be the administration office, I felt as though I had been transformed to another time, even to another world. Unlike other historic structures I had been in, the building had not been renovated to conform to twentieth-century utilitarian demands. The ubiquitous linoleum tiles that adorn the floors of many public and academic buildings in this country were not to be seen. Instead, in the entryway or former vestibule there was a polished gray marble floor, and in the hallways the floors were of worn but well-kept oak.

I walked toward a door which was marked "Admissions" and was almost unaware of where I was and what my purpose was, so impressed was I with the integrity of this building and of all I had thus far seen of the Wharton School for Girls. The hostility I felt toward Leslie Summers was still there, but it was momentarily tempered by all I was taking in. I went into the admissions office and saw an elderly woman sitting at a desk which was surrounded on three sides by tall oak file cabinets. There was something about this woman that suggested she was an original fixture in this building. I don't mean that in a degrading sense—rather I mean if I had somehow traveled through time to the eighteenth century and found myself in this building in a circumstance similar to or identical to the one I was in in this year of 1967, I would have expected to come face to face with this very woman. At first glance, there was nothing particularly striking about her. She was probably in her mid-sixties and had gray-white hair which appeared to have been recently coiffed. She was a little on the heavy side and wore a comfortable-looking, yet reasonably formal, black dress with circular white designs on it. It was clear that she wore glasses because of the faint indentations on the bridge of her nose, but the glasses were nowhere in sight. I detected a slight odor of perfume, which I recognized as Shalimar, because that was what my mother had worn.

The woman stood up from her desk and asked, "May I help you?"

She came to the counter where I was standing, and I realized what had caught my attention. She was wearing a cameo on a chain around her neck, and the finely sculpted mother-of-pearl face, surrounded by a delicate frame of filigree gold, was the face of Leslie Summers. My expression must have been grotesque, because the woman said, "Are you all right, young man?"

I finally managed to say, "Thank you, yes. I'm fine."

It was obvious that she didn't believe me, or that she didn't believe my face, so I said, "I was taken by your cameo. It's identical to one my mother used to wear," I added, lying.

She gave me a quizzical look and said, "This has been in my family for nearly two hundred years. Was your mother's an old one or a reproduction?"

"I really don't know," I replied, trying to take my eyes away from hers. "She had it for as long as I can remember." I wanted to slap my face or splash cold water on it, anything to transform the image in the cameo.

"Would you like to take a closer look?" she asked, and I realized she was as curious about me as I was about the piece of jewelry.

"No, no, that's all right. It just surprised me, that's all."

She smiled in a way that caused me to feel naked, or strangely disarmed. It was as if something I had said about my mother's identical cameo had let this woman in on a secret that I couldn't have been aware of, and I was sorry I had told the lie, sorry I hadn't said the face reminded me of a girl I knew.

She said, "It's interesting that my cameo caught your attention."

"Why's that?" I asked, confused.

She backed away from the counter and turned toward one of the filing cabinets near her desk. Opening a drawer, she said, "Because the image on my cameo strongly resembles one of our former pupils."

I almost blurted out, "Yes, I know," but I remained silent, hoping she would tell me more before I had to ask.

She pulled a file folder from the open cabinet and frowned. She then took a form from the folder and peered at it for a few moments before removing a photograph which was inside its fold. As she held it toward me, I said, "It's Leslie Summers, isn't it?"

She opened a desk drawer and put a pair of wire-rimmed glasses on. As I stared at the photograph of Leslie, the woman said, "I knew your mother didn't have a cameo like mine."

"Oh," I replied, embarrassed at being caught in my lie. I looked directly into her eyes, which I expected were judging me harshly. I was relieved to see understanding in them instead.

She removed her glasses and placed them on the counter. Then she examined the cameo. "The image is of my great-great-grandmother, who was, as you can see, a beautiful young woman. Beautiful in the same way Leslie Summers was and undoubtedly still is." She held the cameo tightly and affectionately in her hand.

"Yes," I replied, "they are beautiful in the same way." Leslie and the face in the cameo had the same high cheekbones and finely sculpted features.

"Now," she said, dropping the cameo to hang from its chain, "why have you come here to inquire about Leslie?"

"She's my wife. At least, she was."

A sympathetic expression crossed the woman's face, but still it wasn't one that showed she believed me. I had the eerie feeling that I wasn't the only person who had come to the Wharton School for Girls asking about Leslie Summers, and this suspicion was confirmed when she said, "Leslie is the sort of girl who will always have admirers. They were numerous when she was a student here. But never mind—you say you're her husband?"

"We've been married for a little over three years, and . . ." I didn't know whether to tell her the whole truth or to improvise. Finally, since I hadn't gotten away with the lie about the cameo, I told the truth, explaining that I had gotten home from my mother's funeral early that morning and had found Leslie and Audrey gone. I then took Leslie's note from my pocket and offered it to her, saying, "This is what I came home to."

She accepted it reluctantly and, as she read it, I could see the concern on her face. "Mr., Mr. . . ."

"Noble," I said, realizing I hadn't introduced myself.

"Mr. Noble, I don't know what to say. That is, I don't know how I can help you. This places me in a difficult position."

"How do you mean?"

"Leslie was a student here, but she's also my grandniece. Her father is my nephew."

I was startled, not only by the coincidence but by the mention of Leslie's father, and as I fumbled for words, she said, "It has been several years since I have seen Leslie or Franklin. We're not a particularly close family, especially since . . . since Leslie left Wharton."

"You mean since she got pregnant and had to leave?" I said boldly.

Her face flushed. "Yes." She picked up the photograph, which I had placed on the counter, and returned it and the form to the file folder.

"Then you don't have any idea where Leslie might be now?"

"No, I don't."

"Will you tell me where her parents live?"

A pained expression came to her face. "Surely Leslie has told you her mother and father were never married."

"No, she never told me that. She seldom talked about her parents, but when she did, she said they lived somewhere here in Westchester County. She said her father had an apartment in the city and came up here on weekends." Both impatience and anger were building up in me. Once again, I felt stupid and heavy, not only because of the lies I had fallen for, but also because of the things Leslie had conveniently deleted from her life. "There are a lot of things Leslie hasn't told me."

The woman seemed not to hear me, lost as she was in her own thoughts.

I felt awkward as she stood there in silence. I wanted to ask about Leslie's father, not just about where he lived, but about who he was. I wanted to know what kind of man could have sex with his own daughter. I didn't, of course, know how much this woman knew about the circumstances of Leslie's early pregnancy, and I held my tongue so I wouldn't risk breaking this small bond we had formed.

"Mr. Noble," she finally said, "as an employee of this school, I'm not at liberty to give out information about students or former students. I can understand your predicament, as I'm sure you can understand mine, but I really don't know what I can do to help you."

Her tone was sympathetic, yet firm, and I knew I wasn't going to get any more information from her, at least not until she'd had time to think and probably until she'd had a chance to contact Leslie's father. I was tempted to ask if she knew who had fathered Leslie's first child, but decided against it, knowing that could turn her against me, if out of nothing but family pride. If necessary, I thought, I could always bring that up later.

"I understand," I said, discouraged. "Maybe I could call you in a day or two if I don't find them by then, just in case . . . I don't know, in case you hear anything."

"That would be fine," she replied. There was a slight tremor in her voice, which I thought was a good sign. "My name is Mrs. Bullard, Catherine Bullard."

We shook hands as I said, "My name's John, John Noble." I then said, "I'm sorry if I put you in a compromising position."

"Not at all, Mr. Noble."

I turned to leave, but looked back toward her and said, "You must think I'm crazy to have been married for over three years and to know so little about my wife and her background."

"No, I don't think you're crazy. Maybe a little desperate under the circumstances, but definitely not crazy. I hope you find Leslie and your daughter."

"Thank you." I left the office, and when I stepped out of the building into the brilliant early afternoon sunlight, I felt faint. All I wanted to do was sleep, and then when I was rested try to sort this out.

I went to my car, and as I drove toward the center of town, I realized I didn't know where I was going next. I had an urge to turn around and go back to the school and spill the whole story about Leslie and her father out to Mrs. Bullard, with the hope that she would be sympathetic or shocked into telling me how to find Leslie's father, but something wisely told me the timing wasn't right for that. I thought again of the apartment on West Seventy-fourth Street in the city, but going there didn't make sense anymore. I knew I had to find Leslie's father's address, and I also felt I had to find out who her mother was and where she lived, but I didn't know how to do it without Mrs. Bullard's help.

I drove through the center of town toward the highway that led to the thruway. As I was trying to decide whether to go on to New York or back to Woodstock, I saw a Holiday Inn sign and decided that the best thing I could do was sleep and try to get my senses back.

I rented a room, and as I lay on the bed, drifting in semisleep, I realized my hatred of Leslie was spreading like a cancer. I wanted more than to find Leslie and Audrey. I wanted revenge, not only from Leslie, but from her father as well. He was the one, I thought then, who was really responsible for what I was going through. He had made Leslie the way she was. I resolved to find him, not only because he might be able to help me in my search, but also so I could punish him with his guilt.

I thought of the time Leslie had disappeared in Boulder and how fruitless my search for her in the Manhattan phone directory had been, but this time it was different. I had to be methodical and follow every lead, no matter how slight the chances of success. It was then, as I finally drifted into an uneasy sleep, that I made up my mind not to wait for the possibility of help from Mrs. Bullard. I decided to go back to the Wharton School for Girls later that night. I had noticed that despite the overall good condition of the building I had been in, there had been some heaving of the sills over the years and the doors and windows didn't fit as well as they might have. I knew it would be easy to get into the building, where I could take a look at the folder Mrs. Bullard had put back into the filing cabinet.

XX

I did go back to the Wharton School for Girls that night, and I got in and found the file folder without incident. To my surprise, Franklin Summers lived on East Eighty-first Street in New York, as Leslie had said three and a half years earlier. I copied his address and phone number in a pocket-size notebook I had bought that afternoon and then looked through the folder for the name of Leslie's mother, but it wasn't on any of the forms.

After returning the folder to the cabinet, I climbed back through the window I had jimmied open and went to my car, which I had parked behind the jungle animal topiary. Even though it was a warm July night, I felt a chill as I approached the car. The huge animal-like shrubs, by the light of the moon, cast shadows that seemed to be threatening me with vague warnings about pursuing Franklin Summers.

I got into my car and decided to go back to the Holiday Inn and call him. As I started the car, I noticed the headlights of another car as it came up the hill toward the school. I left my lights off as I slowly pulled forward and watched as the car stopped in front of the administration building I had just broken into. I then heard doors slam, and in the headlights I saw two policemen approach the main entrance. I realized I must have set off a silent alarm, and panic almost took hold of me. I didn't know if I should simply drive up to the cops and identify myself and tell them what I was doing or just try to get away. I was sweating heavily and nausea was taking hold of me as I watched the cops, now with flashlights on, walk around the side of the building. I was perhaps a hundred and fifty yards from them, and I realized I could probably get past them when they got to the back of the building, where I had jimmied the window.

I killed the car's engine and began to coast past the topiary and down the gently winding drive toward the building's entrance. The cops were now out of sight, and I was thinking I was safe when I happened to glance in my rearview mirror and saw the red glow created by my brake lights. Nausea attacked again as I cursed my stupidity and took my foot off the brake.

The car continued to coast, and my terror was excruciating as I became aware of the noise being made by my tires on the driveway. I then saw the flashlight beams shimmering from the far side of the building and knew I was going to be seen. Without hesitating, I turned the ignition key and popped the clutch. The car roared in response and the rear wheels squealed as I shot forward. I fully expected to see flashing red lights and to hear the booming of pistols being fired at me as I floored the accelerator. I was still going around sixty-five when I got to the center of Croton-on-Hudson. I braked for a stoplight, and only then did I look into the mirror to see the police car wasn't behind me. Not yet, anyway, but that didn't mean it wouldn't be. I paused at the red light long enough to see there wasn't other traffic, and then I ran through it and turned right on the next side street, where I hoped to lose the cops. As I started to pull to the side of the street and turn my lights off, I saw another police car in front of me, and panic seized me again as my brain created two-way radio messages being passed on from the cops at the school to the cop in this car. I resigned myself to being stopped and arrested, but the second police car turned at the next corner. I went straight, expecting the other car to turn around and pursue me, but it didn't.

I must have driven the side streets of Croton-on-Hudson for

fifteen or twenty minutes before I finally got my bearings and headed toward the Holiday Inn. I was still going to go back and try to call Franklin Summers, but the paranoia that had attacked me at the school took another swipe and told me every cop in the area was going to be out looking for me. I exaggerated the nature of my crime to murderous proportions, and in my mind I saw the cop who had earlier in the day given me directions to the Wharton School for Girls and knew that he would have no trouble remembering me and my car. I thought of the shoulder bag, which was still in the motel, and felt an almost desperate need to go back for it, not because of the clothing it contained, but because the stuffed rabbit I had bought for Audrey was still in it. I was thankful that I had my traveler's checks and the joint passport in my jacket pocket and knew I could always buy more clothing for myself and Audrey, but I wanted the rabbit. It seemed then to be the only link I had to my daughter.

But I did not go back to the motel. I was too frightened, and as I drove out of Croton-on-Hudson toward the thruway and New York City, my fears expanded geometrically until I was sick to my stomach and had to pull to the side of the road.

It was close to midnight when I got to the city. I hadn't the slightest idea where I was going to stay, but then I thought of the Plaza Hotel, where I had begun my search for Leslie and Juan Lanzo Ernesto three and a half years earlier, and decided that even though it was probably the most expensive hotel in the city it had brought me good luck before and might again. I was fortunate to find a parking space on Fifty-eighth Street behind the hotel, and that alone was enough to bring on a new sense of optimism.

It was with considerable skepticism that the desk clerk rented me a room for the night, not only because I hadn't any luggage, but also because I was greatly in need of a shower and a shave and because my clothes were wrinkled and dirty. Thinking the worst, that the police in Croton-on-Hudson had somehow anticipated my destination and had already managed to alert all the hotels in the city, I lied to the clerk, explaining that I had gotten dirty fixing a flat tire and had planned to go on home to Woodstock that night, which was why I didn't have luggage, but that I didn't trust the spare tire. I doubt he believed me, but he finally agreed to let me have the room, provided I paid for it in advance, which I willingly did.

It isn't yet dawn and I'm lying in bed with Kay sleeping at my side. I'm feeling the worst depression I have known in a long time. I think I'm halfway between sleep and consciousness, trying to fall back or break free, but I can do neither.

In my dream, Kay and I are in Denver in Crown Hill Cemetery, where my mother is buried, and we're walking among trees and tombstones toward a great white tower which is a crematorium and mausoleum. I'm angry with her, but I don't know why. She's silent as we make our way to the huge building. We walk up a steep flight of white stone steps, and I seem to expect to see my mother come out of the doors of the great tower to greet us, but when we get to the landing, Kay is led away by a short, middle-aged man with oily black hair. I try to go inside the mausoleum, but two large men stop me. I stare out at the graveyard and at the snow-covered Rocky Mountain peaks to the west and wonder where my sons are. I start to run and, hearing the sharp slap of my shoe soles against marble floors, I realize I'm running along the corridor of the mausoleum. I run faster, but the goons are catching up with me. I come to two massive wooden doors and try to open them, but they're locked. I tug on the brass doorknobs and they pull loose, sending me into a backwards somersault. I fly between the two goons and hit my head on another door. I grasp a doorknob, and this time a door opens. I twist my body and manage to get through the door, which slams shut.

I hear the men shouting and banging, but I feel safe now, until I realize it's pitch black where I am. I try to stand, but my legs won't permit it. I try to yell out to Kay, but the words won't come. I feel resigned to the blackness of death, then see a faint light far across the room. Now I can stand, and I feel myself being propelled toward the light. As I glide forward, I bump into something and realize it's a ladder. Now the light is above me, and I begin climbing. I get higher and higher and feel the rungs and sides of the ladder growing rough and crusty with something I can't identify. Then I'm aware of a stench and realize the ladder is encrusted with bat guano. I'm repulsed by both the texture and the stench and want to climb back down, but I can't. I'm inching up the ladder toward the light, which is growing brighter and taking on form. There's a plaintive voice coming from the light, but I can't understand it. Slowly, I climb. Now the light has disappeared. I reach up, and a trapdoor gives under the force of my push. The door arcs up and slams open against the flat roof of the tower. As I climb onto the roof and wipe the guano from my lips and eyes, I see daylight. The sun is brilliant, hanging over the mountains and the western afternoon sky. I squint, only to realize it is drifting away, and reach out toward it. I feel as though I'm going to be lifted off my feet, as if I'm going to be pulled from this tower toward the star, which is now growing dim as it retreats from the solar system. The sky, the mountains and the city are turning gray now as I feel my feet leave the surface of the roof. I'm prepared for flight, or death, or whatever this is, when I hear a woman's voice shouting, "John, John, come back!" I look down, and far below the tower I see Kay running through the cemetery. I want to jump or fly down to help her, but I can't. My feet, which only seconds ago were the weight of air, are now leaden, and when I look down at them, I see they're encrusted in guano. I grab on to the railing that circles the top of the tower and try to pull free so I can go after Kay, so I can save her and our marriage. But something slaps me hard against the side of my face, and as I drift into unconsciousness, I hear a giggle and then a recognizable feminine voice which says, "She can't have you."

My head's throbbing when I open my eyes and see Leslie standing over me, naked and with her legs spread. I try to move away from her, but she places her feet on my hands and says, "It's too late."

It's dark now, and the only light I can see is coming from Leslie's body. I can smell her sex, which at first is alluring, but then it combines with the stench of the bat guano, and I feel sick. I try to pull my hands from the weight of her feet, but I can't, and I'm terrified as she begins to lower herself toward my face. I feel dizzy, as though I'm about to slip into unconsciousness. She gets even closer and opens wider, and I see inside the moist walls of a huge cave. I'm being drawn inside, and I can feel myself trying to resist the suction which is pulling me deeper and deeper into this sexual cavern. I know now that I'm in Leslie's womb, and one part of me is loving it, while the other part is fighting to swim away. I know I'm dying, but I no longer care. I close my eyes in resignation, but a brilliant light forces itself through my eyelids, and I see a vaguely familiar form. My eyes open, and I recognize the shape. It's the stuffed toy rabbit I bought for Audrey after my mother died. It's running along the cavern, deeper into Leslie's womb, and I know it's imploring me to chase after it, to follow it to the heart of her womanhood, where I will find my daughter.

Hours seem to pass before I finally catch up with the rabbit, and when I do I'm so exhausted I can hardly see or think. But then I see Audrey. First she's an adult who looks strangely familiar, but as I get closer, she becomes a small child. As I reach toward her, she says, "Daddy, where have you been?" I start to answer and pick her up, then I hear Juan Lanzo Ernesto laugh and say, "I warned you, my friend, I will take her away from you if I can." "No!" I shout. "That was Leslie, not Audrey!" But I'm too late, for he picks her up and disappears in this fleshy cave with her.

I wake to the sound of my own screams and feel hands touching me and trying to comfort my body, which is covered with sweat.

"It's all right, John. Everything's okay. You had a nightmare." I'm trembling as I open my eyes and see Kay leaning over me.

"It's all right," she says again.

"Jesus, it was so real."

"I know." She tenderly kisses my forehead and repeats, "I know. You were talking in your sleep."

"What did I say?"

She kisses my forehead again. "Nothing. Nothing we have to talk about now. Just try to go back to sleep."

I want to talk now, but the temptation of sleep is too great, and as I slip back into it, I know that in searching for Audrey, I'm also trying to find Leslie Summers, and now Kay knows, too.

XXI _____

I lay awake that night in the Plaza Hotel, plotting schemes for getting to Franklin Summers the next morning. I wanted to be courageous enough to confront him, forcefully if necessary, and get what I thought of as the upper hand from the beginning. But what if I called and he simply brushed me off? What would I do, skulk around his apartment building and approach every middle-aged man who went in or out? Or worse, what if Leslie and Audrey were with him? A phone call would ruin everything. Maybe one already had. What if Catherine Bullard had called and told him I was on the prowl?

Everything in my head was muddled. I didn't have any answers. I didn't even have sensible questions. I wanted to sleep, hoping things would be clearer when I woke later. But sleep wouldn't come. I thought of my mother and realized she had been dead for exactly a week.

At nine o'clock the next morning I dialed Franklin Summers's number and was startled when a man's voice answered on the second ring. "Hello."

"Mr. Summers?"

"Yes?"

"My name is John Noble."

168

"I know who you are. I've been expecting to hear from you."

"Mrs. Bullard called?"

"Yes."

"May I talk with you? I mean about Leslie."

"I think we should talk. Do you know where I live?" He laughed, nervously, I thought. "Of course, you must."

"Mrs. Bullard told you . . ."

"She knows you broke into the admissions office last night. It's all right, though. She didn't tell anyone. Other than me, that is."

I made arrangements to meet him in an hour, at ten o'clock.

After I hung up and began dressing, I was nervous for different reasons. He had sounded too friendly. Too eager to talk with me. Was this a setup? Had he been in on everything from the beginning? Were he and Leslie still *lovers*? (The thought disgusted me.) Was I walking into some sort of trap?

What could be worse than the trap I was already in?

I tried to brush wrinkles from my shirt, jacket and trousers, and I buffed my shoes on the Plaza bedspread. I wasn't going to make a good impression in these clothes, but that wasn't what I was meeting Franklin Summers for.

It was with a temporary sense of power that I took the elevator down to the lobby, where I inhaled the strong, sickening perfumes and after-shave lotions of other hotel guests who were sipping coffee and eating warm croissants in the open Palm Court in the center of the main floor. I was conscious of my shabby appearance, and I headed quickly for the Fifth Avenue exit. When I got outside, I was assaulted by the high humidity and the heat radiating from the pavement. Almost immediately, I felt moisture in my armpits.

It took me a little over half an hour to reach the block where Franklin Summers lived on East Eighty-first Street. Even without confirming the street number I had copied the night before at the Wharton School, I knew I was approaching the right building. It was the largest and most impressive building on the block. There was a blue-and-white canopy that stretched from the entrance to the curb, and leaning against a wall inside the foyer, reading the *Daily News*, there was a bored doorman. He was wearing an uncomfortable-looking navy-blue uniform with yellow stripes running down the trouser legs and a blue cap with a shiny military bill, which was pulled over his brow. Both the building and this man fit the descriptions Leslie had given me nearly four years earlier in Boulder. I opened the heavy plate-glass door slowly and quietly, hoping the doorman would be so engrossed in what he was reading that he wouldn't notice as I made my way past him to the wall of mailboxes and the building's register, but I wasn't surprised when I heard a gruff Bronx- or Brooklyn-accented voice demand, "Who ya lookin' for?"

Aware again of my appearance, I said, "Summers. Franklin Summers. He's expecting me."

The man came toward me. There was an inferior yet vicious look on his face when he said, "What kind of shit you tryin' to pull, pal?"

I stepped back. He was an older man, probably around sixty, but he was still intimidating. "I just spoke with Franklin Summers, and I'm supposed to meet him here."

"Ain't no Summers here." He opened the heavy glass door and said, "We don't want no trouble here."

"But he lives in this building." I took the notebook from my pocket and looked for the number. "This is two eighty-one, isn't it?" Even as I said it, I looked up and saw the number 293 above the building's entrance. I went through the open door, murmuring apologies.

As I walked back toward 281, which I had passed on the way to this building, I felt a new sense of rage toward Leslie Summers. The building I had just been in was the one she had described, but it wasn't the one her father lived in. Franklin Summers's building was a modest-looking five-story red-brick rowhouse, which looked like most of the other buildings on the block. The building I had been in was the one she had wanted her father to live in.

I went inside the ground-level entrance and saw Franklin Summers's name next to a button labeled 2-A. I pushed the button, and there was an immediate buzzing sound and a click, which unlocked the door. I went up the worn carpeted stair treads toward the second floor and heard another door lock click.

I did have preconceptions as to the sort of person Franklin Summers would be. In my mind's eye, which had been influenced by Leslie's early descriptions of her father, he resembled the Hathaway-shirt man, who had been ubiquitous in magazine ads for as long as I could remember. He was middle-aged, or slightly beyond that, trim and fit, suave and cultivated, and he wore a black patch over one eye, which I suppose made him into something of a gallant warrior figure to the men, or their wives, who purchased dress shirts. I don't know why I had envisioned Franklin Summers as a sort of Hathaway-shirt man without the eye patch, but I suspect it had to do with Leslie telling me he was an advertising executive and my associating that with the highly successful Hathaway advertising campaign. On the other hand, it may have been much simpler.

But when I saw Franklin Summers for the first time that July morning in 1967, standing in his open doorway on East Eighty-first Street, he was not the Hathaway-shirt man. He appeared to be close to fifty, he was maybe five-ten, and he was overweight— not exactly fat, but his midsection was full. He wore what I've always thought of as an Amish beard, which is a full beard without a mustache. It was dark brown with prominent gray streaks on either side of the chin. His dark brown hair was long on the sides, but not too long for the times, and he was balding on top. There was about him both a jovial and an intelligent look. It was a look that put me at ease, but also warned me to be on guard. His dark eyes, high cheekbones, and sculpted nose were Leslie's, as well as those of the face in Mrs. Bullard's cameo, and there was no doubt in my mind that Leslie had told the truth about this man's being her father. He was wearing wrinkled khaki trousers, a nondescript polo shirt and leather sandals, all of which, combined with his own features, gave him a sort of casual, professorial appearance—a reasonably accurate assessment on my part, for I learned later that morning that he was a high school English teacher.

His greeting was friendly and slightly nervous. He reached for my hand and said, "Frank Summers."

I was glad it was Frank and not Franklin. I shook hands and was impressed with his firm grasp. "Hello. I'm John Noble."

The apartment, like the man, was not what I had envisioned from Leslie's descriptions. It was small—a fair-sized living room, a tiny kitchen and a bedroom at the rear—and plain. There was nothing to suggest wealth; however, there were two walls of bookcases (not mahogany as I seemed to remember Leslie saying, but unfinished pine and crudely put together), and there were several prints on the other walls—two Picassos, which I recognized, and four or five others I didn't know. The couch was not the one Leslie had described when telling me about the "rape." It was of uncomfortable-looking Edwardian design and badly in need of new upholstery. There was a plain metal office desk, which was littered with papers, and there was an overstuffed armchair. The room was one of a bachelor, and it was comfortable-looking, but nothing more.

"Why don't you sit down while I make some coffee," he said. "You like it regular?"

"No," I replied. "I'd prefer it black with no sugar."

Instead of sitting down, I went to one of the bookcases. I was impressed by his collection. He had most of the classics as well as a large number of contemporary novels by authors I admired. There was very little nonfiction. I took a copy of *The Ginger Man* from the shelf and began thumbing through it. "You like Donleavy?" Frank asked, coming into the living room with the coffee.

"Yeah, I discovered him when I was in college. He's a funny writer."

"Have you read *A Singular Man*? It's probably his funniest."

"No. Only this one."

He set the cups down on a liquid-stained coffee table and took a copy of *A Singular Man* from the shelf. "Here, take this. I have another copy."

"Thanks," I said, taking the paperback book and glancing through it.

"What did you study in college?" he asked, returning to the coffee table and picking up a cup and handing it to me.

"Journalism."

"And you ended up being a contractor. I started out as a chemical engineering major and ended up with an English lit. degree."

So he did know something about me. Leslie had kept in touch. I felt a little chill go through my body.

"I haven't gotten my degree." I felt uncomfortable about that.

"You're still young. I was thirty before I got mine."

I almost liked him for putting me at ease. "Thirty, huh? How'd you happen to wait so long?"

"I got hung up in the war, the Second World War. By the time it was over, I was already twenty-five." He paused, as if trying to decide whether to offer me a confidence. Then he added, "And I had responsibilities of a sort."

I was sure he was leading up to Leslie, and I said, "You mean you had a child?"

"Yes and no." He sipped his coffee and said, "Here, let's have a seat." I sat on the old sofa, and he sat across from me in the easy chair. "I mean, Leslie was born shortly before the war was over, but her mother and I were never married. Of course, she's probably told you this."

"No, no she hasn't." I started to say it was Mrs. Bullard who had told me he and Leslie's mother hadn't been married, but I decided against it. "To tell you the truth, I don't know much about you and Mrs. Summers, I mean Leslie's mother, at all."

"That doesn't surprise me." He sipped his coffee again. "When I said I had responsibilities after the war, I was referring to Leslie. I offered to marry her mother, but things weren't exactly right."

I shifted uncomfortably on the couch. As much as I wanted to hear anything he would tell me about Leslie, I still felt uneasy hearing it from this man who was a stranger and was the father of both Leslie and her first child. I felt caught between abhorring and genuinely liking Franklin Summers.

"My aunt told me why you'd be getting in touch with me, and I know you hope I'll be able to help you find Leslie and your daughter."

"Yes," I said uneasily. I hadn't expected him to come to the point so quickly.

He leaned back in the chair. "I'm not sure I'm going to be able to give you much to go on."

"Anything would be helpful," I said. "I don't know if I really expected you to know where they are. I had my hopes, but I guess I'm not really surprised. Leslie hasn't talked about you much. And she has never talked about her mother. Frankly, I don't know much about her past at all." I noticed a quizzical and almost relieved expression on his face, but it faded when I added, "I do, of course, know about her first baby, Michael."

"Yes, you would know that," he replied. "You probably see me as some sort of sex maniac because of that?"

I wasn't prepared for this directness, but I did say, "I don't know if I thought in exactly that way, but, yes, I have thought of you in, I guess you'd say, unpleasant terms."

I still couldn't understand or forgive him for what he'd done with Leslie, but there was something about his openness that I couldn't hate.

"I can't say I blame you for thinking of me in, as you say, unpleasant terms. But don't misunderstand. I don't go around wallowing in self-pity. I've made mistakes, and I have to live with them."

I felt uncomfortable. "Look, Mr. Summers . . ."

"Frank, please."

"I don't expect you to tell me these things. I mean, I know a little of what happened several years ago between you and Leslie, but . . ."

"But you're polite enough not to want to pry?"

"Something like that."

"I want to try to explain a few things to you, to help you understand Leslie. When she was born, I was still in France. It was only after the war that I learned I had a child. You see, in the summer of 1944 I was home on leave. I had seen a lot of action, which is to say I'd seen a lot of people die, and while I was never hit, I was still suffering from a sort of shock. To make a long story somewhat shorter, I came back here on a thirty-day leave, knowing I'd have to go back overseas and thinking I'd probably be killed. I'm not telling you these things so you'll feel sorry for a worn-out soldier. At least I don't mean it that way. Anyway, after I'd spent a few days here in the city with my family, I decided I had to get away, somewhere by myself, just so I could think and somehow enjoy myself. I borrowed my father's car and began driving around New England. I went up to Boston and then to Maine, and then I drove west and ended up in Stockbridge, Massachusetts. You probably know where that is. It's not too far from Woodstock."

"I know. I've been to Great Barrington a few times."

"This may sound absurd," Franklin Summers continued, "but I went to Stockbridge for—not exactly sentimental reasons—well, yes, for sentimental reasons. When I was in France, we frequently got copies of The Saturday Evening Post, and I always liked Norman Rockwell's covers. Not because they're great art or anything like that—God knows, they aren't—but because of his way of, I suppose you'd say, his way of evoking the American scene. I know this sounds old-fashioned and dusty these days, but back then Rockwell's pictures were special to me. They made me homesick, but at the same time they made me feel good, in a sort of mom-and-apple-pie way. I knew Norman Rockwell lived in Stockbridge, and I thought I might be able to meet him, just to tell him how much those Saturday Evening Post covers meant to me and a lot of other GIs."

Listening to Franklin Summers talk about Norman Rockwell and his covers, I realized he was like Leslie in that he seemed unable to stop a story once he had started it. He was the sort of person who told too much, as if an accretion of detail would set everything right.

"Of course, I never did get a chance to meet Rockwell, but I did find one hell of a good bar in West Stockbridge." He laughed. "I think it was called Grundy's Bar. No, it was more romantic than that. It was Grundy's Roadside Inn. That's right. It was actually a run-down pool hall and juke joint that sold liquor. And that's where I met Elizabeth, or Lizzy, as everyone called her. She's the girl who became Leslie's mother. You can pretty much guess what happened from there."

Listening to him, I had the eerie feeling that I had heard this story before, and then I realized I was thinking of the drawn-out story Leslie had told me that snowy night in the Skyways Motel, of catching her father in the kinky rubber sex costume and being raped by Juan Lanzo Ernesto. I felt embarrassed, not by Franklin Summers's story, but by what I was remembering.

"Lizzy wasn't exactly the town goddess of virtue, but she certainly was the prettiest girl I had seen in a long time. She was only seventeen, but she looked older, in much the same way Leslie did at her age. And she acted older. She chain-smoked Lucky Strikes, and she could down her liquor as well as any guy in the place could. And, God, as I said, she was pretty. There must have been fifteen guys hanging around her, buying her drinks, trying to get her to dance, that sort of thing. The guys who hung out in this place were what I guess would be the equivalent of Hell's Angels today. Maybe not exactly. They were actually pretty harmless-looking, but they all rode big Harleys. Anyway, as luck would have it, I was wearing my uniform. Actually, it wasn't luck at all. In those days wearing a uniform was like walking a cute puppy across a college campus. It attracted girls, and being the horny bastard I was then, I was into attracting girls. And that's what happened. Lizzy ended up with me that night."

"And that's when she got pregnant?" I asked.

"Who knows? We spent the next several nights together. Not

exactly together—she still lived at home with her folks—but we spent every evening together in the fleabag motel room I'd rented, and, yes, she did get pregnant, but as I told you, I didn't know about it until a year later when the war was over."

"How did she know where to find you?" I asked, realizing I was getting as caught up with his story as I had with Leslie's a few years earlier.

"She had my address. I had given it to her. I wasn't in love with her, but I certainly wanted to see her again when I got home, if I got home. I wrote to her a few times from overseas, and she wrote to me, but then the letters stopped coming. I attributed it to the war, and it wasn't until I got home in the fall of '45 that I learned differently. Frankly, by that time I had pretty much forgotten Lizzy Ford. There were a lot of girls here in New York who loved us, the conquering heroes, and it was easy, well, not to think of Lizzy Ford. But then one day I did get a letter, and that was when I learned I was a father."

As I sat there listening to Franklin Summers, I drifted in and out of his story. Part of this undoubtedly had to do with my exhaustion, but mostly I think it was related to the parallels that were being created. In his story he was a young man with the pregnant girl and then the young daughter. I wasn't sure if he was really talking about himself, though, or telling me something about myself. He hadn't loved Lizzy Ford, and that didn't sound like me. I had desperately loved Leslie Summers. Leslie Summers was the daughter, the baby, he was talking about. Somehow, that didn't make sense to me. Leslie Summers was my wife. The daughter was Audrey. Franklin Summers never saw Lizzy Ford again, and he didn't see his daughter until she was fourteen. I didn't want to hear that. What if I couldn't find Leslie and Audrey? Could I live if I knew I wouldn't see Audrey again until she was fourteen? Franklin Summers had wanted it this way. He said he had offered to marry Lizzy Ford—that's the way things were done in 1945—but she had turned him down. "She just wasn't the sort to settle down. Neither was I. We were young." Then he added, "I did send money, though, when I could."

Would that be my future with Audrey, sending money when I could?

His voice wasn't the same as it had been. Before, it had been even and precise. His consonants had been clearly enunciated (just as Leslie's always were). But it changed. The nuances shifted just enough to catch my attention, to let me hear entire sentences without confusing me with my own life, my own history. Franklin Summers was telling me about the time he first saw his daughter, when she was fourteen. She had written him a letter, "a bright and perceptive letter." She had written to say she wanted to meet her father (will Audrey write such a letter to me one day?), and he wrote back, saying he wanted to meet her, too. "What else can a father say under such circumstances?" I wanted to say. "You should have known her way before that." I was angry with him, but I also felt a vague sense of compassion. What would I say to Audrey after fourteen years?

He told me how Leslie had come to New York on a bus. He met her for the first time at Port Authority Bus Terminal. I wondered how many fathers meet their children for the first time at Port Authority. As I was thinking this way, thinking about the terminal being a nursery in the seedy Eighth Avenue section of midtown Manhattan, Franklin Summers began telling me how Leslie had grown up in both financial and emotional poverty just outside Stockbridge. But she was bright. It was clear that he was proud when he said "bright." That was the first thing he noticed about his daughter. She wanted to live with him. "How could I say no?" Even though he taught in the New York public school system, he couldn't send his daughter there. She was too "bright and fresh" for that. But he had an aunt who had worked for over two decades in a prestigious school in Westchester County. She could probably help Leslie get a scholarship.

He got up from the comfortable chair and went to the kitchen. "Would you like an ale?"

I glanced automatically at my watch. It wasn't quite noon, but I said, "Yes, I think I would."

He came back with two bottles of Molson. "Hope you like this Canadian stuff."

I took the ale and said, "You know, I am, of course, curious, but I didn't really come here for this. I mean, what's happened has happened. My interest now is in finding my daughter."

He sat back down and stroked his beard thoughtfully. "What are you going to do when you do find her?"

His question sounded sincere, but there was still something about his easygoing attitude that I didn't trust. "I don't know, not exactly. If at all possible, I'd like to work things out with Leslie and put things back where they were. If that can't happen, I don't know. I guess I'll have to find them first."

"I do want to tell you about Leslie and me," he said. "As one man who loves Leslie to another who does."

That sounded almost vulgar coming from him, and he seemed to pick up on my thought. "I mean as a father who loves his daughter." He took a sip of ale. I was too uncomfortable to respond.

"When Leslie came here, I was, to say the least, unprepared. I wanted, somehow, to be able to make up for the time we hadn't spent with each other, but I didn't suddenly want to become good old Dad. I didn't feel like a father. By that I mean the only history we had in common was that of blood. As I've told you, I hardly even knew her mother. But to get to the point, Leslie moved in here the summer before she was to enter the ninth grade. I did talk to Lizzy, her mother, of course, and she said she was happy that Leslie and I were finally getting to know each other. It was also clear that she was delighted to be free of the responsibility of caring for a teenage girl. So that's how it began. There were no formal arrangements. I simply said she could stay here and that I'd get her into a good school.

"I don't know exactly how to describe Leslie as she was then. She was very much a young woman in both body and mind."

I took a long swig of ale and more or less braced myself for the sexual side of his story. I have always been edgy about discussing sex with men; even locker-room sex talk bothers me.

Summers seemed to sense my uneasiness. "I didn't have ulterior motives when I said she could live with me that summer. I had never put much stock in Freud's Oedipus or Electra complex. What I honestly wanted to do was try and be a decent and responsible father, and that feeling was magnified when she told me about the kind of life she had lived with her mother. She told me they lived in a run-down house in Lenox, a town just outside of Stockbridge. I knew the house, because it was where Lizzy had lived when I knew her. She said both of her grandparents had died when she was little and that her mother had always hung out with lots of different men. She wasn't saying Lizzy was exactly a whore, but she made it clear that she was a woman of questionable virtue. She told me these things, not in an accusatory way, but rather in a way that made it clear that she needed a change. As I told you, and as you know, she was, despite everything, an extremely bright girl, and I looked forward to her intellectual companionship as much as anything else.

"We got on very well that first summer. We did the things you might expect a father and daughter to do in New York City. We went to the Statue of Liberty, the Empire State Building, the museums, Coney Island, the Staten Island Ferry, Jones Beach and all that sort of thing, and we also went to the theater and to moderately fancy restaurants. I have certainly never been particularly well off financially, but I think to Leslie I was the richest man in the world. She actually told me the first month she was here that she had never eaten in a restaurant in her entire life. That made me feel bad, and I went out of my way to, well, make things a little glossier than they really were."

His eyes, dark and intelligent, like Leslie's, did not seem to be asking for sympathy, but they were somehow telling me he was trying to explain things in the best way he knew how. "As you know, she did end up going to that fancy school in Croton-on-Hudson, and she adapted readily. She made straight A's with ease, and she fit in with the other girls. When she'd come back here during school vacations, and sometimes on weekends, she'd be full of stories about her friends up there and would thank me again and again for making her life so much better. Often we'd sit together on the couch and talk about how things were going with her. But there was never anything even remotely sexual in this contact. We were a father and daughter sort of making up for lost time. I was happier than I had ever been, and I believed she was, too.

"Things began to get a little funny during her sophomore year at Wharton . . . in the way she behaved at school."

"You mean her grades began to drop?"

"No, that was never a problem with Leslie. School was never a problem in an academic sense, not even when she lived with Lizzy and her various men. By funny things, I mean there were a lot of exaggerations. I wasn't aware of them at first, and maybe I never would have been if my aunt hadn't let me know what was happening. Needless to say, most of the girls at the Wharton School for Girls were from prominent families, and they had social histories that Leslie couldn't begin to compete with. It was mostly snobbish bullshit, as it usually is at such schools, but still it affected Leslie, and she began making up a past that wasn't hers. At first, I didn't take it seriously. I mean, I could understand why she would want to polish the rough edges of the life she'd had with her mother and even those of the life she had with me. But things did eventually get out of hand."

"How do you mean?" I asked. I knew exactly what he was talking about, about Leslie's way of "polishing," but I wanted to know what she had done to go too far.

"It wasn't a single thing. She built stories on top of one another. Each story by itself would have been harmless enough, but she built them into entire histories. And she was smart enough not to get caught in inconsistencies. But there were those at the school, the teachers, the headmistress and my aunt, who saw what was happening and tried to talk to her about it. Without much success, I'm afraid. I tried to talk to her, too, but she would have none of it. She didn't deny anything. Actually, she was quite sophisticated with her reaction. She said she was only playing the game that the other girls there played but that she was playing on credit while the others used hard currency."

Franklin Summers stopped talking and gazed around the room. He then stood up and went into his miniature kitchen. I heard him opening two more bottles of ale. Waiting for him to return, I found myself wishing he could have been the Hathaway-shirt man, not for his sake, but for Leslie's. If he had been, maybe she wouldn't have felt compelled to invent so much. Maybe she would have been satisfied with that "second life" which had been there for her. I realized the hatred I had felt for her since I had returned to our house on Camelot Road the morning before was waning. There was a sadness about her that I had never allowed myself to see or feel. In the time we had been together, I had known only the strong, beautiful and intelligent young woman I had fallen in love with, and I hadn't bothered to consider that her frailties were as prominent and legitimate as those of anyone else. Or maybe I hadn't been capable of such a consideration, so busy was I tasting the sweetness of this immeasurable love I felt.

Even with these thoughts, I still wasn't ready or able to forgive her for what she was doing. It didn't matter how much she had suffered (if suffering was what had caused her to bolt with Audrey), she had no right to do what she had done.

Summers seemed to know what was going through my mind, for after he handed a fresh bottle of ale to me and settled back down into his chair, he said, "Leslie is capable of creating this idyllic world for herself, and even for others, but I don't think she has ever been entirely comfortable in it." He took a long drink, looking at me with those eyes that could have been Leslie's. "I don't think she ever truly left her mother's house up there in Lenox. I don't mean I think she wanted to return to the uncertainties of the life she had led there, but I always felt she wanted to go back at least for a while. First, to flaunt this new side of herself, this sort of princess side, so she could show her mother and the various men around her that she was better than they were, but also so she could, in a sense, rescue her mother from the circumstances that had made her what she was. I don't necessarily mean that she was even conscious of this, but I do think she has such a deep-seated hatred of men that she is driven to be not only her own protector but her mother's as well." He paused uncomfortably and then added, "And the protector of her daughter, your daughter."

"I'm not sure I understand what you mean," I replied. "At least in terms of Audrey I don't. There has been nothing to protect her from." I felt myself getting angry, not only because of what I perceived as his amateurish psychological assessment of Leslie, but also because I felt he was building some sort of protective shield around himself. I didn't hate him as I had thought I would, but I did think he was exaggerating or reshaping reality every bit as cleverly as Leslie had. There was something about his almost homey countenance that didn't ring true.

"Leslie, for obvious reasons, had a lot of admirers. According to my aunt, boys were constantly hanging around Wharton, trying to get Leslie to go out with them. But Leslie wasn't interested in these boys. She seemed, Aunt Catherine said numerous times, to feel she was too good for them, and in a sense there was more than a little truth to that. She was intellectually superior, and there was also a sexual superiority. My aunt was concerned, not so much because Leslie consistently rejected the attentions of the boys who asked her out, but because she did it so condescendingly, so viciously, or as Aunt Catherine put it, 'She would make Scarlett O'Hara blush.' It was as if she saw through all their pretensions, which I'm sure were abundant. That, by itself, would have been all right, considering her age and background, but she didn't stop there. I didn't know it then, but when Leslie came here to spend time with me, or at least when I thought she had come to see me, she was making her own set of friends on the other side of town, on the Upper West Side, which, as you may or may not know, isn't exactly the jewel of Manhattan."

Thoughts of the West Seventy-fourth Street apartment assaulted me again, but I didn't have a chance to ask him about it or about who Leslie had been staying with there when I had found her after my trip to Puerto Rico.

A melancholy tone crept into his voice when he continued. "I know I'm not good at abridging stories, but in this case I'll do my best. She met a young man, a Puerto Rican boy, over there, late in her junior year, and she began bringing him here. Not when I was home, though. Don't misunderstand me; I probably wouldn't have objected. But Leslie was sneaky, or maybe I should say circumspect, about her involvement with this boy."

"You're talking about Juan Lanzo Ernesto, aren't you?" I said.

"So she hasn't kept everything from you?"

"I've met Juan."

A look of surprise came to his face. "How did that happen? I wouldn't have expected it."

I told him about the trip I'd made to Puerto Rico when looking for Leslie nearly four years earlier. When I said that was where I had seen Michael, he said, "Yes, we've come to that, haven't we?"

I nodded, embarrassed for both of us.

XXII _____

Kay and I are drinking our morning coffee in bed and talking. Because of what has been going on the past several weeks and because I had the sexual dream last night and talked in my sleep, she has (I can tell) decided to take action. She's not the sort of person who will sit around and let fate simply have its way with her or those she loves. Not without a fight. When she was in high school in a small farming community south of Topeka, Kansas, she woke one morning to learn from her tearful mother that her father had been arrested the night before for embezzling money from the state treasury, where he was an accountant. Her mother told her she thought it would be best if she and her two younger brothers stayed home from school that day, because the story was on the front page of the morning paper and she didn't want Kay and her brothers to be tormented by their classmates. The boys stayed home, but Kay refused, saying, "It's not going to go away just because I stay home." Years after we were married, Kay's mother said, "She got us out of that family crisis. Her father was techni-cally guilty, but not in the way the press made it sound, and it was Kay's stubborn determination not to let the opinions and gossip of others tear us apart as a family or internally as individuals. It was her resolve that gave her father the courage to stand up for himself publicly and privately and eventually to win a pardon from the governor." Her mother laughed and went on to say, "Tom always called her 'the colonel' because of her straightforward way of getting things done. After the governor's pardon, he promoted Kay to general."

It's this same sense of resolve that I see in Kay this morning. She has known since we were married, a little over sixteen years ago, that I have been divided between wanting to know Audrey and not wanting to interfere with her life. This was relatively easy when Audrey was young. I had fought a battle with Leslie and had lost. It didn't matter how badly I wanted to be with my daughter, I couldn't be, not if I wanted her to have a chance at a reasonably happy and stable life. That had already been resolved in my mind when Kay and I met. I did keep in touch with Franklin Summers until he died when Audrey was eleven or twelve. By then, Mike and Jack had been born, and Kay and I, with the boys, had settled into our own family routine. I didn't forget Audrey, but neither did I think of her every day.

But things changed when Rob Dawson exhumed his daughter's grave.

Kay looks at me thoughtfully. There's a no-nonsense expression on her face, which makes it clear she's not about to let me drift into an emotional backwash and cloud the issue. She teaches history at the local community college, and once again I'm reminded why she's such a good teacher. "John, we have to deal with this."

"I know it," I say. I can tell from her "teacher's tone" that she has already thought this out.

She adjusts the pillows behind her head and takes another sip of coffee. Then she looks at me. She's fifty-two, but she doesn't look it, except for the weight she has put on since she quit smoking four years ago. "When we were first married and when you would call Audrey's grandfather . . . do you remember?" She doesn't wait for me to answer. "I didn't understand what a loose end this was for you."

"What?" I ask. I don't think I heard her right. "What did you call it?"

"I said 'loose end.' You were searching for Audrey, not in a literal sense this time—it was internal. But you were looking and keeping in touch with Franklin Summers out of a desire to complete your life. But I didn't understand that then. I couldn't look beyond our own family. When you would call Franklin Summers, it was something that wasn't quite real because it seemed so far removed from *our* lives. It had happened to you so far in the past from my perspective that even though I knew it was there, it was something I'd never had to deal with. There was something, some vague thing in my mind, that said you had a daughter in California, but it didn't really register, partly because she was so far away and there was absolutely minimal contact. I mean, only what you could get from Franklin Summers once or twice a year."

She pauses to sip her coffee and, I think, to see how I'm taking this.

"Usually you'd call when you were a little in your cups. It was always around Audrey's birthday or Christmas. I'd see you beginning to feel melancholic. It always showed. But there was nothing I could do. Then you'd call Franklin Summers and ask him about her, to get a sense of what was happening, to know if she was all right and where she was in her life."

This is strange, hearing Kay talk this way. Strange the same way it was that night three months ago when Rob Dawson was telling me my own story. Kay and I have always been open with each other, but I've never heard her talk quite like this. Of course, we've never been this direct about my "loose end" before. I ask, "How did you feel when I called Franklin Summers?"

She frowns. It's the sort of frown that comes to her face when she's uncomfortable about something she's going to say or do. I've seen this expression appear countless times when she was about to reprimand one of our children. "Usually, when you'd make your calls, I'd go away to another room. I'd be aware of what was going on, but I wouldn't really be right there beside you, I think for two reasons. One, it seemed sort of inappropriate for me to be hanging on you right then . . . because it was a part of your life I'd had nothing to do with, and if I'd been there, right there with you as you talked, I'd have felt like an intruder. And the other reason is that it did make me feel uncomfortable. I just felt better if I was in another location. Not right there in the same room."

I think she's going to say something about Leslie, that maybe she was a little jealous or uncertain about where she stood when I made contact with my "other life." I ask, "Would you have preferred it if I hadn't kept in touch with Frank?"

"I would have just as soon seen you let it go in the sense that it was going to disrupt our lives as a family . . . in the sense of it disrupting my life, I would have liked to see it go away, but I understood your strong need to follow up on it and know where Audrey was and what was happening and also, I think, to let Franklin Summers and Leslie know you were still around and cared.

"Now, about you getting in touch with Audrey? Personally, I have no expectations one way or the other. If it works out, I know you'll be happy, and I'll be happy for you. If it doesn't . . . I can't say. I'm not worried now about how it will affect *me*. I'm not deliriously happy with the prospect for myself, but I am interested in your well-being. I am, I suppose, a little nervous, because I can't help wondering what will happen, say, if she's not interested in meeting you, or if she's a monster. What if she's like her mother, or grandmother, for that matter? This is where I see all of this as harmful, maybe even devastating, but on the other hand, I don't see where you, or we, have much choice in the matter. Things have gone this far, and there doesn't seem to be any stopping them. The point is that you have to act, but you also have to be prepared to take a loss and recover from it. But until there are losses, if there are any at all, you should be optimistic. I could quite easily put all this out of my mind and go on with our lives, but I know you can't."

I'm glad Kay is saying these things, but I can't simply tell myself to be optimistic. My problem at the moment isn't that I don't know how to get in touch with Audrey. I have an address and phone number. It's that I don't know how to do it. I have the same fears

Kay has mentioned. What if Audrey refuses to have anything to do with me, or what if she is a monster, as Kay put it? There's another thing that bothers me, too: In getting in touch with Audrey, I may have to come into contact with Leslie. I ask Kay how she feels about that.

"What are you getting at?" she asks with a kind of coldness in her voice.

"To tell you the truth, I'm still a little afraid of Leslie. She almost destroyed me over twenty years ago. I came close to suicide."

"Wait," Kay says impatiently. "I don't really understand your question."

"I mean, well, you know because of the dream I had last night that I haven't gotten her entirely out of my system."

"Okay, but what are you trying to say?"

"You know I love you, but there's something about Leslie that still haunts me. I don't know if you feel threatened, but I can't help but think you might be."

Kay's getting edgy. "What are you asking me?"

"What do you feel?"

With a tone of both understanding and indignation, she says, "Let me tell you something, John. No, I do not feel threatened by Leslie. Maybe I did in the beginning, but not now. At fifty-two, I'm not a kid anymore, which may be my way of saying I have confidence in myself and in our marriage. But I'll tell you what does worry me. It's that you have never been able to let her go."

"What's that supposed to mean?" I feel defensive.

"You just said yourself that she still haunts you. Well, in my opinion, she has always been the true nightmare of your life. Leslie is so firmly rooted in you that you'll never be free until you confront her, knock her down and show her, to yourself, as the cheap little hustler she is and always has been. I don't feel threatened by her; it's you and your obsession with the past that bother me. You know, you call yourself a carpenter. Well, that's what you are. You've developed a damn fine skill, but you're not the real carpenter, not the true shaper and maker of things. Leslie has that rank. She's a born carpenter. Do you understand that?"

I'm sorry I brought this up and I shake my head no.

Kay continues. "She's a born carpenter because nothing she has ever done has come from training or a desire to please. Her skills, from all you've told me, are natural and spontaneous. She shapes and manipulates the world to suit herself. Everything she does, every little finishing touch, is flawless. Can't you see that? You haven't seen her in over twenty years, yet she still not only has a hold on you, but has you bolted to the foundation she created for you in the beginning. You've asked how I feel about you finding your daughter, and I've told you. You have to find her and get to know her if you can. But you also have to find Leslie so you can, once and for all, exorcise her from your life. Neither of us can live in her shadow anymore. I was afraid of the hold Leslie had on you. I was distressed when Rob Dawson came to you with that ridiculous belt, but it wasn't because I wanted to keep you to myself or keep you from Audrey. It wasn't that at all. I did want to protect you—and us—from your obsession with Leslie. I wanted to shield all of us from those demons you've always been so hung up with. Don't you know what those demons are? Your demons, or whatever you want to call them, aren't under your sole proprietorship. I have them. So do Mike and Jack, and I suspect Audrey does, too. But yours have a hold on you, because you keep them prisoner. When you were a child, after your father was killed, it was natural for you to see yourself somehow being kept from him. But now it's not. You're a builder, the master builder who has constructed a wall that's so high and solid and dark that even the most ferocious of your demons can't contemplate escape. And you'll never be free of them if you don't get through that wall now and evict them forever. Leslie still has the key, and if you don't confront her, you're doomed. You're doomed to remain her little lab rat."

Kay gets out of bed and begins to dress, but she hasn't finished. "Does that answer your question?"

I start to say yes, but she stops me with a stern gaze and says, "As far as Audrey is concerned, yes, I do see this as something which is going to have a direct effect on my life, but, okay, you know what I'll do if she says she wants to come here. I'll clean the house. I'll want everything to look good. I'll want everything to look as neat and tidy and pleasant and appealing as I can possibly make it. But I'll also worry about whether or not we're going to get a druggie or a crazy or what. I'll worry about how I'll cope if some crazy person shows up on our doorstep. But I won't worry about Leslie. That's something you have to deal with. I've told you what I feel about you meeting Audrey. I hope you do and I hope everything works out beautifully. Christ, what do you want me to hope? John, just do it. Do what you have to do, and I'll tell you how I feel then. You can start by writing a letter. Just write a goddamn letter."

XXIII _____

Franklin Summers did tell me how his sexual involvement with Leslie had begun, and his story, of course, was nothing like the one she had told.

She had come home unexpectedly on a Friday night and had found him in bed with a woman. I had an urge to ask about the kinky rubber sex things Leslie had mentioned, but modesty or something prevented that, and he didn't volunteer anything. He said he and the woman were simply making love when Leslie came into the apartment. They were, naturally, embarrassed, and he got rid of the woman as smoothly and quickly as he could.

He told me that after she left, he intentionally got drunk on martinis. The only part of the story that matched Leslie's was the bit about the martinis. She had several, too. He said that instead of being upset, Leslie had been "provocatively curious" about the sexual scene she had interrupted. "Her curiosity was disarming and arousing," he said, "and it eventually led to what you're thinking." The culpability he felt seemed apparent as he told me how the "affair" had begun. He didn't say this in so many words, but I was left with the impression that it was Leslie, and not her father, who had instigated things. Several times he mentioned

192

"sexual teasing," and that was something about Leslie Summers that I understood very well.

I asked about the time he walked in on Leslie and Juan Lanzo Ernesto and heard yet another version of the "rape" story.

"It was several weeks after Leslie and I had begun our involvement. It's difficult for me to explain this, but I had fallen in love with her, obviously in a way that wasn't fatherly. I don't think I believed this myself, but for the sake of conscience, I invented a story about her not actually being my daughter. It was easy to do, considering what I knew and had subsequently heard about Lizzy, her mother. But never mind all that, I came home early from a faculty meeting one night and found Leslie and this Juan naked in my bed. I heard laughter when I came inside the apartment, and I sneaked up on them. They weren't actually making love. In a way, it was worse than that. At least, to me it was. Maybe I mean it was more embarrassing. She was sitting on his chest and masturbating him. I don't know which part of me took over then, whether it was the jealous lover or the outraged father. It was probably a little of both, but whatever it was, I went berserk. I rushed into the room, grabbed Leslie's wrists and threw her off the bed. I can still see her, frightened and huddled up against the corner of the room, looking like a naughty child. I don't know exactly what happened during the next several seconds, but by the time I focused on the boy again, he had his pants on and was struggling to zip the fly. I grabbed a heavy chain that was hanging around his neck and slammed him into the closet door. He recovered enough to get past me and into the kitchen, where he picked up a knife. I lunged at him and knocked the knife from his hand. As he reeled backward, I grabbed a beer-can opener from the counter and attacked him. I managed to cut him rather badly. When I saw the blood gushing from his neck, I more or less came to my senses. I first thought I'd gotten his jugular and had probably killed him. He was stunned, frightened by all the blood, and was as docile as a baby when I held a towel to his throat and chin. As it turned out, the wound, while deep, wasn't dangerous." Summers raised his head and touched the soft, fleshy area between his jawbones and behind his chin. "The opener made quite a puncture, but the bleeding didn't last long, and I knew he was going to be all right."

He paused, and a distant look came to his face. "This is hard to explain, but after I came to my senses and as I was bandaging Juan's wound, I looked up and saw Leslie standing there." He pointed to the space between the counter that separated the kitchen from the living room and the wall. "She was just standing there, holding a towel around herself. I remember wondering how she'd had time or presence of mind enough to go into the bathroom, open the linen closet and carefully wrap a towel around herself while the fight had been going on in the kitchen. I sensed Juan was wondering the same thing. There was . . . I don't know how to describe it . . . almost a mischievous quality to her expression as she stared at us. It was as if she had been the one who had walked in on us and who had calmly watched as we fought. Even now, I can visualize her expression. It was . . . not one of the bad little girl who had been caught doing something wrong."

I knew the expression he was trying to get across. I had seen it on Leslie's face twice before: the night she had given me the hot enema in my sleep and the day she had left the gas on and the oven exploded.

Summers went on to tell me that after he had bandaged Juan's wound, he sent him into the bedroom, where he finished getting dressed. Then, he said, Juan left the apartment, dazed and without a word to either him or Leslie. I told him this was the third version I'd heard of this story, and when I said Juan had told me that he, Franklin Summers, had raped Leslie after the fight, he shook his head and said, "No, that isn't what happened. That may be what she told him, but it isn't true. I never touched her again after that. I was too disgusted with her and with myself."

I wanted to believe him, both because of his solemnity and because he seemed to have no reason to lie, but there was still something all too pat about this and almost everything else he had told me. It sounded rehearsed.

It was about six weeks later, Summers said, that Leslie called him from the Wharton School and told him she was pregnant. "I wanted to believe it was Juan's child she was carrying, but even then I knew it probably wasn't. Still, I asked, 'How do you know it's mine?' and she coolly replied, 'Because you're the only man who has ever been inside me, Daddy.' I felt sick. It was, and still is, a kind of shame that I can't describe.

"I said we'd get an abortion, but she wouldn't even discuss it. She said flatly that she was going to have the baby. I argued that because of the nature of her pregnancy, that because I was the father, there was a chance the baby would be genetically deformed, either physically or mentally, or possibly both. She stopped me cold by saying, 'That's all right, Daddy. Taking care of a deformed child will give you something to do in your old age.' I don't know what I would have done then if we'd been talking face to face instead of over the phone. I've thought about this several times over the years, and I honestly think I would have killed her and myself.

"Leslie, at my insistence, agreed to come back here the next day. It was the first time she had been here since the incident with Juan. Since she had refused to have an abortion, I suggested that she go to a Florence Crittenton home for unwed mothers, but that infuriated her. She had already decided what she was going to do, and she neatly laid out her plan to me. She was going to stay at Wharton until she showed, which wouldn't be until the first semester had ended, and she was going to take extra courses so she could graduate early. That, for most people, would have been an almost impossible task, but for Leslie it was easy. Then she was going to go upstate, where I had a cabin. You, of course, know about that."

I nodded, knowing he was referring to the small house Leslie and I had lived in until we built the house on Camelot Road.

"She said Juan was going to move to Woodstock with her. She then told me that if I would deed the cabin and land over to her, she would see that the baby was born in Juan's name and that no one would ever know who the real father was." I noticed a slight, twisted grin on his face when he said, "Despite everything, I had to hand it to her. She was very businesslike when she made her proposal. Of course, it didn't stop with the cabin. I also had to agree to support her, Juan and the child. What choice did I have? As I've said, I'm not a wealthy man, far from it, but the cabin wasn't particularly valuable, as you know, and I did have some money set aside."

Franklin Summers got up from the chair he'd been sitting in for so long. He stretched and asked, "You want a drink, something a little stronger than the ale?"

A drink sounded good, but I said no, for I'd had an idea while he talked, and I knew I had to stay sober to implement it. As he went to the kitchen and began mixing a martini, I watched and thought, You haven't learned a damn thing.

He had looked almost boyish, in a guilty, solemn way, when he told me about his "shameful past" (his words), but when he had come back into the living room and knocked down half of his drink, he was clearly more relaxed. It was as if, in telling me all he had, he had lifted a great weight from his shoulders, or conscience.

"You obviously know what happened from there on," he said. "I mean, from the time Michael was born. She decided to go to school in Colorado, at my expense, of course."

"Of course," I heard myself repeating. "But what about Juan?"

He laughed. It was a small, sympathetic laugh. "You know, I felt sorry for that poor bastard. He was so in love with her that he would have done anything. I never saw him again after that incident here, but I did speak with him on the phone a few times. He didn't stay up in Woodstock with the baby, as Leslie had more or less instructed him to. Instead, he came back here to the city and stayed in a friend's apartment on the West Side, and got his old job back at the Plaza Hotel. Later I guess he moved back down to Puerto Rico."

It was clear that the ale and gin were taking effect. I couldn't help but feel some pity for him, not because I forgave him for what had happened, but because I recognized that Leslie had ruined his life in much the same way as she was ruining mine.

"Well," he said, "I guess that's about it. I wish I could tell you where Leslie and your daughter are, but the truth is I don't know."

I believed him. "After what you've told me, I have a thought."

A puzzled look came to his face.

"I have an idea that after all these years, maybe Leslie has finally gone home."

He ran his forefinger around the rim of his glass. "What do you mean, home?"

"I know this is a long shot, but . . . do you think she might have gone back to Stockbridge, where her mother lives?"

A strange pallor came to his face. "It's Lenox, just north of Stockbridge." He took another drink, and the color returned. "Yes, I think that's possible. Maybe even likely."

After leaving Franklin Summers's apartment, I went back to the Plaza, not to the room I'd stayed in, but to a pay phone in the lobby, where I called information in Lenox, Massachusetts, and got Lizzy Ford's number. I didn't plan to call, because I knew that could have ruined everything, but I did at least know that Leslie's mother was real and still lived there. I asked the operator for the address and was told that it was on Furnace Street, but there wasn't a street number listed.

My spirits were up when I went back to my car, certain I'd be with Audrey by that night.

As I drove up the thruway toward the Massachusetts Turnpike, I decided it would make sense for me to stop in Kingston and at least talk with my lawyer, Jeff Morgan, before heading on to Lenox. I realized that even if I did find Leslie at her mother's house, there was going to be the serious question of how I would get Audrey away from her. I was aware of the reality of courts and custody suits in New York State in 1967, and I knew it would be almost impossible for me to win one, simply because I was the male parent. In the back of my mind there was still the hope that Leslie and I might be able to resolve our differences (whatever they were), but I didn't have a lot of faith in that remote possibility. Neither did I have any concrete plans for what I'd do if and when I found Audrey, but I was thinking of somehow disappearing with her and beginning a new life somewhere.

Jeff Morgan was as lawyerly as anyone in his profession can be, but he was not without compassion. When I barged into his office and past his secretary, who protested, saying he was "in conference," I found him alone at his desk working on the Sunday *Times* crossword puzzle.

"In conference, huh?" I said, trying to sound lighthearted.

He placed the *Times* magazine on his desk and took his dark-framed glasses off. Grinning, he replied, "Just trying to keep my mind alert." He glanced up and saw his secretary, who had followed me in. "It's all right, Beth. John here is obviously in the middle of something important." He faced me again and said, "You look like shit. What's up? You got a well-heeled city couple on the line for a quick closing?"

I sat in a chair across from his desk. "I wish it was something that simple. Listen, I apologize for breaking in here like this, but I've got a problem."

He leaned back in his chair and said, "Shoot. The *Times* can wait."

After I explained what had happened, he said, "It's a rotten way of doing things, but my guess is that her lawyer . . . do you know who he is?" I shook my head. "That her lawyer told her to disappear with Audrey until he's able to serve you with a divorce and custody summons. From what you've said, I gather you haven't received one."

"No, I haven't been around long enough to get one." I then told him where I'd been and that I had reasons to believe Leslie was in Massachusetts with her mother. I also told him about Michael and how Leslie had given him up to Juan Lanzo Ernesto.

"That might work in our favor, but it could backfire on us, too. A judge might feel sympathy for her because of, you know, the nature of that birth. We'll have to play that by ear as things go along. At the moment, the fact is that the male parent is always at a disadvantage in situations like this. Your case, if it comes to that, is compelling, because she left you without any warning at a time when you're under considerable duress—I mean, in terms of your mother's death—but still, ninety-nine out of a hundred judges are going to decide in her favor."

I stood up and said, "I know the odds are against me, but what can I do? I mean, what makes sense in real life now?"

He pressed his fingertips against his temples and looked away from me. "If you think you can find them up there in Massachusetts, do it and get physical custody of Audrey, but make damn certain you do it peacefully. If you have physical custody of the child at the time of the proceedings, your chances won't be great, but they'll be better than they are now."

"Right," I said, knowing I had no intention of ever leaving this in the hands of the courts, "but how do I do that? I mean, Leslie isn't simply going to hand Audrey over to me and say, 'Here, John, I'm sorry.' And what about Audrey? She's not even three yet, but she certainly won't feel great if Leslie and I have a tug-of-war with her."

Jeff stood up and came to where I was standing. He put his hand on my shoulder and said, "I wish to hell I could be more helpful, but there's not much I can do, as a lawyer, that is. As a friend, and as a father who would be as hurt and pissed as you are if my wife pulled anything like this, I can say this: Go up there and look for them. If you do find them and can't get Audrey without a fight, call a lawyer there and have him serve a summons on Leslie." He leaned over his desk and flipped through an address book. "What did you say the name of that town is?"

"Lenox. It's just north of Stockbridge."

"I don't know anyone right there, but I do have an old buddy in Pittsfield, which is close." He wrote a name and number on a slip of paper and handed it to me. "Give Shel a call if you need help up there. He's a good guy."

"Thanks," I said as I headed for the office door. "I'm going to go back to Woodstock to get a few things. A couple of changes for myself and a new rabbit for Audrey."

He looked puzzled. "Rabbit?"

"Oh, nothing. Just something for her."

"Listen, John, I don't think that's such a hot idea. Going to Woodstock, I mean. Stay away from your house. The last thing you want now is for a summons to be served on you. That would put the ball irrevocably in her court."

"Yeah, you're right," I said. As I went back outside and headed toward my car, the optimism I had felt during the drive up from New York had faded into a depression that, along with my exhaustion and the late-afternoon heat, was rapidly weighing me down. My old demons began taking swipes at me, telling me that Franklin Summers had had second thoughts and had called to warn Leslie.

XXIV

Friday, January 29, 1988

Dear Audrey,

I have tried several times (six to be exact) to write this letter. This time I'm determined to finish it and put it in the mail before I begin to have second thoughts (or sixth thoughts) about something I've said. Before I get into the "meat" of this letter, I want to comment on the enclosed belt. I wonder if you remember it, if it has any meaning to you. It belonged to your childhood friend Myrna Dawson. Her father, Rob, gave it to me a few months ago because he thought you would like to have it.

I don't know if this is the absolute truth, but Rob told me it was given to him in the forties by the actress Shirley Temple when he was a young circus performer. He said you and Myrna used to fight over it (in a friendly way) when you were little girls. I vaguely remember this, too. Instead of being important because it had belonged to a once-famous actress, it seemed special to you and Myrna because it had been Rob's and he had been in the circus. You surely won't remember this, but you used to chastise me for never doing anything as exciting as being in the circus. Whatever,

201

the belt is enclosed, and I hope it will spark a few pleasant early memories.

It probably goes without saying that writing this, my first letter to you ever, is an unusual experience (I started to say "strange experience," but that isn't exactly what I mean). It's probably as unusual from your point of view as it is from mine.

Now, for the "meat" I mentioned.

I'm married to a woman named Kay. She's fifty-two (but honestly doesn't look over forty) and I'm forty-nine (alas, I look it, but I still have my hair—ha ha). We have two sons, Mike, who's fourteen, and Jack, who's ten. I don't know if this is news to you or not. I say this because I used to be in regular contact with your grandfather until he died when you were eleven or twelve. He always told me about you and how you were getting along, but I don't know how much, if anything, he told you about us. Kay and I have been married for sixteen years. She teaches history at the local community college, and I'm a contractor here in Woodstock. Both of the boys are avid athletes. Soccer is their big sport, but they're good in baseball and basketball, too. Mike has just become interested in football and wants to go out for it when he gets to high school next fall. I'm trying to discourage him, because I think it's a dangerous sport (I broke my arm six times when I played high school football), but I suspect he'll end up playing, regardless of my protests. Speaking of sports, your grandfather used to tell me what a good swimmer you were. Is this an interest you kept up with? I'm enclosing a snapshot of the four of us, just so you'll be able to get a general idea of who we are—at least of what we look like (yes, I'm the one with gray hair).

Coming out of nowhere like this, this letter will, I suspect, catch you off guard, as the expression goes. I mean, it will probably be surprising. I can certainly understand that. I could probably go off on a tangent and explain why (or at least part of why) I haven't written before now, but this doesn't seem to be the appropriate time for that. I hope I'll be able to explain it all to you in person one of these days.

This brings me to the heart of this letter. I would like to be able to meet you and get to know you, and I would like to do it by coming out there to California or by you coming here. Have you ever been to New York (I mean, since you were a young child)? Woodstock is a small, rather "artsy" community in the Catskills and is about a hundred miles north of New York City. I think you would like it.

I have a million different pictures of you inside my head, but I don't know how to choose among them. I also have an actual photograph of you, a school picture taken about ten years ago when you were thirteen or fourteen. It's the one you sent to Myrna Dawson then.

I know you'll need time to think about all of this—about this letter and the idea of us getting together—so I won't hold my breath in anticipation. Of course, I hope you will feel comfortable enough to write back, but I'll understand if that's not the case.

I look forward to hearing from you.

                                                            John Noble

XXV

It took just over an hour for me to get from Jeff's office in Kingston to Great Barrington, Massachusetts, where I rented a car. I didn't want to drive to Lenox in my Volvo, because I was afraid Leslie, if she was there, might spot it and get away before I was able to make my play for Audrey. I also bought a new stuffed rabbit to replace the one I had left in the motel in Croton-on-Hudson, as well as a few Matchbox cars. I wanted to buy some fresh clothing for myself, but couldn't find an open men's shop.

When I got to Lenox around seven that evening, I had no trouble finding Furnace Street. It appeared to be the main thoroughfare in this section of the small town. Most of the houses, while attractive enough, were simple in design and had undoubtedly been constructed for the laborers who had worked at a large sooty-red-brick textile factory that dominated the south end of the street. The factory was long abandoned, as evidenced by its shattered windows and sagging roofline, but the houses were still inhabited. As I drove, clandestinely in the rented beige Chevy, along the street, I understood why the operator had been unable to give me Lizzy Ford's exact address. The houses weren't numbered.

I cruised up and down Furnace Street, which was eight or ten blocks long, for several minutes, hoping I'd catch sight of Leslie's car, or better, hoping I'd see Audrey playing in the front yard of one of these houses. But luck wasn't with me.

As I was trying to think of a way to determine which of the houses Lizzy Ford lived in, I noticed a small clapboard corner grocery store, which appeared to be open and which had a telephone booth out front. I stopped and went inside, where I saw an old man with a walker, laboring along a narrow aisle, and a younger man in patched overalls, scuffed work boots and no shirt, who was, it seemed, trying to make an impression on a teenage girl who was sitting on a stool behind an antique chrome cash register. She was wearing pale green shorts and a sleeveless white T-shirt, which revealed tattooed biceps and forearms. I edged past the man in the walker and was glancing at the dusty shelved goods, as if I knew what I wanted, when the girl called out, "What's it yer wantin', mister?"

I turned to face her insolent grin and blackened teeth and said, "I'm looking for Pampers."

"Ain't got no Pampers," she replied, turning her attention back to the young man. "Have ta get 'em over at that new 7-Eleven on Route 7A."

"Oh, right, thanks," I said as I turned and made my way back past the old man and out the door. I headed toward the car, then noticed the pay phone again. I decided to call Lizzy Ford's house. If Leslie or Audrey answered, I'd hang up. If someone else picked up the phone, I'd say I'd gotten a wrong number.

The phone was answered on the first ring by a young child whose voice I didn't recognize. When I asked if Ralph was home, there was a long silence and then the receiver was slammed down. I stood in the phone booth, holding the dead receiver to my ear for a moment, and then I silently congratulated myself. I didn't know which house Lizzy Ford lived in, but I at least knew someone was home. Now all I had to do was find out where that was.

I sat in the car for several minutes and tried to decide what to do next. I thought of going back inside the store to ask the people there if they knew which house Lizzy Ford lived in, but thought better of that. They might tell me, or if they knew her, they might tell her some stranger was asking about her. I couldn't afford to take any chances.

I started the car and patrolled the length of Furnace Street one more time before turning off on a side street. As I drove, I noticed a reasonably well-kept stone building, which housed both the town's library and the police station. I decided to try the library, reasoning that the librarian in a town the size of Lenox was bound to know almost everyone. I wasn't to find out, though, because when I went inside the one-room library, I was greeted by a stony silence. There wasn't a soul in the room. I had turned to leave when I saw an index card on the librarian's desk which read: "Upstairs, feeding the baby. Ring bell if you need help." I was touched by that and decided not to disturb the mother and her child.

I sat down in the library to wait for feeding time to end, but when I heard a phone ring on the other side of the entryway in the room that served as the police station, I decided to go there and ask whoever was on duty if he or she knew where on Furnace Street Lizzy Ford lived.

The police officer behind the high counter looked up, seemingly surprised to see me walk in, and said into the phone, "Hold on a sec." Then to me, "Something I can do for you?" He was a cheerful-looking man, in his early thirties, with pale skin and bristly red hair.

After I told him I was a friend of Lizzy Ford from New York and couldn't locate her house, a wide, knowing grin came to his face and he spoke back into the phone. "Hang on a couple of minutes, hon. Got a little business." Still grinning broadly, he said to me, "I've got to hand it to old Lizzy, she picks them younger every day."

I knew he was making some sort of in-joke, probably at my expense, but I tried not to show my discomfort when I said, "I'm just passing by on my way to Boston and thought I'd stop by and say hello. I was going to call her," I added, "you know, to ask for directions, but, well, I sort of want to surprise her."

The policeman laughed, but he bought my story and said, "Go back over to Furnace, the south end by the old factory. You know where that is?"

"Yeah, I was just over there."

"Well, just down the street from there you'll see a little store, Peg's Market."

"Yeah, I know where it is," I said.

"You can't miss Lizzy's house then. It's directly across the street. You can't miss it. It's the worst-looking place on the street." He laughed again. "It's white, 'least it used to be, with peeling paint, dead flowers and high weeds in the yard. Might be a red Jeep there, too. That's what Lizzy drives. And motorcycles, maybe. Old Lizzy has a thing for bikers. You see her, say hi from Ned."

I thanked him and went back outside, where I felt the blood draining from my face. Not only had I passed the house several times, but I'd been standing directly in front of it when I'd made the phone call. I was furious with myself for being so careless, and I was certain Leslie had seen me and taken off with Audrey.

I decided not to go back to Furnace Street until after dark. If Leslie had seen me, I was too late anyway. If she hadn't, then I'd be better off to wait until I had the cover of darkness before I went back.

I drove to Route 7A and found a diner, where I ate supper and drank coffee until dusk finally slipped into darkness.

When I did return to Furnace Street, I was surprised to see how alive it seemed with lights glowing from the windows of the small houses. I drove slowly along the street and parked in front of Peg's Market, which had closed. There were no lights on in Lizzy Ford's house.

After about half an hour of waiting for someone to come home, I worked up the courage to approach the house. I knocked on the front door, and as I had expected, no one answered. I tried to see through a window if there were any traces of Leslie or Audrey inside, but the house was too dark. I had started to walk away when I noticed the outline of a garage set at the back of the side yard. Taking a cigarette lighter from my pocket, I approached the side door. I opened it and flicked the lighter, and I saw two motorcycles and Leslie's white Nova.

"Son of a bitch!" I said aloud. "I've got you now."

I went back to the car and waited for Leslie and Audrey to return to the house.

It was fortunate that I had asked the policeman at the station for directions and had told him I wanted to surprise Lizzy Ford with my visit, because every fifteen minutes or so a patrol car drove past me. The first couple of times the patrolman waved, and after that he ignored me.

I had been waiting and watching for well over two hours when a car with three men in it pulled behind me. They got out and one of them asked what I was doing there. I told them the same story I'd told the policeman, that I was waiting for Lizzy and wanted to surprise her.

They laughed in a way that left me feeling they knew something I didn't, something almost lascivious, but they at least seemed to believe my story and left me alone. Still, I felt uneasy and guilty as I imagined them talking it over, going to the police and telling them they suspected I was up to more than I had told them. I began cursing the fact that this was such a small town and any move I made was bound to be observed by someone. If I don't find them tonight, I never will, I thought. By tomorrow, the whole town would be talking about this stranger who was looking for Lizzy Ford.

As I waited, I tried to imagine what this street must have been like in 1944 when Franklin Summers was seeing Lizzy Ford. Maybe he had been in a car with her in the very spot I was parked in when Leslie was conceived. That thought depressed me.

Until around eleven-thirty I was able to make myself believe that Audrey, Leslie and Lizzy had probably gone out to dinner or to a movie, but as time passed and as the lights in the other houses went out, I began to realize they weren't coming back. It didn't make sense that Leslie had left her car in the garage unless she had seen me standing in the phone booth or unless Franklin Summers had betrayed me and called to warn her.

As I brooded over these possibilities, my demons crept out of the darkness and told me something had gone wrong with Leslie's plans. She and Audrey might have been in an accident in Lizzy's Jeep. Maybe they had been killed. Maybe the Jeep had broken down. Maybe they had been kidnapped. Maybe . . . anything could have happened.

My fear expanded to the point where I wanted to go back to the police station and tell the true story, with the hope that the policeman I had talked to would issue a missing-persons report and somehow find Leslie and Audrey. I didn't care then about Leslie's motives or that she was trying to have a summons served on me. I didn't even care where they were, but I was desperate to know if Audrey was safe.

I kept the house under surveillance until after one, but finally gave up and went to a motel in Pittsfield, where my demons frolicked throughout the remainder of the night.

XXVI _____

I'm sitting in the Duck & Dog, talking to Pat O'Ryan. It's not quite noon and the regulars won't be in for at least another half hour or so, which means Pat and I can talk for a while without being interrupted. Pat is the quintessential bartender in that he's both a good listener and a good talker.

"How's the house comin', Johnny?" he asks, handing me a mug of Guinness. "Your fancy city lady still tellin' you how to hammer nails?"

I laugh. "Now she's showing us how to make them."

"Real expert, huh?"

"Same old story," I say. "Everything's great at the beginning. Framing goes up fast, doors and windows pop in, roof goes on, and the partitions seem to grow on their own. Owners come up on weekends with their Nikons, slap me on the back and take photos back to their disbelieving friends, who have told them all contractors are a bunch of no-good bastards, out to milk the city folks."

"Then they turn on you, right?" Pat says, drying a glass and putting it in the slip above the bar.

"It never fails. Every time I begin a project I tell the owner not to get excited when things slow down, when we begin the finishing work, and every time that's exactly what happens. They get anxious and can't understand what's taking so long. You'd think I'd learn to roll with it. But I don't."

"Dear Jesus, when I hit the lottery, you can build me a house. I won't bitch." Pat pours what he calls a breakfast beer and leans on the bar in front of me. "Know what you need, don't you?"

"What's that?" I ask, realizing I'm about to get a dose of Irish advice.

"Time to yourself, man. Don't be jumpin' into the next house. By all that's holy, I'm tellin' the truth when I say you look like shit, Johnny Noble. Now, don't get me wrong, but when did you last take a little time off? Just sit on your arse and take things easy? I've known you at least ten years and I've never seen a time when you weren't workin'. You must have put a couple of dollars aside. Be sensible, man. Take care of yourself. No one else will."

I hold my empty mug up and say, "I am thinking about taking some time off after this project."

He tips the mug under the Guinness tap and says, "And don't you know, you owe it to yourself, too. By God, Johnny, why don't you come over to Ireland with me next month? Could we have the time of our lives! Isn't a pub in Clare that wouldn't be home to the likes of us."

"I'd like that," I say, "but I've got something else in mind. Maybe I'll go out to California for a while. Nothing's certain. I'm just thinking about it."

"California, mind you. Never been there, but I hear it's full of lovely lasses. Aw, God, wish I was twenty years younger, and I'd go with you. So what you gonna do out there, just tip a few and lie in the sun?"

I hadn't planned to talk about Audrey, but the stout and Pat's good nature make me want to. "You've probably heard I have a daughter out there," I say.

"I've heard rumors. You know, the usual bar talk. But I didn't know it was the truth. Is it?"

"Yeah, it's the truth. I haven't seen her since she was a baby, over twenty years ago."

212 · *Thom Roberts*

"The old nestin' instinct gettin' to you?"

"What do you mean?"

"Aw, shit, I don't know. Guess I mean, you know, middle age catchin' up with you, tellin' you to gather all your chicks under one roof."

I like the way he puts it. "Yeah, I guess that's what you'd call it. I've spent most of my life gathering money and all the stuff it buys, but I've missed some of the important things."

"Bullshit! That's what livin' in these times is all about. Try bein' a decent human being without money. No one gives two shits. You've done the right thing, Johnny. I've never seen Kay and your boys in rags with holes in their shoes. You've done the right thing. What's a man expected to do?"

"Thanks."

"So old Rob Dawson, rest his pitiful soul, this is some of his doin', I'm willin' to wager."

"You're a perceptive son of a bitch."

Pat chuckles. He takes his glasses off and wipes the lenses on a bar napkin. They aren't dirty, but this is his way of pausing for thought. "What's Kay think 'bout all this?" he finally asks. "I mean, 'bout you goin' out West, lookin' for her?"

"You know Kay. She's with me."

"And what of the girl's mother?"

I'm embarrassed, I think out of loyalty to Kay. "In a way I guess I'm still infatuated with her, but it's a weird infatuation. I'm not in love with her or anything like that. If anything, I hate her more than I ever did, but it's a different hate. It's not for the things she did then. Time has taken the edge off most of that. It's not even because of all the years I've missed with Audrey. Sure, there's some of that, but it's really because of what I've done, or haven't done. I mean, God, I don't know how it happened, but I somehow managed to put blinders over my brain. I kept in touch with her grandfather for years, but after he died about twelve years ago, I almost forgot I even had a daughter. There have been times, of course, times when I've let her surface, but then I've always buried her again. I guess it's been a sort of self-imposed amnesia. Then Rob Dawson comes along, and he somehow brought her back, I mean right to the top of whatever it is in my mind that knows I miss the hell out of Audrey and always have. I guess to the top of my fatherhood. Rob Dawson, of all people."

Pat regards me silently. It's the first time I've seen him at a loss for words. Finally, he says, "So Rob, he brings your daughter back, and he drags the mother along with her. That's a strong dosage, I'd say. What you're sayin' is, you were lettin' sleepin' dogs lie and then they suddenly sprung up and started nippin' at your heels."

I nervously pick at my fingernails. "I hadn't thought of it that way, but that's good, it's what's happening."

"So you've decided to go ahead with it—I mean, go to California and find *them?*"

His emphasis on "them" bothers me. I start to protest, but end up saying, "Yeah, them. But don't get me wrong, it's not what you think. I'm not thinking of trying to start anything with Leslie, Audrey's mother, again. Nothing like that. I love Kay and the boys too much. It's just that I need another glimpse, I guess so I can get Leslie out of my system for good. What do you think—does it make any sense at all for a man almost fifty years old to go running off for one last look at a woman he loved nearly a quarter century ago?"

Pat grins and rolls his eyes back. I can almost see him transforming into a boy as he says, "By Jesus, not only is it normal, it's necessary, Johnny. I'm even slippin' back myself. Aw, what a glorious time. My mother and father, they've taken me across the water for the first time, you know, to Wales, and I'm walkin' along the River Dee, watchin' barges on the water and holdin' hands with the prettiest lass you ever did see. Love at first sight, it was. Me, a poor Irish lad, and an English lass in Wales on holiday, and we're in love, don't you see." He closes his eyes and drifts even further. "And don't you know, my parents and hers, you can't imagine the ignorance. It was black and white all over, the same old thing, it never changes. There was nothin' lower than the

Catholic Irish to the English, and it was the same the other way round. Oh, what fear and hatred. But do you think that stopped us for a single minute?" He grins broadly, and I see dimples surface from beneath the wrinkles in his face. "God in heaven, it was hate that caused us to part, but, oh lovely, it was this very same hatred that made our young love so powerful. It was, don't you know, Romeo and Juliet all over again. We'd never have loved each other so much, and I might say, so completely, if our parents hadn't feared and hated one another so damned thoroughly. Oh, dear, I'll never forget lovely Vandra Thorndike, you know. And Johnny, by all that's holy in me, I'd go back. I'd go this very minute if I thought there was a chance in creation that I'd get one last look. That doesn't mean I'd toss over dear old Kathleen and take off on a fool's fantasy. No, not that a-tall. I'd give my left testicle for another look, but still I'd save the right one for Kathleen. One is a dream, a very pretty dream indeed, but the other's my life. And that, I'm sure as I'm standin' here, is what's happenin' with you, Johnny. Take a peek, but don't run away, man."

I feel a sort of intimate glow after hearing Pat's story and wonder if most men have a Leslie Summers or a Vandra Thorndike buried in the layers of their pasts. "You know," I say as the first of the lunch crowd come inside the Duck & Dog, "I wish I could take that trip to Ireland with you. Maybe some other time. Maybe next year."

He winks at me before going to the end of the bar to take lunch orders. "But first you got to take that peek."

XXVII _____

Thinking back on that third day of my search for Audrey in July of 1967, I can clearly see Lizzy Ford's house on Furnace Street and the house on its right. At one time, they were almost identical. Built, I would say, in the early to middle thirties, they were simple rectangular one-story frame houses with nondescript hip roofs. There was originally nothing wrong with them, nor was there anything distinguishable about them. However, by the time I saw them, they were vastly different from each other. One had been cared for and had over the decades acquired a certain kind of dignity, a dignity resulting from the quality of life that had been lived within it. The other, Lizzy's house, had not. It was, as the police dispatcher had said when giving me directions, an ugly little white house with peeling paint, surrounded by dead flowers and high weeds. Unlike the house next door, it reflected a poverty that was both financial and emotional. Instead of boasting a modest pride, as the house next door did, it radiated despair. This was the sort of house that I, as a builder, would have razed or burned in order to start a new one from scratch. Neither its character nor its structural integrity was worth saving.

I dwell upon Lizzy Ford's house not out of scorn but because it told me as much about Leslie as Franklin Summers and my experiences with her had. It reflected both the spiritual and the financial deprivation she had gotten away from. It explained what Juan Lanzo Ernesto had tried to tell me four years earlier in Mayagüez when he said Leslie was someone who'd had to invent a life in order to live. Lizzy Ford's daughter might have grown up in the poverty of this house, but the Leslie I knew had not. She had made certain of that.

I almost felt a new sense of compassion for Leslie when I pulled up in front of the house at seven the next morning. Leslie's roots, I realized as I stared at the still-vacant house, had not had enough life in them to bother with nurturing. Somewhere along the line, presumably when she was fourteen and went to New York City and then to the Wharton School for Girls, she had seen the futility of clinging to anything that had been her life. To survive, she'd had to create new roots, improvising as she went along.

I said I almost felt a new sense of compassion. But the bitterness overpowered it, and I realized that while I might be capable of caring for the girl who had grown up here, I would never be able to let go of the hatred I felt for Leslie, the liar and cheat who had stolen my daughter, and my resolve to find Audrey and take her away from Leslie became even more urgent as I stared at the ugly little house on Furnace Street.

I knocked on the front door again, not expecting an answer and not receiving one, and then I checked the garage, to make certain Leslie's car was still there. This time I noticed a coloring book in the backseat and picked it up. I felt a little weak in the knees when I saw that most of the pages had been hurriedly scribbled on with a red crayon. It was Audrey's favorite color. I took the book with me, and then I saw the keys were in the ignition. I took them, too, not for any reason other than to frustrate Leslie or whoever eventually came for the car.

I had started back to the rental car when I heard a child call out from the house next door, "Can Mike and Audrey play today?"

I looked at the house and saw a five- or six-year-old girl standing behind a screen door. "Mommy said I can play with them."

I approached the front porch and saw a young woman appear behind the girl. "Something I can do for you?" she asked cautiously.

I saw her lock the screen as I stepped up onto the porch. "Yes," I said, "maybe you can. I'm looking for your neighbor, Lizzy Ford."

She pulled her daughter away from the door and said, "Missy, you go on back to the kitchen and finish your cereal." Then to me she said, "She's not around."

"You have any idea when she'll be back?"

She laughed weakly. "Who knows about Lizzy? She kinda comes and goes as she pleases."

I nervously cleared my throat. "Actually, I'm looking for her daughter, Leslie. Do you know her?"

She scrutinized me before replying, "Yeah, I know her."

"I noticed her car's in the garage and wondered if you know where she is or when she'll be back."

"Who are you, anyway?" she asked. "I've never seen you around here before."

"I'm . . ." I started to say I was her husband, but I changed it. "I'm a friend from New York. I'm on my way to Boston, but thought I'd stop by here, you know, on the way, just to say hi."

I realized I was still holding the coloring book I'd found in the car. I held it out and said, "I brought a little present for Audrey."

For the first time, the young woman smiled. "Didn't you bring something for the boy, too?"

"Boy?" I said, without thinking.

She frowned. "Leslie brought both her kids."

I shrugged, but then it hit me. "Oh, yeah, Mike. I've got a couple of Matchbox cars for him. Didn't figure he'd be interested in coloring."

"You're the guy who was hanging around out front last night, aren't you?" asked the woman. "For just passing through, you've spent a lot of time here."

"Yeah," I said. "I was here last night, you know, hoping they'd come home. When they didn't, I decided to stay over in a motel and get a fresh start this morning. I don't want to bother you or anything. It's just that Leslie's a good friend, and I thought . . ."

More suspiciously than before, the woman said, "You Leslie's friend or her husband's?"

"Last I heard she'd broken up with her husband," I said.

"Well, if she did, she picked up a new one right away."

"What do you mean?" I asked, confused.

"Listen, I don't know who you are, but you'd better get your stories straight before you come around asking questions." She turned and started to shut the solid front door.

"Wait a minute," I said. "Please wait."

She faced me again.

"Could I talk with you, for just a couple of minutes?"

There was clear hostility in her voice when she replied, "Just what is it you want to talk about?"

"It's important that I find Leslie. I didn't know she was here with anyone other than her daughter. I lied to you a moment ago. Audrey, her daughter, is my daughter, too."

I noticed the look of surprise on her face behind the screen door. "What do you mean, your daughter, too?" she finally asked. "I don't know what's going on. All I know is Leslie and some guy, a guy named Juan or something, who she says is her husband, and their two kids have been around the last few days. That's it. Their kids and my little girl played. That's all. I don't know anything else."

"Juan?" I asked, astonished. "You're sure it was Juan?"

"He was some Spanish-looking guy. That's all I know. She said he's her husband. Who am I to question?"

"Juan Ernesto?" I asked.

"I think that's right. Sounds right. Now listen, I don't want to get mixed up in any of this. I knew Leslie all her life, before she took off for New York to live with her father, but to tell you the truth we never were the best of friends, if you know what I mean, so I don't want to get involved."

"Wait," I said. "Sure, I can understand that. But listen, please. There's more to it than I said."

I don't know if it was what I said or my tone of voice that caused her to soften her attitude a little, but she said, "Okay. You a jilted lover or something?"

Her directness, combined with the mention of Juan Lanzo Ernesto, left me feeling vulnerable. "You might say that," I finally replied. "I'm her husband, and Audrey's my daughter."

She laughed cynically and said, "Leave it to Leslie to have two husbands. Are you putting me on? You're really her husband?"

I nodded and said, "Yes."

"Boy, like mother, like daughter," she said.

"How do you mean that?" I asked.

She finally unlocked the screen door and stepped out onto the porch. I was struck by her plainness. She was neither attractive nor unattractive. Her light brown hair showed traces of early graying, and tied as it was in a careless ponytail, it made her look older than she probably was. She was a little overweight and had muscular arms and thick hands. Her face, though slightly plump, had fine features which made her look as though she was the sort of person who wasn't interested in nonsense. "Let me tell you something about Lizzy Ford," she finally said. "She's not exactly what you call the typical small-town, churchgoing woman."

"I gathered that."

"She's not exactly the best neighbor in the world, either," said the woman. "Don't get me wrong. I don't have anything personal against her, but I've lived here all my life, and there are, well, just things I don't like a whole lot, if you know what I mean."

"Yeah, I think I know."

"I'm not saying she's a floozy or anything like that, because that's not exactly the case. It's just that she hangs out with what I'd call questionable men. Always has. Don't get me wrong, I know this is the sixties, and I'm not exactly a prude. What I'm saying is, my folks and I always felt, you know, a little sorry for Leslie. That's the thing I never understood or liked about Lizzy. Leslie's been on her own since she was a little kid."

"What about her father?" I asked. "Did you ever know him?"

"Father. That's a laugh. Until she went off to New York about ten years ago, I don't think she even knew who her father was. God knows how she found out about him, but I'm glad she did. Let me tell you, there's been a string of guys about ten miles long going through that house, long as I can remember. Lizzy, far as I know, hasn't ever had time to settle down with a husband. Like I said, I always felt sorry for Leslie, and that's why I was so surprised when she showed up a few days ago with two kids and this guy she said was her husband. She's the last person I ever expected to see married. When she took off years ago, I didn't think I'd ever see her again. That's the kind of rotten life she had. You know?"

"To tell you the truth, I didn't know," I said.

A confused expression crossed her face.

"Do you have any idea where they are?" I asked. "I was out of town last week, and when I came back home a few days ago, Leslie and our daughter were gone. All I want to do is find them and see if they're all right."

She let out a sigh. "Listen, I really don't know anything. All I can tell you is that she and the kids and the guy she said was her husband left in kind of a hurry yesterday afternoon. They took off in Lizzy's Jeep. That's all I know."

"How about Lizzy?" I asked. "Any idea where she might be?"

The young woman frowned and replied, "No, no idea. She left on a motorcycle with one of her friends the day Leslie and her brood showed up. There's never any telling when she'll get back."

I said, "I don't want to bother you any more than I have, but if I give you my number, would you mind calling me if Leslie does show up again? I know you don't want to get involved, but this is very important to me." I took my wallet from my hip pocket and handed her a business card.

She reluctantly took the card and replied, "Well, I guess it wouldn't do any harm. If you're really her husband, I mean." She shrugged. "I guess those kids didn't look to me like they had any Spanish blood in them."

"Thanks a lot," I said. "Well, I might as well be going."

"Good luck," she said.

I thanked her again and went back to the rental car, which was parked across the street.

I returned to the motel in Pittsfield where I had spent the night and called Jeff Morgan to tell him how I had just missed Leslie and Audrey. I also told him about the neighbor, Juan Lanzo Ernesto, and the child, Michael.

Jeff said, "I think you'd better come back here right away."

"Why, what's happened?"

"Nothing yet, but it's time to stop messing around. You should get in here as soon as you can. I want you to dictate a writ of habeas corpus. It's about time we tried to reverse this little game Leslie and her friend are playing. You've done what you could, but now we've got to do more, and we don't have any time to lose. Get back here as fast as you can."

I returned the rental car in Great Barrington, and it was a little after ten when I got to Kingston. When I went inside the law office, Beth, Jeff's secretary, said, "Go on in. He's waiting for you."

She followed me into the office, and Jeff and I dictated the writ to her. While she was typing it, he explained that this would force Leslie's hand—that is, it would legally force her to produce Audrey—but he added that we still had to find them before the document would have any formal meaning. He then told me he had checked around and learned that Leslie's attorney was a lawyer named Pete Sickler. Jeff said he had tried several times to call him, without success, but he did say that when he last called, a few minutes before I arrived, he learned from Sickler's secretary that he was in court. He got up from behind his desk and said, "Let's, for the hell of it, take a stroll across the street and see if he's there with Leslie and your kid. It's a long shot, but why not check?"

As we walked across the street to the courthouse, my spirits and optimism grew, and I asked, "If they happen to be there, should I try to get Audrey to come to me? I mean, should I still try to get physical custody of her?"

"I doubt they'll be there," he said, as if trying to dampen my unfounded optimism, "but if they are, sure, do whatever you can."

We walked up the stairs to the second floor, where family court was, and Jeff held the door for me. I walked through to the hallway outside the courtroom, and before I saw anything, I heard a voice I knew well scream, "Oh, no!"

It was Leslie, and Audrey was standing in front of her. Juan was sitting on a bench next to her, with Michael on his lap. When Audrey saw me, she cried out, "Daddy, where have you been?" and started toward me. I reached for her, but Leslie grabbed her by the shoulders. Juan pushed Michael from his lap onto the bench, and both he and Sickler lunged toward me. Jeff stepped between us, and he and Sickler began shouting at each other.

Juan faced me, and I could see the fury in his eyes and in Leslie's as she continued to hold Audrey, who was struggling to pull away. She cried, "Let me go, Mommy," and reached for me again.

Juan threw a punch at me, but was stopped by Sickler, who grabbed his forearm, even as he and Jeff continued to shout threats at each other. I kneeled in front of Audrey and said, "It's okay, sweetie. Everything's going to be okay." Leslie glared at me, and Audrey asked again, "Where have you been, Daddy?"

"Looking for you, sweetie. Looking for you."

"I was with Mommy. Didn't you know that?"

"Yes, I knew. I was looking for both you and Mommy."

She looked at the backpack I had taken into Jeff's office and then brought to the courthouse. It contained the stuffed rabbit and other toys I had bought for her, as well as our joint passport and my traveler's checks. "What's in your pack, Daddy?"

"Oh, just papers and some things for you."

She laughed and reached for me again. She extended an index finger and shouted, "Shooter, shooter, bang! Got you, Daddy."

I edged closer, and she grabbed my hands and broke away from Leslie.

Both Leslie and Juan tried to grab her, but I picked her up as I got to my feet and backed away toward the door Jeff and I had entered through. Jeff and Sickler saw what was happening and hurried toward us.

I saw a blur of people in the hallway and heard angry voices, but I couldn't understand what was being said. I held Audrey close. People were shouting, and I saw Leslie's red and angry face over Audrey's shoulder. All I could understand was Audrey as she repeated, "Daddy, where have you been?" I couldn't talk. I held her tight and kissed her over and over.

Juan backed us into a corner, away from the door. I could see Sickler and Jeff, but still I couldn't understand what they were saying. Leslie was shouting, but I couldn't understand her either. Juan glared at me with his fists doubled and his teeth clenched. I could see the hatred in his face and in Leslie's, but it didn't make any difference. Audrey was in my arms, talking, trying to tell me everything that had happened. Even with all the shouting, she didn't seem upset. She didn't even seem to be aware of it. I noticed a small cut on her nose and lightly kissed it. "That's my hurt," she said. "I fell off a motel bed where Mommy and Juan took me and Michael."

She kept asking where I'd been. As I tried to explain I had been looking for her, I edged toward an elevator, but Sickler and Juan blocked it. Juan started to take another swing at me, but stopped when I said, "You once said you'd take Leslie away if you ever had the chance. Now's your chance, but you're not taking Audrey." He glanced at Sickler and backed off.

Leslie grabbed for Audrey again. I dodged her and yelled, "Try taking care of your son!" I turned and finally made it through the door and down the stairs. Once outside the courthouse, I started across the street toward Jeff's office, followed by Leslie, Jeff, Sickler and Juan, who had picked Michael up. Audrey asked again about

224 · *Thom Roberts*

the backpack and about the things I had in it for her. I told her about the rabbit and Matchbox cars. While she was begging me to let her see them, Leslie shouted, "You're mad, you bastard!"

Audrey and I made it first to Jeff's reception room, and I yelled to Beth, "Be a witness!" She stared blankly as the others followed me inside. I took Audrey into Jeff's office, and Leslie followed us.

Outside, in the reception room, I heard Sickler shouting, "I'm going to get a cop to take us all back to court. We're going to have a hearing. Now!"

I shut the door between the reception room and Jeff's office and sat down with Audrey. She asked again about the toys and the rabbit, but I said, "Let me talk to Mommy for a minute. Then I'll give you the toys."

Audrey hugged me as Leslie said, "You're stupid, you know. You'll never get away with this."

"Get out of here!" I shouted.

"What's wrong with Mommy?" Audrey asked.

I glanced at Leslie and said, "I guess she doesn't feel very well."

"You'll pay for this, you mediocre piece of shit," she said, positioning herself directly in front of us. "I promise you'll end up paying dearly."

Before I could respond, she opened the door and ran back into the reception room. I heard her shouting at Sickler.

Audrey kissed me again and again and asked if she could see the rabbit and toys. I opened the pack and put her new things on Jeff's desk. She grabbed the rabbit and held it to her face. "I'm going to call him Daddy Rabbit," she said.

"That's a great name."

Still hugging the rabbit, she said, "Daddy, I don't want you to go away ever again."

"Don't worry," I said. "I'll never go away again."

Jeff came into the office, and as Audrey played with Daddy Rabbit and the Matchbox cars, he said, "Sickler's insisting we have a hearing now to determine who will have temporary custody until this can be brought to court."

"Do I have a chance?"

He stared at me. I hadn't shaved, and my clothing was dirty and wrinkled. I knew what he was thinking.

"Even under the best of circumstances, the father, as I've told you, has little chance, especially in these preliminary hearings."

"I can't face a hearing now," I said. "Look at me. I'm wiped out. I'd kill any judge who said I had to hand this child back over to her."

Tears came to my eyes. Audrey noticed and asked, "Do you hurt, Daddy?"

I picked her up again and held her close.

Jeff said, "Your daddy's okay. He just has something in his eye."

I wiped my face and said, "Sorry. I can't go to court now. I can't face a judge or anyone else. I can't stand the thought of having to turn her over to Leslie. Not after all this. Not even if it's only temporary."

Jeff went out to talk with Sickler again, and Audrey and I talked and played "race" with the toy cars. I showed her the photograph of the two of us in the passport and said, "Hey, look at this funny picture."

"Who's this baby?" she asked, pointing at the photograph of herself. "It doesn't have any hair."

"That's a little girl named Audrey," I said. "It was taken when you were just a few months old."

We both laughed. Then Jeff came back into the office. "Sickler won't back down."

"What happens if I just walk away with Audrey?" I asked. "I haven't broken any law."

"He'll call a cop, who'll have no choice but to take you all to family court."

I glanced at a door that led directly to the street. "Can we get out through there?" I whispered.

Jeff stared at the floor and replied, "I'm not going to stop you."

I got Audrey to help me put the rabbit and cars back inside the pack. I slipped the passport into my jacket pocket and picked

Audrey and the pack up. Then I went to the door and slowly opened it. Before going outside, I glanced back at Jeff, but he crossed his arms and looked away from us.

When we were outside, I was temporarily blinded by the bright sunlight. Audrey asked, "Where are we going, Daddy?"

I wiped my eyes and said, "You want to see how fast a bunny rabbit can run?"

"Yes, yes! Are we the bunny rabbits?"

"The fastest in the world." I ran across the street with Audrey in one arm and the backpack in the other. Remembering I had parked several blocks away because of congestion around the courthouse, I cut between two old houses across from Jeff's office and noticed one of the buildings was where Sickler had his offices. Sweat began to sting my eyes, but I couldn't wipe it away. I got a better hold on Audrey and kept on running, praying Leslie and the others hadn't caught on yet and weren't chasing after us. We had run maybe two blocks when I stopped and looked for my car. "Daddy, are we going to run some more?"

"Just a little more," I said.

"I'm tired," she said. "Let's walk."

I put her down and said, "Okay, for a minute, but then we'll have to run again. You don't want that old turtle to win the race, do you?"

She asked, "What turtle?"

"You know which turtle."

She giggled. "Oh, yeah, the one in my storybook."

"Right," I replied as we walked across the street toward my car, which was still half a block away. I glanced down the street and didn't see them after us, but I was sure they would be soon. I picked Audrey up again and said, "We'd better get on with the race."

She laughed and said, "We have to beat old Mr. Turtle."

When we got to the car, I didn't even look up to see if anyone was after us. I threw the pack through the window on the driver's side. Then I opened the door and lifted Audrey to the bucket seat on the passenger side. I got in and fumbled for the keys and struggled to get the right one into the ignition. As we pulled away from the curb, I glanced behind the car. Still no one was after us.

I cursed every red light until we finally made it to Washington Avenue, which led to the thruway. As we slowly made it through traffic, Audrey asked, "Where are we going, Daddy?"

It came out automatically. "Would you like to fly on an airplane?"

"A big airplane?" She giggled.

"A very big and fast jet," I said.

"Oh, goody. We get to fly!"

I drove onto the traffic circle, which led to the thruway, but decided that wasn't such a good idea. In my mind, I saw every cop in New York State looking for us. I knew, or at least part of me knew, that this was paranoid exaggeration, that it would take a while for Leslie and the others to get their bearings, but still I was afraid. I had my daughter and I wasn't going to take any chances.

I passed the thruway and drove toward another highway, which was an indirect route to New York City. Audrey quickly fell asleep, and as I glanced at her, something within me insisted, "Go on. You've got to have time to rest and think."

I headed for New York, but then changed my mind. The city, I thought, would be the first place Leslie would think of, and if it occurred to her that I'd try to get far away, she'd have her lawyer do whatever he could to have the airports blocked.

After driving for an hour or so, I noticed another highway, which led west toward Pennsylvania. Convinced that most of the New York state police were looking for my car, I thought we'd be safer in another state. We could go to Scranton, which wasn't far, and then take a shuttle to any big city, to Pittsburgh or Philadelphia, and then get a flight to . . . I didn't know, to anywhere where we'd be safe.

As we headed toward the Pennsylvania line, I was afraid even to stop for gas, but I had to. I watched nervously and suspiciously as the attendant filled the tank, sure he was going to notice or sense something was wrong. I broke into a sweat as paranoia dulled my wits. Every cop in the state was after us. Even service station attendants.

We got back onto the highway, and I struggled to keep the car at sixty-five. All I needed was to be stopped for speeding.

I glanced at a map as I drove and realized I had missed the first chance to cross into Pennsylvania. I tried to backtrack, but got lost, and as the frustration built up, I couldn't even find my way back to the main highway. I drove aimlessly for several miles and then saw a "Welcome to Pennsylvania" sign. As we crossed over from New York, I felt as though we had passed from a totalitarian country to one that offered new freedom and a new life.

When we finally got to the Scranton airport, Audrey woke and asked, "When are we going on the big airplane, Daddy?"

"We're in the parking lot now," I replied, as I pulled into a parking space. "We'll be on a plane soon. First we're going to fly on a small one, but later we'll go on a great big jet."

"Can I have Daddy Rabbit?"

"Sure you can." I untied the cord at the top of my backpack and took the rabbit out for her. I then put the parking ticket in the glove compartment, thinking I could ask my friend Will Paulson to pick the car up.

The next shuttle flight from Scranton was to Philadelphia. It was scheduled to leave in around thirty minutes. I bought tickets under phony names, and then we went into a bar, where I had a drink and Audrey had a Shirley Temple. We still had time after finishing our drinks, so I decided to call Jeff, first to let him know we were all right, but also to see if he thought I was crazy to be taking off with Audrey. He was calmer than I imagined he would be, and when I told him I didn't know where we'd end up, he said he understood. He then told me Leslie had filed a writ of habeas corpus herself. I asked what that meant, if it made me liable for arrest. He let out a little laugh and said, "Not if they don't find you." He then suggested that I at least keep Leslie informed as to Audrey's well-being and said I could do it through his office.

Once the small plane was in the air and on its way to Philadelphia, I felt a sense of freedom, even security, as I held Audrey on my lap. She was excited as she pointed at the mountains, cars and houses below and explained to Daddy Rabbit that they weren't really as small as they looked. "When are we going to get to the big jet, Daddy?" she asked.

"Soon," I replied. "After we get to Philadelphia."

"Where are we going on the big jet?"

"It's going to be a surprise," I said, truthfully.

When we got to Philadelphia, I looked at various flight schedules. I had thought about going to Colorado, but quickly dismissed that idea, knowing Leslie would think to check there. I thought of California and even remote places such as Utah, Nevada, Montana and Wyoming, where no one would think to look for us, but decided a father and young child would stand out in places such as those.

I then thought of other parts of the world. I still had well over seven thousand dollars, and I had traveled enough in the Merchant Marine to feel comfortable in foreign countries. If I left the States, I was sure it would be very difficult for Leslie to find us, and it was with this in mind that I checked the international flight schedules. The next overseas flight was to London, and it was due to leave in just under an hour.

Without giving it any more thought, I booked passage on BOAC. I had to use our real names because of the passport, and that worried me, because I didn't know how far Leslie and Sickler would go to find us. I could only put myself in her position, where I had been a few hours earlier, and I knew there was nothing I wouldn't have tried.

After buying our tickets, I took Audrey to a snack bar for sandwiches. I then bought a carton of Pampers and a pad of paper and some colored pens for her. We sat in a corner of the waiting area, where she drew pictures and I told her stories. She was rested from her nap in the car and was in good spirits, but I was exhausted and couldn't wait to get on the plane and sleep. Every time I saw a policeman in the airport, I experienced the same panic that had assaulted me since Audrey and I had run from Jeff's office.

It wasn't until we were well over the Atlantic that the magnitude of what I was doing began to sink in. Until then I had been running only on gut instinct, but when I began to feel safe, I allowed myself the luxury of trying to sort things out so I could plan ahead. I didn't regret the fact that I was burning a lot of bridges. Audrey was with me, and that made it all worthwhile.

Audrey slept peacefully on the plane, but I didn't. Other passengers didn't seem to notice my scruffy appearance, and the woman sitting across the aisle from us seemed to see no more than a father traveling to London with his little girl.

I held Audrey as she slept, and with every breath she took, I marveled at the miracle of her existence. There were no words for it, but I understood love then.

As we got farther and farther from the United States, I began to look at myself almost as I was looking at Audrey. From outside. I was on a plane with my daughter heading for another world. But were we really on that plane, or was I watching a three-dimensional movie made during another lifetime? Or was I dying at that moment and being forced to review my life? Was I only one of billions of amoeba-like actors on a cosmic stage? I felt drugged, but happy, perhaps happier than I had ever been, and as I stroked Audrey's fine blond hair, I wanted to cry. This was the rawest emotion I had ever experienced. But there was a sadness, too, a heavy feeling of guilt. What right had I to run off with my daughter? How could it possibly be fair to her? What was Leslie going through? She had to be the most miserable person in the world at that moment when I was the happiest. I knew I needed sleep, and the airplane was taking care of time and distance, but fate, as kind as it had ultimately been, would not let me rest. Why couldn't I be content to hate Leslie Summers and then get on with my life and Audrey's? Why couldn't I simply block her from my mind? Did Audrey realize what was going on? Would she miss her mother as she had missed me? Would she hate me when she did understand?

The plane rushed on toward an English dawn, and its other passengers, most of whom were sleeping, were only extras hired to make the scene realistic. As daylight began to filter through the cabin, and as I saw the weight in my arms and lap begin to take on human form, I swayed between consciousness and unconsciousness. I saw Leslie Summers and Juan Lanzo Ernesto with policemen and private detectives. I saw an embarrassed ticket agent apologizing for selling plane tickets to a deranged kidnapper. I saw Jeff Morgan apologizing for his role in all this. I saw the headlines in the Woodstock and Kingston papers: *Maniac Kidnaps Daughter*. I saw Interpol agents waiting for us at London's Heathrow Airport. Someone in a gray trench coat was pulling a crying little girl away from me. Photographers were all around us, and airport security guards were holding back crowds of people who wanted to kill me.

But I also saw a pleasant thatched cottage in the Devon countryside. A little girl in a short skirt, argyle stockings and a wool sweater was running up a path toward the door, shouting, "Daddy, Daddy, look what I found!" She showed me a rounded, stream-polished stone. I saw the happiness on her face, and I knew I wasn't the unconscionable man police all over the world were looking for.

But then I saw Leslie Summers, gray and sickly, sitting in a wicker rocking chair, waiting to die, knowing death was a long way off. She was clutching a photograph of her young daughter. It was the photograph of a distant memory. How could I hate this pathetic old woman? How could I feel anything but compassion? Was she the same woman who had taken Audrey away from me while I was at my mother's funeral, who had done what I was doing now?

There was Myrna Dawson. How could I tell Audrey we'd never see Myrna again? How could I tell her she'd never see her mother again? How could I tell her she'd never sleep in her own room on Camelot Road again?

I was startled from these images when the seat-belt sign flashed on and a cabin attendant announced we were preparing to land at Heathrow.

Audrey stirred some as I strapped her back into her seat, but she slept through the landing. As the other passengers stood and reached for belongings in the overhead compartments, I gently shook her awake.

She rubbed her eyes and asked, "Are we still on the big jet?"

"Yes, but we've just landed. We're in England."

She looked out the window toward the terminal and then back at me. "Is England like New York? Does it have a 'pire State Building?"

I laughed and kissed her on the forehead. "No, there isn't an Empire State Building here, but there are lots of other interesting things."

She looked back out the window, not convinced I was right. "What kinds of things?"

"Oh, there's a huge clock called Big Ben and there's a tower and there are great buses, red double-decker buses. If you ride on top, you can see all sorts of things."

She clapped her hands and said, "Let's ride on one when we get off the jet. I like England, Daddy."

"I think you will. Did you get a good sleep?"

"Daddy Rabbit and I both sleeped good." She stood up on the seat next to mine and said, "Let's go ride a big bus."

It was around seven-thirty or eight when we got inside the terminal. As we waited in the customs line, Audrey asked, "Why are all these people opening their suitcases when they aren't even home?"

I laughed. "Sometimes when people go to a different country they bring things they aren't supposed to have, and the customs people have to check their suitcases."

"Will they check our pack?"

"I imagine they will."

"They won't make me give them Daddy Rabbit and my new toys, will they?"

"No, they won't do that."

She squeezed my hand hard and stood behind me, away from the customs inspectors. "Daddy," she said, "why don't we have a big suitcase like that man?" She pointed to a man in front of us who was struggling with the lock on his suitcase.

"Well," I replied, "we didn't have much time to plan this trip."

"What will I sleep in? I don't have any jammies in England."

"Don't worry, sweetie. After we've had some rest, we'll buy jammies and a whole bunch of clothes. Maybe some more toys, too."

XXVIII _____

Saturday, February 13, 1988

Dear John,

Just for the record, this is my third attempt at responding to your letter. As you said, this is an unusual experience, but it's also exciting, from my point of view, anyway, to realize I have another "family" on the East Coast. (No, I have never been to New York— except when I was a baby, that is.)

It was especially interesting (and a little weird) to learn that I have a second brother named Mike. Was that planned, or did things just happen that way? I'm also glad to have a brother named Jack. Is his full name John, after you?

Now, to the belt. I'm staring at it as I write. I think I remember it. I'm not trying to be vague, but it's all a little strange. I don't know if I really remember it or if what you said about it (belonging to Myrna's father and being given to him by Shirley Temple when he was in the circus) makes me think I do. For some reason, it makes me think of geese. Does that make any sense?

Yes, it makes sense. When you were very little, I sometimes took you and Myrna to a pond here in Woodstock, where you fed the geese. They were greedy, insistent birds, and they would flap their wings and chase

234

after the two of you. You and Myrna thought this was great fun. I don't remember the belt in this context, but it obviously has some association for you.

I do, of course, remember Myrna, but we lost touch, probably about the time I sent her the school picture you mentioned. I think her parents were getting divorced then. Anyway, I never heard from her again. If you see her, tell her hi from me and say I might be seeing her before long. (Yes, I would like to come to New York and meet you and the rest of my "other family"—more on this later.)

It's strange—at least to me—that I never knew you lived in Woodstock. I always thought you lived in Denver, Colorado. In fact, when I was fifteen, I went to the telephone company here and looked through the Denver directory for your name. I'm not sure, but I think Mom always said you lived there. Did you once?

I wonder why she's asking me. Why doesn't she ask Leslie or Juan?

You said you kept in touch with my grandfather until he died. I never knew him, and Mom never talked about him. I'd like to ask you about him someday.

"Mom never talked . . ." She uses the past tense. Is she being intentionally mysterious? Is she alluding to—I don't know—is she saying (or not saying) that Leslie's dead or that she, Audrey, doesn't know where her mother is? Did Leslie leave her and Juan and Michael? It wouldn't surprise me. This is strange—I have never considered that Leslie might be dead.

You asked if I'm still interested in swimming. I'm glad my grandfather told you about that; I'm glad he knew. Swimming has always been a sort of passion with me. I swam on my high school team and then on my college team for four years. I once considered training for the Olympics, but decided against it because it would have taken too much study time.

Now that I've told you about my swimming, I might as well tell you a little more about myself. I graduated from college in Long Beach a year ago last spring. I have a B.A. in business. (Not very exciting, but I majored in business in a prelaw sense.) I'm working in a law office here in L.A., as a sort of glorified legal secretary, and I plan to go to law school next fall. As I tell everyone, I'm getting a little "life experience" now, which really means I'm saving money for school next year. (I have a scholarship, but there will be other expenses.)

I thought it was going to be hard to write this letter (actually, it was when I first tried), but now it's easy, almost as though I'm writing to my oldest friend. Maybe that's because you sent the picture of yourself, Kay, Mike and Jack. You're right, Kay does look a lot younger than fifty-two. You look younger than you are, too. I would never have recognized you if you hadn't said you're the one with the gray hair—ha ha to you, too.

I keep looking at this picture, trying to find a family resemblance between myself and you and the boys. So far, I haven't really been able to do it. Well, we'll have to check that out when I come to New York.

That leads me to the "meat" of my letter. I would love it if you were to come out here, but to tell the truth, I would rather come there. First, I want to meet all of you. Second, I'm just being selfish. As I've said, I haven't been East since I was a baby. I would like to see New York City and Woodstock, too. Now, here's the problem: I work in a small office, and I can't get away from work very easily. I could take a Monday or a Friday off and have a three-day weekend there, but that seems too short a time. I have given some impulsive thought to quitting my job, which I'm not terribly fond of, and then looking for another one when I get back, but that wouldn't be a responsible thing for a future lawyer to do (don't get me wrong—I'm not known for either my lack of impulsiveness or my sense of responsibility). Anyway, here's what I'm thinking now, and I'll welcome your thoughts on this. How would it be if I waited until the Easter-Passover holidays in April? One of the good things about working in a Jewish-Christian-heathen office is that there are more and longer holidays. I could probably get a full week off then.

I want to tell her to come now. She doesn't have to work. I'll send all the money she needs, to live on now and to get through law school. But she's not asking for that. I have to keep from acting impulsively, too. Don't push, John. Everything's just fine, so don't do anything which could scare her away.

If this is all right with you and Kay, let's keep in touch and make plans for then. Okay?

I'm really glad you wrote to me.

Audrey

P.S.: Thanks for sending the belt. It means a lot to me. I don't know exactly why, or how, but it is bringing back little pictures.

"Little pictures." That's the way Leslie Summers would have put it. Why hasn't she said anything about Leslie or Juan? Just be patient. There's plenty of time.

I'm floating, first through the house I live in with Kay and the boys, then through the house on Camelot Road where I once lived with Audrey and Leslie, and finally through the thick woods of Overlook Mountain. There's a sort of red haze in front of me. It makes me think of the way taillights look in a heavy fog. I'm gliding, maybe just centimeters above the forest floor, toward this haze, but it always stays ahead of me. I know I want to catch up with it and somehow become a part of it, but I don't understand why. It's as if something infinitely greater than I am is beckoning me on but at the same time refusing to let me join it. I'm glancing around and listening intently, expecting to see and hear my demons, expecting them to lead me again to that high black wall, and wanting them to because I feel stronger than I ever have before. I want them to dare me one last time, because this time I know I can make it. I know I can defeat them and make it safely to the other side. I have discovered their sinister little secret. They want me to believe, as they always have, that once I'm on the other side I'll be reunited with my father, who has been dead for over forty years. I have always believed them, but now I know better. I know he is dead and always will be. But now I know something else, too, something the demons can't suspect. I know it's really Audrey who's on the other side of the wall. I know she's alive and waiting for me. This I know for a fact, and it's this knowledge that is at last going to let me prevail.

I'm still floating, gliding toward the red haze. It could be a spacecraft in the distance, hovering just above the earth's surface, as I am at this very moment. I hear dawn awakening to the sounds of countless birds, chirping in the forest around me, where the first morning traces of blue are appearing through the trees and merging with the red haze. The sounds of the birds are clear and musical. There's nothing haphazard about this early-morning concert. There is, in fact, a sense of mathematical order I have never before known. I am aware of a heavy but clean and sweet odor as I take in each breath, and I feel a slight chill as this mountain air passes by and through me as I, still gliding, get closer to the red haze. I don't see the wall, but I know it's there, and I look forward to this final confrontation.

Someone else is with me now, and although I can't see him, I know it's Rob Dawson, and knowing this, I feel safer and more confident than I ever have. I know he's dead, but more than that, I know he's with me. It strikes me briefly as odd that in death I know him much better than I ever did in life, that in death I can love and trust him without reservation. There are little jabs of thought all around me now as I continue toward this haze in the forest. My mother and father are with me, too. This is too important for them not to be. Death has brought them and Rob Dawson closer to me than life ever could have.

There is no passage of time. Only sensations, and I know this is what has always been important. Something is telling me this is a dream, which it is, but letting me know that's good. This is important. It's what I'm about.

Now the wall is visible through the trees, which are giving way to form as their silhouettes begin to take on the color of day. The red haze is lifting, too, and leaving in its stead a pulsating red sun, or something that appears to be the sun. I am drawn to it, free of the restrictions of gravitational pull, and I know where I'm going. The wall is directly in front of me, and no longer is it high and imposing. I don't need anything to help me catapult over it. It's nothing. There is absolutely nothing intimidating about it now. All I have to do is step over it. The only caution I have to take is not to crush it as I cross to the other side, where I know I'm going to be reunited with Audrey.

I feel myself back on solid ground, and as I lift my right foot to step over this little wall, I hear (the birds, my demons, Rob Dawson?) whispering: "Fate is merely performing its obligation to creation."

It's not quite three in the morning. I'm awake now and sitting at our long pine-plank kitchen table, rereading the letter I received from Audrey nearly two months ago, and I'm thinking about the phone conversations we've had since. I find it almost impossible to believe I'm going to be meeting her at La Guardia later this morning.

I love my dream with its whispered message: "Fate is merely performing its obligation to creation." I'm not clever enough to understand it entirely, or what I suspect its meanings are, but I know it seems right as I sit here, enthralled by both realities of my existence, sipping coffee, thinking about Kay, who is still determined to clean the house, and the boys, who are asleep in their rooms. What is it going to be like meeting Audrey for the first time in her memory? What will it be like for me? For her? For my sons? For Kay? The first time we talked, she repeated what she'd said in her letter. "This is weird, but it's exciting, too." Weird and exciting. That seems a fair assessment, but I wonder how that will change in the next few days. What will our memories be in a month, in ten years? These memories, these pictures of something that hasn't even happened yet, will trail along with us for the rest of our lives. They will be a large part of this precious fate, of this collective fate of ours.

I'm still amazed that the red belt brought back memories of geese to Audrey. Geese and a red patent-leather belt are the things joining me with my daughter as I sit in the kitchen on this unseasonably warm April morning, thinking about both the past and the future—the future that is going to begin in a few hours.

I'm thanking you now, Rob. I don't know where your wisdom, or basic goodness, or whatever it is came from, but it worked, and I'm grateful to you. Wherever you are, old friend, the next bottle of hooch is for you.

XXIX _____

It's still hard for me to make sense of Audrey's and my time in England. Everything happened so quickly. The physical things are reasonably clear—that is, I can see the bed-and-breakfast house we stayed in on Culford Gardens in Chelsea. It was owned by an elderly woman named Mrs. Brighton. I can remember our room, which Mrs. Brighton called the Queen's room because it had a private bath. It looked out over a garden, which hadn't been tended for years, and its pale pink walls were chipping so badly that I laughed at the idea of the Queen staying there. I remember trying our first day there to bribe Audrey with candy, toys, Cokes and french fries to rest or play quietly so I could get some sleep, and failing. I recall riding with her on double-decker buses and then taking her to Victoria Station to watch the trains. I can see us in our room, playing the Great Gambini, a game where I got on my back, brought my knees to my chest, balanced her on my feet and catapulted her into the air and onto the bed. This was a game, she told me, that she and Myrna sometimes played with Rob Dawson.

There were endless questions about Myrna. "Can we go get Myrna so she can ride a big bus with us? Can Myrna come to England and play the Great Gambini with us?" And there were questions about her mother, Juan Lanzo Ernesto and "my new brother, Michael." "Can Mommy and Juan and Michael come here? Can we all sleep in this big bed?" I clearly remember that her questions and her eagerness to bring her entire world to us brought me to tears. But what I don't remember is what actually caused me to break down and lose virtually all perception of what was going on around me. My memory has somehow warped. The parts are there, but they don't fit together.

These are the things I do recall. We became friendly with Mrs. Brighton during the three days we stayed in her house. She was openly interested and curious about our circumstances and about the fact that we didn't have Audrey's "mum" with us. I told her the truth, everything from beginning to end, and that turned out to be the undoing of all I had accomplished by finding Audrey and making off with her. On the morning of what was to be our last day in Mrs. Brighton's house, she urged me to talk with her solicitor, a Mr. Malcolm Farley. I was reluctant to tell anyone else what was happening, but Mrs. Brighton convinced me that I would have to do something about our legal status in the U.K. Our joint tourist visa was good for only three months, and if I was going to settle in England, I would have to do something about working papers.

I went to see Mr. Farley while Mrs. Brighton watched after Audrey. Sitting in his office, I remember feeling as I had a few days earlier in Jeff's office in Kingston—trapped and afraid. He listened politely as I told him the story, and after I had finished, he said I was in a precarious position, and he added that it would probably be only a matter of time before Leslie and her lawyer traced us to England. He then asked if I believed I could ever feel secure, running and hiding as I was. I should have realized then that I had been betrayed, but while I may have suspected it, I didn't actually believe it. I'm sure this refusal or inability to see what was happening had to do with my exhaustion and overwhelming sense of guilt.

I'm not sure how long I talked with Mr. Farley, but I know I was terrified by the time I left his office. He said that if I decided to stay in England and was located by Leslie or her agents, as he referred generally to American authorities, it was likely that Audrey and I would be forced to return to the United States simply because

British authorities wouldn't want to get involved in a foreign domestic issue. He added that it was possible that British ports had already been blocked to us. When I asked what that meant, he explained that if Leslie or her agents had learned we had come to England, which they could have easily done by checking airline records, they could have notified British authorities to be on the lookout for us. That, he said, would mean they would, in all probability, stop us at any embarkation port and make it impossible for us to go anywhere but back to the United States.

Mr. Farley was direct and honest with me, but I didn't comprehend all that had been left unsaid or implied. I knew something was wrong, something more than my uncertain frame of mind, but I couldn't identify it, and when I left the solicitor's office, I felt the way I imagined people did in their last seconds of life. I could see what was going on around me, but I couldn't feel anything. It was as if I had been covered with a leaden blanket that had had eyeholes cut out of it. I walked slowly and heavily through the streets of London, but I couldn't raise my arms, nor could I turn my head from side to side. My vision was clear but narrowed. I remember people staring at me as I made my way through them, and I remember cars and buses honking as I crossed streets with no regard for them.

I don't know how long I plodded along the streets of London before I finally made it back to Mrs. Brighton's house, but I do know it was dark and that I felt dizzy and sick when I finally knocked on the front door. My mind's eye can catch only little patches of what happened next.

I was sitting on a worn overstuffed sofa in Mrs. Brighton's living room with cats all around me. Audrey was somewhere in the room, but I don't remember where. I can hear bits of talk between her and Mrs. Brighton, but I can't make out the words. I can see the color in her new pajamas, but I can't see her. It's almost as if the pajamas are filled out not with a little girl, but with the ghost of a child who is long dead. Mrs. Brighton is across the room, preparing "tea," which is really a concoction of gin and something else. She's saying something to me, I think about the importance of a child being with her "mum," but I can't put the words or their meanings into a pattern that makes sense. I can hear the cats purring loudly as they compete for my affection, but they are only furry patches of color. Suddenly the cats stiffen and leap from the sofa and my lap to a window that faces the street. I hear grinding sounds of brakes outside, and then I hear footsteps clomping up the steps to the front porch. There's a wild look of surprise on Mrs. Brighton's face. I pick Audrey up and bolt toward her as Mrs. Brighton tries to hand me the drink she has just prepared. Glass shatters as I knock into Mrs. Brighton, and I hear Audrey shouting, "Daddy!"

The door knocker raps, and I stand frozen with Audrey in my arms.

Mrs. Brighton opens the door.

Leslie, Juan, Pete Sickler and two other men come into the vestibule.

Audrey slips from my grasp and runs to Leslie.

There's a sort of satisfied look of self-righteousness on Mrs. Brighton's face, and I know she's responsible for this.

Leslie is glaring at me.

Sickler is standing next to her and in front of me with an insipid grin on his face.

One of the other men is saying something about being a British immigration officer.

The other man is trying to hand papers to me.

Leslie is moving slowly, almost floating. She's handing Audrey to Juan, telling him to take her outside.

I feel the immigration officer's grasp on my arm.

The other man is still trying to hand the papers to me. I want to hit him, but the immigration officer is holding tight.

I hear Sickler saying something about extradition and about a restraining order in New York.

The man with the papers is still trying to hand them to me. I swing at him with my free arm, and the immigration officer forces the other arm behind my back.

I twist out of his grasp and fall to the floor.

Leslie's teeth are glistening, threatening, blinding. She leans down and whispers, "If you ever try this again, I'll kill *her*."

I get to my knees, knowing she means it. The hands are coming close. I crawl away from them and toward Leslie, who is going out the door.

From outside, I hear a plaintive voice calling, "Daddy!"

The papers are on the floor in front of me.

I hear the ominous chugging of a taxi's diesel engine.

The only person here with me now is Mrs. Brighton. I hate the interfering, pious old bitch, knowing she snooped through our things and found our address in the passport and then called Leslie.

I get to my feet and go outside, but the taxi has already gone. I can see only the hazy glow of its taillights.

When I got back to Kingston late the next afternoon, Jeff told me Leslie had already received temporary custody from the family court judge, and he explained what I already knew: that I didn't have a chance when the formal hearing came up.

I go out the door Audrey and I had escaped through four days earlier.

I'm in my car, driving as fast as the Volvo will go toward our old house upstate.

What happened in Easton is more or less as Rob Dawson told it a little over five months ago in the Duck & Dog. What he didn't get right, because he couldn't have known, was why I didn't kill myself. It wasn't because I suddenly came to my senses or because the two policemen showed up and took me to the county fair. It was because, as I lay naked on the cushions with my head in the oven, I realized that I was completing the job Leslie had begun over a year earlier when she turned the gas on and told me to light the oven. I wanted to die then, but I wasn't going to allow her that victory.

Part Three

Hussong's Cantina

XXX

We're sitting at a small table in the back of Hussong's Cantina, a dimly lighted, almost Mexican bar and restaurant on Columbus Avenue in New York City. Both Audrey and I are a little drunk, which I think is good, because it's allowing us to feel more comfortable with each other.

We have been walking the streets of Manhattan all day—her plane arrived at La Guardia at seven-forty this morning. Audrey is smart, the way her mother was. This frightened me at first, but now it doesn't. This daughter of mine, this stranger, doesn't have the need to hide behind fabrications as Leslie did. At least I don't think so.

We're staying in the Plaza Hotel. It still works magic on me, not in the way it did twenty-odd years ago, but because it is what it is: an elaborately ornate and expensive hotel, which deserves to be expensive. I reserved two rooms, but when we got to the hotel this morning, we discovered only one was available. Audrey laughed and said, "What better way for us to get to know each other." I shuddered at this. But then Audrey said, "It's not so weird for a father and daughter to share a hotel room."

"You're right. I'm still adjusting to the idea of having a daughter."

"Yeah, aren't we both."

We settled into our room and then went to SoHo—Audrey had brought a list of places she wanted to see. SoHo was on top, because a Los Angeles friend had told her there were a lot of Art Deco shops there. Art Deco isn't my style, but she loves it—everything from jewelry to furniture to painting. I tried to buy some jewelry for her, but she said she didn't want to own it. "Looking's enough."

We did the normal touristy things—World Trade Center, Staten Island Ferry, Chinatown, South Street Seaport and the East Village—and now we're doing what we're really here for. We're getting acquainted. It's not as difficult as I thought it might be, but still there's an edge of reservation. I keep looking for the little girl who was snatched away from me in London so long ago, but she's not here. Instead, I'm with a beautiful and smart young woman who could almost be Leslie. I find myself staring at her constantly, especially now that I'm a little drunk. The physical resemblance is there, but there's a lot more than that. I see myself there, too. She is not a carbon of Leslie, but something entirely her own, something better. I'm seeing Leslie's beauty, but it's not hers anymore. It's Audrey's, and it's almost as if all that once made Leslie attractive and exciting has passed from her and into Audrey, filtering out all the crazy parts.

Audrey's asking me something above the din of other patrons and the canned Mexican music. I know I have a shit-eating grin on my face as I ask, "What?"

She's not grinning now. "I asked why you and my mother didn't have an abortion when she got pregnant." Now she's smiling. "I mean, I'm glad you didn't, but I've always wondered."

Why would she have wondered? Did Leslie tell her we got married because she was pregnant? Did she say that was the only reason? God, I hope not. Has Audrey ever asked Leslie this question? How can I answer it? Honestly?

"There was never any question about an abortion," I finally say. "You weren't exactly planned, that's true, but abortion never entered my mind. I loved your mother more than you can imagine, and there was nothing I wanted more than, well, than what we got. *You.*"

"My mother said she almost had an abortion, but didn't because you talked her into marriage."

Jesus, why would Leslie ever have said that? "That isn't exactly the way it happened. She did think about an abortion at first. She was here in New York and I was in Colorado, and she was afraid. She was only eighteen and had already had one child." I don't know if Audrey knows the circumstances of Michael's birth or not. I hope she doesn't. "But," I add, "when I got here, we loved each other as much as ever and immediately decided to get married. Not because we had to, but because we wanted to."

"Am I making you uncomfortable with my questions?"

"No, not at all." I'm half lying, but I'm trying not to. I'm trying to lighten up, to feel comfortable. She has a right to any answer I can provide.

God, she's beautiful. She is everything I ever imagined to be good between Leslie and me. She's what I wanted to believe in in Leslie. What Leslie should have been.

"Do you know how scared I was about coming out here?" she asks.

I place my hand on hers, but then remove it. "Yes, I know," I reply. "I felt the same way. I still do. A little, anyway."

She puts her hand on mine now and leaves it there. We're looking into each other's eyes. (Did we ever do this when she was a child? I can't remember.) I hope I don't look as drunk as I feel. She's laughing. "You want to know how I rationalized coming out here?" she asks.

I don't know if the question hurts or not.

"I don't mean that in a cruel way," she says. "I mean, when I got your first letter, I was afraid, not of you, but of us. That maybe you wouldn't like me or that I wouldn't like you. Am I making sense?"

I feel my hand trembling under hers. "Yes, you're making sense."

"After we had talked a few times, I felt better, but still there was that question, the big one: Would we like each other? So I had to invent another reason for coming here. I had to look at the whole thing in a different way. Almost detached, I'd say." She's frowning now, and looking to see how I'm taking this. "I had to tell myself that even if none of this worked out I was at least getting a free trip to New York. Do you know what I mean?"

I laugh now. "Of course I know. I had similar feelings. The only difference is that I didn't get a free trip." We haven't talked about Leslie or Juan yet. I want to, but am afraid to rush things.

It's almost as if Audrey is reading my mind. She says, "I wasn't going to tell Juan I was coming out here."

What about Leslie?

She takes her hand from mine and looks away from me toward the end wall, where the head of what appears to be an antelope is mounted. I stare at the animal's glass eyes, too, as my daughter says, "I didn't want to hurt Juan's feelings, but that was silly. It turned out to be silly, anyway."

"How's that?" I ask. What about Leslie? I almost want to scream it out, but I don't.

"When I told him I was coming here to meet you and Kay and my brothers, he was genuinely pleased. I think I could even say delighted. He told me to tell you hello." She faces me again, and a wide grin crosses her face. "So, hello from Juan Ernesto."

We both laugh, and I order two more frozen margaritas from the waiter. Just what I need.

"How's he doing?" I ask. Of course, I want to ask how he and her mother are doing, but I hold off.

"He's all right. Not great, but all right," she says. "I haven't seen a lot of him since I went away to school a few years ago. I mean, sure, I've seen him over vacations, but that's different. I haven't seen him the way I used to, when I lived at home. He's an amazing person. I have never understood him, why he, I guess you'd say, why he more or less sacrificed his life for Mike and me."

"How do you mean, sacrificed?" I have to know now. I have to know what happened to her mother, to Leslie.

"When my mother left . . ."

Jesus! I guess I'm not surprised, but . . . but what? I don't know what I'm thinking, what I expect to hear her say.

"When she left, Juan just stayed on. I mean, he remained . . . he stayed with us. With Mike and me." She sees the confusion on my face. "I'm sorry. You didn't know about any of this, did you?"

"No," I say. "I didn't know anything." I feel numb all over. "When did your mother leave?"

She rests her chin on her clasped hands. "It's not exactly what you're thinking. My mother, as you probably know, has never been particularly stable. I guess it goes back to her own childhood—I don't know. But for as long as I can remember, she has been running away. Sometimes she's gone for a few days, sometimes for months at a time. Juan has always said she's a depressed sort of person, that she can't help being this way. And I guess that's true. She has these extreme highs where everything's great and beautiful and close to perfect. But then she sinks down into a sort of hell. I never understood it when we were growing up. I still don't. I don't know if you can understand this, but when I was a little girl, I thought my mother was a movie star or something. I know that sounds weird, but I really did. When she was home, she was almost always in great shape, most of the time, anyway. She'd come back from wherever she'd been, loaded down with presents for Mike and me and even for Juan. And we'd do all these great things, like charter boats and go deep-sea fishing. Once we went all the way to Alaska. And she'd buy us these incredible things—toys when we were young, and later, great clothes and watches and TV sets, stereos—all that sort of thing. And we'd just lap it up. I mean, Mike and I would. Juan wouldn't. He always went into a sort of shell when she was around. That, of course, was because he knew this sort of magic world wouldn't last."

I can't help myself, so I ask, "Where did all the money come from? Or did Juan sponsor these extravagances?"

"Oh, no. Juan has never made much money. He was a waiter for years, and he went to night school and finally got a degree in accounting. I guess he had a dream about making a lot of money someday as an accountant, but that has never happened. He works for a lumber mill in Sonoma County, just north of Guerneville, where he and Michael have lived the past four years." She brushes her long, baby-fine hair from her eyes, just as Leslie Summers used to do. "No, my mother has always managed to get money when she needs it. Not only when she needs it. Whenever she wants it. But it isn't because she's a movie star. That's a laugh."

I think I know what she's going to say, and it's breaking my heart. I hold her hand in both of mine now. I want to hold her and somehow let her know everything's going to be all right.

There are tears in her eyes. "I can't believe how stupid I was. How stupid I was for such a long time. I always thought the gorgeous Leslie was a great star, and then I found out what she really is. What she *was*, anyway. I don't want to say it."

Oh, Jesus, I don't want her to tell me any more. Not now. I don't want her to have to. How she has managed to turn out the way she has seems a miracle. But it's more than that, I know. Thank God for Juan Lanzo Ernesto. I want to thank him one of these days.

"Listen," I say, "let's walk back to the hotel. A little fresh air would do us good."

I stand up, and she looks at me. She's smiling. A good sign. "Yeah, I guess a walk would be good. I hope you don't think I drink like this all the time."

"I hope you don't think I do," I say, helping her to her feet.

We're walking along Columbus Avenue, holding hands. It's strange and sobering, but my feelings are clearer than they've ever been. I can almost touch those old demons of mine as they slip away. After nearly half a century, they're being evicted from the only residence they've ever known. They have become, like Leslie, their own victims. I feel younger, healthier, happier than I ever have. I wish we weren't staying at the Plaza tonight. I want to get back to Woodstock as quickly as possible. I want to run into our house with Audrey and shout, "Here! This is *our* home. This is

Kay, these are your brothers, Mike and Jack. And I'm your father! Everything is okay! Everything's great!"

I stop walking, and so does Audrey. The street is brightly lighted, and a lot of people are out, probably staring as we embrace. I love this girl, and I know she's going to love me, too. It's the kind of love I feel for Kay and our sons. It's the kind of love I once felt for Leslie Summers. It's the kind of love I felt for the little girl who was taken away from me nearly twenty-one years ago.

Who knows what will happen next? Are we going to go to Woodstock and live happily ever after? Is everything finally over? No, that's not right. Is everything finally beginning?

Audrey kisses me on the cheek. "Thanks," she says.

"For what?" I ask.

"For Shirley Temple's belt."

I pull away from her and see a sort of twinkling in her eyes. I know she's all right. I know I am, too.

About the Author

Thom Roberts is the author of many books for children. He and his family live in Woodstock, New York.